Brilliant Re...

A Clara Fitzgerald Mystery
Book 26

By
Evelyn James

Red Raven Publications
2022

© Evelyn James 2022

First published 2022
Red Raven Publications

The right of Evelyn James to be identified as the Author of this work has been asserted in accordance with the Copyrights, Designs and Patents Act 1988.

All rights reserved. No part of this book may be reprinted or reproduced or utilised in any form or by any electronic, mechanical or other means, now known or hereafter invented, including photocopying and recording, or in any information storage or retrieval system without the permission in writing from the author

Brilliant Chang Returns is the twenty-sixth book in the Clara Fitzgerald series

Other titles in the Series:
Memories of the Dead
Flight of Fancy
Murder in Mink
Carnival of Criminals
Mistletoe and Murder
The Poisoned Pen
Grave Suspicions of Murder
The Woman Died Thrice
Murder and Mascara
The Green Jade Dragon
The Monster at the Window
Murder on the Mary Jane
The Missing Wife
The Traitor's Bones
The Fossil Murder
Mr Lynch's Prophecy
Death at the Pantomime
The Cowboy's Crime
The Trouble with Tortoises
The Valentine Murder
A Body Out of Time
The Dog Show Affair
Worse Things Happen at Sea
A Diet of Death

Chapter One

Another year had trickled away like sand through fingers. 1923 had been full of changes and adventures, but Clara considered that overall, it had been a successful year with many good things to recall.

Clara Fitzgerald – private detective. Remarkable for both being a woman and under the age of thirty, and yet embarking upon, and successfully achieving, a career in a job most would consider a man's business. People underestimated Clara, and she liked to think that was one secret of her success. They saw a young woman, respectably dressed, dark hair in plait or bun, not bobbed or shingled like a starlet's, and they mistook her for someone who was unworldly and could not possibly solve a mystery. Time and time again, Clara had the satisfaction of proving them wrong.

She stood in the back garden of her home, late on the 29 December and looked up at a starry sky. The clouds had dispersed after several dull days and the stars glowed brightly above them. She tried to make out certain constellations, but her memory for astronomy was not what it once was and after finding three arrangements of stars that could have been the Big Dipper, she decided to give up on the effort.

She was feeling rosy-checked and a little light-headed after a party at Captain O'Harris' Convalescence Home for Former Servicemen. It had been a good evening, spending lots of time in the handsome captain's company while the men under his care provided entertainment in the form of piano recitals, comedy skits – and one musical arrangement that had not been approved for the party and involved a rather risqué song that had to be curtailed swiftly before the ladies at the event were heartily offended.

The evening had been, to Clara's way of thinking, perfect. She had a soft smile on her face and was feeling that life in that very moment was rather good. The night might be cold and icy, but it did not penetrate her woollen coat and even if it did, she would not have noticed; a warm, cheerful glow burned within her.

Clara shut her eyes and took a long, deep breath of the wintry air. Filling her lungs with satisfaction and making a silent promise to herself to always remember this evening.

"Hello Miss Fitzgerald."

Clara let out a sharp yelp at the voice beside her and nearly tumbled over. She spun to her left and realised there was someone stood beside the garden fence. She could make out little more than an outline of a figure, but they were smoking a cigarette and the tip glowed in the dark.

"Who is there?" Clara demanded, alarmed someone had slipped into her garden and taken her by surprise.

Clara prided herself on being alert to trouble at all times, and her failure to notice a visitor dented her ego.

"Never fear, Miss Fitzgerald, I am not here to cause harm," the person moved forward and came into better view.

"Brilliant Chang," Clara groaned as she recognised who it was.

"You sound disappointed to see me," Chang said with humour in his voice.

Brilliant Chang was Chinese, though he had worked hard to largely mask his accent and develop an upper-class British twang to his diction. He was shorter than Clara, (which had always somewhat amused her) dressed expensively and was a despicable criminal leader who dabbled in whatever illegal activity took his fancy and made a good return.

He was not someone Clara was pleased to see in her garden.

"I was just thinking what a lovely Christmas I had had, and then I find you here," Clara said, not masking her displeasure.

Brilliant Chang chuckled.

"If it is any consolation, this was the last place I wanted to come," he said.

"Then why are you here?" Clara asked.

Chang was silent a moment. He dropped his cigarette to the ground at his feet and stubbed it out with his toe.

"You will pick that up," Clara told him. "I don't want your ground out cigarettes in my garden."

Chang probably gave her a surly look, but it was lost in the darkness. Muttering to himself, because no one told Chang what to do, he bent down and picked up the cigarette end.

"I had forgotten how disagreeable you are."

"You are welcome to leave," Clara replied. "In fact, I shall quite gladly show you the way out."

"Could you not be nice for once?" Chang grumbled.

"Could you not be a criminal?" Clara asked. "Let's face it Chang, we are not friends and never will be. We are enemies, occasionally reluctant comrades when a situation demands it, and mostly glad not to see one another. My only regret is that I have yet to have you arrested for something."

"You are such a kind hostess," Chang snorted. "Do you tell all your guests you would prefer to see them arrested?"

"Only the ones who turn up unannounced and who I do not care to keep company with," Clara shrugged. "If you have nothing more to say to me, I shall be going to bed."

She turned away and was almost on her kitchen doorstep when Chang called out.

"Wait, Clara!"

The use of her Christian name, the sudden drop of formality that Chang used as a barrier between them, caused Clara to pause. She had heard the anxiety in his voice. Chang did not display his anxiety, not around her, at least.

She turned around again.

"What is it, Chang?"

"I need your help," Chang said, or rather he spat out the words, hating to have to utter them.

"Not another relative trying to usurp you," Clara groaned. "Brighton has barely recovered from your sister. I have barely recovered. I never want to be involved in your family politics again."

"It is not anything like that," Chang snapped. "My business dealings are flowing smoothly, as it happens. Everything has been going rather well."

"Then, why are you here?"

Chang shuffled his feet in the dark.

"It is awkward. You were the only person I could think to ask. Anyone else will consider me weak for it."

"Now I am curious," Clara took a pace towards him. "Is someone after you?"

"Not in the way you mean," Chang said. "This is not some gang rivalry that has gotten out of hand. It is…

more personal."

Clara waited for him to say more, allowing silence to open between them. Chang sighed.

"This is very awkward, but you have experience in this sort of thing, and you are very sensible," Chang remarked. "I need someone who I can trust to discover the truth of things for me."

"You have yet to explain what 'things' you are referring to," Clara said. "Could you perhaps hurry up, it is cold out here."

"You are telling me! I was waiting by your rhododendron bush for two hours. I thought I might lose my toes and fingers to frostbite," Chang shuddered dramatically.

"I see this is serious," Clara said.

"It is most certainly serious," Chang sniffed. "I might be about to become a father."

The words fell heavy on the air and were followed by silence. Clara cleared her throat.

"You have lost me. How is this a problem that requires me?"

Chang had shrunk in on himself.

"Well, the first problem is I am not convinced I am the father of this particular child, but the lady in question is insistent I am. The second problem is…"

Chang mumbled something under his breath.

"I did not hear you," Clara said, folding her arms to try to keep some warmth in her body. "Perhaps you could say that again?"

Chang huffed and puffed, battling his own resistance to speaking aloud his troubles.

"You won't laugh at me?"

"I make no promises," Clara retorted. "You have done little to earn my friendship or respect."

"You are a hard woman, Clara Fitzgerald."

"Because I take no nonsense from you? Yes, and

that is why you came to me for help, isn't it?"

Chang muttered under his breath again, then he resolved himself to speak. He had come all this way, after all, stood out in the freezing cold waiting for Clara. He had battled with his natural inclinations towards secrecy to make this journey and speak his thoughts. If he were not so dreadfully concerned, and if it was not for the fact no one else could help him, and he could not help himself, he would certainly not be here.

"I feel a fool speaking it aloud, but I have been kept awake night after night by my fears and I cannot ignore them any longer."

"This is still about potentially becoming a father?" Clara asked.

"It is and then again, it isn't," Chang answered. "I shall speak blunt, Miss Fitzgerald and if you must laugh at me, so be it. It is better than one of my rivals knowing my fears."

"You have my attention," Clara said. "Against my better judgement."

"Hm, I know you despise me, Miss Fitzgerald. I think, in many ways, that is why I have come to you for help. You will do nothing to please me just for the sake of it, but you will be extremely honest with me. That gives me hope. Terrible to think the only person I feel I can trust is a private detective with friends in the constabulary. Even as I say it, I realise how ridiculous I am being, standing here."

"Something must really be worrying you," Clara said.

She did not care for Chang, she found his manners and his business disagreeable, but he was still a human being and Clara could have sympathy for him on that regard. She was not so cold and hard-hearted.

Chang shuffled his feet again. They were like blocks

of ice.

"The gist of it all is that I think..." Chang coughed. "I think I have been cursed, Miss Fitzgerald."

Clara did not speak. She did not laugh. She did not sneer. If anything, she was silenced by the unexpected nature of what he had just said.

"You appear unmoved," Chang said.

"I am... surprised," Clara replied. "You did say cursed?"

"Yes."

"In the magical, spiritual, witches and black arts way?"

"Yes."

Clara allowed this to sink in.

"You appreciate I am not the suspicious sort, and I don't believe in curses, or ghosts or suchlike."

"Precisely why I came to you," Chang said. "I couldn't confide in anyone else."

"You believe in it, then?" Clara asked. "The curse?"

Chang was uneasy.

"It sounds absurd, but I would not be here if I didn't believe in it, would I?"

"Curses are a load of nonsense," Clara said stoutly. "Bad luck happens, curses do not."

"I had your confidence, once," Chang shook his head. "Then life started to become... strange. Things occurred I could not explain, and I have been ill, but no doctor can tell me the cause. These events have been going on for months. I have lost my faith in rationality."

"Sometimes life does seem to be one bad blow after the other," Clara told him. "We all endure those periods, and it can seem as if we have done something to deserve such pain, but most of us have not."

"That was not very subtle," Chang would have glared at her, but the night made it too dark to see his expression. "Especially when I have just bared my soul to you. So, I deserve all this bad fortune?"

"I don't believe in curses," Clara repeated. "I believe that sometimes what we perceive as bad luck is really a result of our poor choices, or poor planning, and sometimes it is just life."

Chang had fumbled in his pocket and retrieved another cigarette. He lit it with trembling fingers.

"I wish I could take things so plainly as you, Miss Fitzgerald, but I grew up in a country where everything was linked to superstition and magic. I might have left that behind physically, but it seems psychologically it is still with me. I generally considered myself too practical for such things, until recently, that is."

"How does this all link to the woman who says you are the father of her child?"

"That is the easy part. She cursed me," Chang shrugged his shoulders and took a long drag on his cigarette. "When she told me she was pregnant and I was the father, I told her to clear off. I had no doubt she was lying. She kept pestering me, insisting I must be the father. I finally grew tired of her and told her never to bother me again. There may have been a few threats involved..."

"Charming, Chang."

"You have not met the woman," Chang snarled. "Anyway, it was then she looked me in the eyes and cast a curse on me. Said that until I acknowledged my responsibility, I should be burdened by ill-fortune, my health would deteriorate and my..."

Chang tailed off uncomfortably.

"The last part was somewhat personal in its implications," he said sheepishly. "Anyway, I was like you Clara and dismissed the whole thing. Then I had some misfortunes with my business, those can happen of course. But then I have these health problems my doctor cannot get to the bottom of. Again, that is not so unusual."

"What of the personal part of the curse?" Clara asked, trying not to smile.

Chang made a sound like he had swallowed his tongue.

"That, unfortunately, has come to pass as well."

"Sounds like your luck has been absent a while," Clara hid her amusement. "But I still do not believe in curses."

"Quite frankly, Miss Fitzgerald, I am relieved to hear that. I need someone who will not respond to this nonsense but will dig beneath it for the truth. I am... most worried."

Chang became quiet and sullen. Clara's amusement faded. He did seem deeply troubled by the situation and that was not like Chang at all.

"I would like to hire you on a professional basis to solve these two mysteries. First, I need to know the truth about this woman's claims. If she is genuine – though I doubt that in the extreme – but, if she is, I will do my duty towards her. Second, and perhaps more importantly, I need you to stop this curse."

"There is no curse to stop," Clara said gently.

"Just humour me on that one, will you? You have not seen the things I have lately. Will you take the case?"

Clara considered for a moment. Her first reaction was to refuse, it was Chang, after all. Yet, he did seem so despondent and that spoke to her professional sympathy. Besides, if this woman were genuine, then she deserved to have support from Chang for her child. Clara ought to determine that, at least.

"I'll take your case," she said.

Chang groaned with relief.

"Thank you, Miss Fitzgerald. You were my last hope."

Chapter Two

Tommy Fitzgerald was Clara's older brother, but he did not always feel as if he was the elder sibling. When Clara was a child, he had looked out for her at school, made sure she was not picked on or tormented by the older kids. She was small for her age and prone to speaking her mind – a trait she had never grown out of – and this could land her in serious trouble at times. Tommy had always been around to make sure she was all right.

Then the war had come, and he had been called up. Something had changed over those four years. Clara had gone from a teenager with too much to say and not always the wisdom to know who to say it to, to a young lady with dignity, decorum, and a sound head on her shoulders.

Lots of things had shaped the Clara there was today during those tumultuous four years. Their parents had perished in a Zeppelin raid in London. He had been crippled and had come home in a wheelchair suffering shellshock. And Clara had done her bit as a volunteer nurse in the local hospital, a challenging role for someone who, at the time, was prone to fainting at the sight of blood. Clara had overcome that issue, thankfully, otherwise it would be quite an inconvenience in her work as a detective.

All of which meant that Clara was now the one who took charge and led the way, even though Tommy had conquered his demons and learned to walk again. He secretly looked up to her a little, though he would never mention such a thing in her presence; it would go to her head.

However, when Tommy entered the morning room first thing the following day and discovered Brilliant Chang perched on the couch silently watching the pigeons who were regular visitors to the back garden, he found himself revising his opinion of Clara's judgement.

He stopped at the side of the couch, staring at the criminal mastermind who had caused him and his sister such bother, all while evading the reach of the law. Brilliant Chang glanced up at him and gave him a radiant smile.

"Good morning, Tommy."

Tommy stared at him a while longer, then turned and marched out of the room.

"Clara!"

Clara was in the parlour, opening the post. There were several New Year's cards from distant relatives who she had completely forgotten to send a card to this year. She was wondering if there was still time to get cards to them.

"Clara!"

Tommy appeared at the door of the room.

"You do not need to shout," Clara said without looking up from the cards. "I know that Brilliant Chang is sitting in our morning room. He has been there since last night."

Tommy opened his mouth, but he could not quite

find the words to express his thoughts. He made a strange noise in the back of his throat, half-strangled cough, half-groan of exasperation.

"He thinks he is cursed," Clara continued, still looking through the cards. She needed to make a list of the names so she could try to send ones back. "He has asked for my help."

"And you agreed?" Tommy asked in astonishment. "Don't you remember the last time we helped him?"

"He caught me last night when it was late, and he was stood shivering in our garden, and I rather felt sorry for him. It was a moment of weakness."

"Then we can send him away!"

Clara gave him a look that said she was not about to renege on her word. Tommy rumbled with disapproval.

"I'm sorry, but I simply can't. It goes against the grain to turn away someone desperate for help, even when they are Brilliant Chang," Clara replied. "Besides, I shall have so much entertainment teasing him about this curse and then proving him wrong."

"Entertainment?" Tommy squeaked. "You do realise the man runs one of the worst gangs in London and has threatened your life in the past."

"I do recall," Clara said with one eyebrow raised. "I also remember stabbing him with a hatpin, which was rather satisfying I must say. But that is beside the point. I have said I shall help him. It might have been done when I was tired and not thinking straight, but it is still done."

Tommy scowled at her, but Clara was unmoving. She had made her decision and she would stick by it. One's word was binding.

"I think Clara is right to do this," Annie said, appearing behind Tommy.

"You too?" Tommy glanced at her, despondent.

"It is the Christian thing to do," Annie said firmly.

"A person in need has asked for her help and no matter who they are, we must offer it. Who else could Chang go to when he is cursed?"

Annie was the Fitzgeralds' friend and, since the summer, Tommy's wife. She also ran their home with military precision and cooked all their meals. Clara and Tommy were banished from her kitchen unless they were there to eat something. She had seen the consequences of their cooking attempts once too often.

"What is this about a curse?" Tommy said crossly, realising he was going to get nowhere with his arguments about Chang's presence in their home, and so changing topic.

"Chang believes he has been cursed. It is as simple as that," Clara explained. "A woman is claiming he is the father of her unborn child. He states he is not and as a result she has cursed him. Chang wants to know if the woman is telling the truth, though I fancy he would prefer if I could prove her lying. He also wants me to find a way to resolve the curse. I tried telling him there is no such thing as curses, but that is not enough to convince him."

"You must not be so dismissive of curses," Annie said solemnly. "They are a serious business."

"Annie, to believe in curses is like believing in magic," Clara replied. "Or fairies and… and…"

"God?" Annie suggested, giving Clara her sternest stare. "I believe in God and the Bible speaks of demons and the Devil. Therefore, I see no reason to discount curses. Of course, they only can affect those people who are not devout in their Christian faith. God protects those who believe in him from such things. I imagine Chang follows some Asian religion."

Clara did not know how to begin unpicking Annie's arguments. She tried not to look too agog that her friend was willing to believe in this curse nonsense too.

"God is one thing," she began carefully, because a battle with Annie over religion might result in no dinner that night. "But curses are not something even a Christian should believe in. They are a psychological device, a way of manipulating a person through the power of their own beliefs. You make a person believe they are cursed and so they are 'cursed' but it is nothing to do with magic."

"My nan was a master of the Evil Eye," Annie said, arms folded across her chest and chin thrust out. "She was well-known for it. People never crossed her for fear of her putting the Eye upon them."

"That seems rather mean," Tommy said, starting to worry his wife might have learned the skill.

"My nan rarely used it," Annie continued. "She was a good person, but if someone tried to do her, or her family, down she would use the Evil Eye on them. She always gave them warning first. The number of people who would sneer and laugh at her, and then she would cast the Eye and it would only be a matter of time before they were back at her doorstep apologising and asking for the curse to be lifted."

"As I said, it is psychological," Clara persisted. "Tell a person they are cursed, and they start to perceive any bit of bad luck or misfortune as a consequence of the curse. They stub their toe, lose their hat in the wind, misplace their keys and it all becomes part of the curse."

"Tell that to the people my nan put the Eye on," Annie sniffed haughtily. "One was the local magistrate. He was corrupt and we all knew it. Well, my nan had an issue with her neighbours. They had put their outhouse too close to where her water pump drew from, and she was sure her water was contaminated. She complained to them and when they refused to move the outhouse, she told them she would complain to the magistrate."

"Why didn't she put the Evil Eye on them?" Tommy asked.

"I told you, my nan only used it when she had to. It is a powerful device, not to be simply thrown around. She would always try other means first."

Clara was trying not to show her disbelief. It was proving hard work.

"Anyway, my nan went to the local magistrate and put her case before him. He said he would take a look at the neighbour's outhouse. Well, he came, and he was all chummy with the neighbours. My nan saw him. He never even looked in their garden, just stopped in for a cup of tea. Turns out he had an arrangement with her neighbour who was a part-time poacher and supplied the magistrate with pheasant, quail, and rabbit.

"My nan realised nothing was going to be done about her water being tainted. So, when the magistrate emerged from her neighbour's house, she stopped him in the road and asked him what he had arranged. He tried to palm her off, and so she put the Evil Eye on him. Told him it would work because of his corruption, and he would come around to her way of thinking. He laughed her off, but a fortnight later he was back begging the curse to be lifted."

"What happened to him?" Tommy asked, becoming engaged in the story despite himself. He liked to think he would never consider a curse real, but a part of him was rather inclined towards the supernatural.

"All sorts of things," Annie replied. "First the wheel fell off his gig as he drove home that day and he nearly ended up in a ditch. Next some important paperwork went missing and turned out to have been blown into the fire by a gust of wind through a window. The cat fell off the top of his wardrobe and smashed a mirror which had belonged to his mother. His wife discovered that every jug of milk in the pantry was off. His roses were destroyed by an unseasonal bout of blackfly and his cook found maggots in the joint of beef meant for the Sunday roast."

"All things that can just happen," Clara said. "In any given week odd little things occur that are such a nuisance. If the milk and the beef came from the same source, then we can suppose whoever supplied them was lax in their food hygiene."

"I hadn't finished," Annie remarked tartly. "Next, the chimneys began to smoke and appeared blocked, but the chimney sweep could find nothing wrong with them. A mouse colony was suddenly discovered in the living room sofa and had eaten a hole through the seat cover. The cockerel fell off the roof of the henhouse mid-crow one morning and was dead as a doornail. The cook could not get any of her bread to rise and the oven seemed suddenly unable to hold its temperature. It either became too hot or was stone cold. Nothing would cook well.

"A stray flock of goats made it into the magistrate's garden and ate what remained of his roses. He slipped in mud trying to shoo them away and hurt his back. He couldn't sleep in his own bed for three nights because of the pain and would sit up in the living room with the smoking fireplace and the quiet scurrying of the mice. He eventually cracked, as you may imagine, and hobbled to my nan to ask her to lift the curse."

"Poor man," Tommy winced at the thought of the misfortune the magistrate had suffered. "She did lift it?"

"After he promised to do his job," Annie said indignantly. "There was nothing poor about him. He had ignored her polite requests and left an old woman with no water to drink. He had it coming. But, yes, he saw that the outhouse was moved, and he even had a man sent to check the pump water was sound to drink. The Evil Eye was lifted, and his home returned to normal.

"The chimneys no longer smoked. The oven cooked as it should. The mice vanished. The milk and meat were fresh and unspoiled, and even his back stopped aching."

"There was a rational explanation for it all," Clara said, earning herself one of Annie's infamous looks.

"You can believe what you wish, Clara Fitzgerald," Annie sniffed. "But the fact of the matter is all those things happened after the Evil Eye was put upon him, and all of those problems disappeared when it was lifted. You ought to be a bit more open-minded to this sort of thing."

"I say, did your nan show you how to use the Evil Eye?" Tommy said, trying not to let any hint of unease into his voice.

"No," Annie said with regret. "My mum would not let her. Said she did not want her daughter being called a witch. My nan was a difficult person, it has to be said, and she did go rather peculiar towards the end. She firmly believed there was a bat living in the clock on her mantelpiece and it would fly out at night and circle the room. It was best not to try and convince her otherwise."

Clara endeavoured not to sigh as this sorry saga came to an end. She hoped she would not have to endure further discussions about curses along the same lines while resolving this case, though she rather feared she would and that many of those discussions would be with Annie.

Tommy was just relieved to know his wife was not capable of throwing the Evil Eye on people.

"I am making breakfast now," Annie informed them. "I shall show Chang the benefits of a good English breakfast to begin the day with. He needs his strength if he is as sick as he claims."

"Chang is sick?" Tommy asked, surprised.

"He says it is another part of the curse and his doctors cannot tell him what is wrong," Clara explained.

"Doctors can never tell you what is wrong," Annie snorted. "Don't need a curse for that."

She departed for her kitchen. Clara gave her brother an apologetic look.

"Sorry, Tommy, I ought to have told you sooner about Chang."

Tommy shook his head.

"Well, we are stuck with him, I suppose. Let's just hope this curse business really is all nonsense."

"Of course, it is!" Clara retorted.

Chapter Three

Brilliant Chang had not slept a wink that night. In fairness, it was not uncommon for him to have sleepless nights and when he did sleep it tended to be for only a handful of hours. There was always so much to do. People did not appreciate the work it required to keep an operation like his going, not to mention the amount of time spent watching your back. He found sleep a nuisance at the best of times and managed quite well with short naps here and there.

For some reason, however, the previous night's lack of sleep had taken quite a toll on him, and he felt utterly exhausted. He could have gladly placed his head in his hands and groaned with weariness, but he was in the house of his nemesis, and he would not show such weakness. He had already revealed his fears about this curse to Clara and that had gone against the grain. If he were not so worried about it, he would never have told her at all, or anyone for that matter.

Chang knew this curse business was crazy and there were people out there who would take advantage of the situation, make a move to take over his dominion, for instance. He would not be taking it this seriously if it were not for the strange illness that had crept over him and was causing him considerable concern.

The illness alone was a secret he had to keep close, for if others knew he was ailing they would soon make the most of the situation. Curse or no curse, Chang was feeling the pressure of his existence and the icy grip of fear that soon it would all be over. He had no illusions on that front of the loyalty he might be able to expect from his followers. If he were lucky, he would just end up an outcast with enough money to see him through. If he were unlucky, every enemy he had ever made would come looking for his head.

It was that dread which had brought him to Clara, the one person he knew would not take advantage of his distress and might actually be able to resolve things for him. It had been a long shot and he had half expected her to send him away. To be in her house and receiving her help, even if she was a goody-two-shoes who would like to see him in prison, was a relief.

He had shut his eyes for just a moment, they felt dry and itchy, a symptom of his illness, when he heard someone enter. He jerked his head up, pretending he had been alert all along. The newcomer was Annie.

"Clara has told me about the curse," she said to him.

He tried to assess her feelings towards him. Annie was harder to read than Clara, who did not mask her distaste for him. Annie looked stern, but there had been a softness to her voice that belied the look.

"I have made a good breakfast to buck you up, and to help you with this sickness," Annie continued.

"Thank you," Chang said. "One of my problems is a lack of appetite. I must apologise in advance, for I am sure your food is delightful."

Chang had remembered from a past encounter with Annie that it was always best to be nice about her cooking. There were few things in this life that could cause her to become more furious than an inference that her cooking was less than divine.

"I imagine that is because you have not been eating right," Annie said firmly. "Once you get some of my cooking inside you, you will be quite well again."

"I admire your optimism," Chang said, a slight grin coming to his face at her self-assurance.

"You will see," Annie replied. "As for this curse business, well, there will be a remedy for that too. We just have to find it."

Chang tipped his head to the side, curious at her words.

"You believe in my curse?"

"I believe in such things, yes," Annie nodded. "Clara won't ever even consider it, of course. She can't allow anything that isn't practical or scientifically proven into her thoughts, but I know there are stranger things out there than what science can explain."

Chang found he was somewhat relieved to hear this. He had begun to feel a touch crazy in the face of Clara's pragmatism. He found he was warming to Annie.

"Come and eat breakfast then," Annie told him. "We all need to hear about this business proper."

Chang rose from the couch, feeling as if the universe was trying to drag him back down. His legs were like lead and he still had a touch of a chill about him from waiting so long in the garden the night before. Adrenaline had driven him to dash from London to Brighton in such haste; that had now worn off and what remained was a man who felt drained and depressed.

He followed Annie to the dining room where breakfast was laid out on the table. Clara and Tommy were both there already, sitting side-by-side on the far side of the table. Annie pointed out the chair she wanted Chang to take, and he obeyed. He was slightly unnerved when she sat beside him because he knew this meant she was going to monitor every bite of food he took. It was worse than having a prison warder watching your every move.

"Start with toast and eggs," Annie informed him. It was not a suggestion; it was an order, and he did not dare decline. "You can work up to the bacon and sausage. I don't make fried bread, however, I consider the amount of grease required hideous. It is quite disgusting."

Clara gave a sad sigh; fried bread was a favourite of hers, but Annie had her 'opinions' and it was best not to argue.

Chang found his plate loaded with buttery toast and scrambled eggs. Everyone began to eat, and he made an effort to show willing, taking a small amount of eggs on the tip of his fork and letting them dissolve on his tongue. They were creamy and peppery, but not heavy or stodgy like some eggs he had been served. He found himself enticed to eat more.

"I am curious about this woman who has caused you such anguish, Chang," Tommy said, tucking into his bacon. "She sounds rather remarkable."

"Her name is Ariadne Griffiths. She is a poet who runs with the London set. She lives a fairly frivolous life existing on her parents' money," Chang explained.

"How did you meet?" Clara asked.

"A literary party hosted by another female friend," Chang explained. "Ariadne was doing a recitation of some of her latest work. It was pretty dire. I recall consuming a lot of alcohol to get me through that night."

"Do you recall doing anything with Ariadne other than listen to her poetry?" Tommy asked pointedly.

Annie gave him a sharp look, but it was a valid question.

"I do not," Chang winced, and the eggs lost some of their delight as he recalled that evening. "As I said I drank a considerable amount of alcohol, though not more than I am used to. I have considered the possibility that someone had spiked it. There comes a point when my memory is a blank of that night. I woke up late the following morning on the floor of a bedroom without any clothing on me. I was the only one there and after finding my clothes I let myself out of the house and headed for my own bed."

"Then, you do not know at all if Ariadne is telling the truth or not," Clara spelled things out for him. "Your denials you might be responsible for her predicament start to sound somewhat hollow."

"I don't know what happened, no, but if there was an encounter, it must have happened while I was drugged and out of my mind. How can I be held responsible for that? Someone laced my drinks, I am sure of it," Chang was angry now. He did not want Clara to take Ariadne's side.

"Finish your eggs," Annie interrupted. "You need something solid inside you to face this mess."

She gave Clara and Tommy sharp looks to indicate they should not ask anymore until Chang was finished.

"Wasn't Ariadne a woman in mythology?" Tommy asked his sister instead.

"She was the daughter of Minos, who gave Theseus the thread that enabled him to navigate the labyrinth," Clara answered. "Seems quite an appropriate name for someone who weaves words into poems."

"There was never a worse poet than Ariadne Griffiths," Chang muttered. "She is trying to get publishers interested in her work. I recall that much from that terrible evening. If she cannot get a publisher, she will no doubt go down the vanity press route."

"We had a case concerning a poet earlier in the year," Annie remarked. "People were divided on his work, as well. I think that is the way of poetry."

"You are not appreciating what I am saying," Chang insisted. "Ariadne should not be allowed near a pen and ink. She tortures words and creates pieces of literature that are too crude to bear that name. She ought to be shot for her assaults on the English language."

"Do you think perhaps your views on her work are tarnished by this curse business?" Tommy suggested.

"No. I think my views are soundly and carefully developed from spending far too much time in one evening listening to her ramblings. It was the literary equivalent of nails being dragged across a slate."

Clara pulled a face, just imagining that put her teeth on edge.

"Well, whether she is a good poet or not, if you spent time with her then you do have a responsibility," Annie said.

"Did you not hear me? I do not remember spending time with her. If I did, it was while under the influence of something and I should not be held responsible for the consequences," Chang pushed away his plate, the eggs unfinished, the toast untouched.

Annie, whose priority was always to have people eating heartily, looked despondent. Chang dropped his head back into his hands. He felt sick to his belly and his head was spinning. He should not have worked himself up, lately doing so worsened his illness. It was a moment before he realised someone had placed a hand on his arm. It proved to be Annie.

"You need black tea with honey, and then you need to lie down in the spare bedroom. You are clearly not well."

Chang was glad someone had at last recognised this.

"Precisely what have your doctors said about your sickness?" Clara asked him, her face serious.

Chang took a shaky breath.

"They have given no real diagnosis. They say my heart is fine and my symptoms are too vague to point to anything in particular. They advised rest and to abstain from smoking and eating meat."

"What nonsense!" Annie declared fiercely. "The not eating meat part, I mean. Well cooked meat is good for you. It builds up your strength."

"Well, none of the doctors' advice has worked so far, and I have seen enough of them," Chang shrugged. "They seem to have no clue what this could be. I think they are waiting to see if I get worse and then they might have an idea of what is wrong."

"When did the illness start?" Clara asked. "You seem convinced it began after the curse incident with Ariadne, but I wondered if it might have actually shown the first signs before then?"

"Sorry to disappoint you, Clara," Chang shook his head. "This sickness began about a week after Ariadne said she had cursed me. I was fit and hale before then. Then, one morning after the final argument with that woman, I awoke with a headache. I rarely get headaches, so I was a little concerned and wondered if I was coming down with something. I spent the day tormented by chills and a fever, one moment shivering with cold, the next burning hot. I assumed it was a cold. As the days continued, the symptoms became more muted but persistent. Weakness, fatigue, lack of appetite, nausea, aches and pains, dizziness, and sometimes blurred vision. I have heart palpitations and sometimes I feel as if I cannot breath. The headache comes and goes, but that is of little comfort when the rest of my symptoms are still there. I cannot sleep even though I feel always exhausted."

Chang groaned as he finished his recitation. Annie was listening intently.

"That sounds like a curse," she said.

Chang glanced at her.

"You know about curses?"

"My grandmother could cast the Evil Eye," Annie

explained, a hint of pride now in her voice. "All these vague symptoms are classic signs of a curse."

"Or of a number of real illnesses," Clara countered swiftly. "Chang, you should rest as much as you can while we investigate this matter. Annie will make you plenty of nourishing things to restore you back to health, never fear."

Annie wanted to refute the suggestion and explain she could not cure a curse, but Clara had laced her words with such confidence and pride in Annie's abilities that she felt she could hardly deny it. Clara had fully intended such a reaction and the way Annie preened at hearing her talents so well-regarded satisfied Clara that she would start to battle this curse rather than carry on about it.

Chang felt a little happier knowing he had them on his side. For the first time in weeks, he felt as if there was hope and he might not be so alone. He was even tempted to nibble at the toast again.

"We shall need an address for Ariadne," Clara informed him.

Chang nodded and reached into his pocket, withdrawing a black leather notebook, which he flipped open to reveal it was an address book. Some of the names Clara glanced as he thumbed through it for Ariadne's, were prestigious and made her raise her eyebrows. She quite expected to see King George himself listed.

Chang paused on a page and turned the book around to Clara.

"When she began to cause problems I discovered her address," he explained. "As far as I am aware she remains in London. I don't think she would dare go home to her parents in her condition."

"She spent Christmas apart from them?" Annie said, surprised.

"Ariadne is the sort of girl who does not care much

for family," Chang shrugged. "You can resolve this, can't you, Clara?"

"I shall determine the truth," Clara told him. "Whatever that might be."

Chang nodded.

"I shall be satisfied with that," he said morosely.

Chapter Four

Clara and Tommy took the dogs, Pip and Bramble, for a walk after breakfast. The dogs needed the exercise and the siblings needed to clear their heads and think about what best to do concerning Chang.

"Do you suppose he is actually sick?" Tommy said. "Really sick, not just cursed sick."

"I have no idea what cursed sick is," Clara replied. "But if you mean, could it be a real illness and not just something in his head, well, that is a strong possibility. Just because a doctor cannot work out the cause does not mean it is something mystical. Doctors often cannot explain why people are sick."

Tommy nodded. He knew that one well enough. How many doctors had told him his legs were fine and he ought to be able to walk, without offering any explanation for why he could not?

"What do we do for him, then?"

"We head to London and talk to Miss Griffiths first," Clara explained. "She is the key to all this. If nothing else, we might be able to convince her to remove this 'curse' and Chang will be happy again and leave us alone."

"Now who believes in curses?"

"Of course I do not believe in curses," Clara tutted. "But as I have explained before, I do believe in the power of a person's mind to convince them of something preposterous and the consequences of that. Chang believes he is cursed, and it is affecting his health. If Miss Griffiths' removes 'the curse,' metaphorically speaking, I think Chang will get better. He just needs to be convinced one way or another there is no curse haunting him."

"And if Chang is actually ill?"

"That is another matter, and I cannot do anything about that," Clara shrugged.

"What do you make of his story that he was drugged at the party where he met Miss Griffiths?"

"Chang is many things, but he is not generally a liar. I also don't think he would admit to something like that without it being true. It is a clear sign of weakness, after all, that he allowed such a thing to happen to him, and Chang is terrified of showing weakness. That is the real reason he is here. He doesn't want any of his people or rivals to know he thinks he is cursed. He realises how that sounds."

They had reached the park where a number of people were taking a walk in the wintry sunshine – blowing away the cobwebs and getting out of stuffy, crowded homes for a little while. They spied Inspector Park-Coombs walking with his wife, having a rare day off from police work. They waved at him, and he waved back.

"I rang up the train station," Clara continued as they edged around the duck pond, which was frozen along the bank, forcing the ducks to congregate in the centre. Children were attempting to throw them bread and were largely missing. "They have day tickets available for today. We leave at ten."

"Wasting no time then!" Tommy chuckled.

"Do you want Chang in our home for any longer than necessary?"

Tommy considered her words.

"Not really."

Bramble suddenly jerked his lead from Tommy's hand and dived onto the ice of the duck pond, after the birds in the middle. He was mildly surprised to discover he was not in water, but that he was sliding slowly forward. He realised his error and attempted to beat a hasty retreat, which just meant his legs slipped out from under him and he tumbled across the ice and into the water with a splash that sent the ducks flapping into the air.

Children shrieked and laughed. Tommy groaned as Bramble emerged from the water and clung desperately to the edge of the ice. It kept breaking and one paw and then the other would slip into the water.

"Daft dog!" Tommy complained as he went to his aid.

"Tommy, you ought to…" Clara fell silent as Tommy placed a foot on the ice and went straight through.

Fortunately, the duck pond was not deep at the edges, and he only sank to his knee. Grumbling to himself, Tommy marched through the pond, breaking up the ice as he went, and rescued Bramble. He was soaked to his waist by the time he was through, and a lot of people had stopped to watch the escapade.

"You and ducks, Bramble!" Tommy berated the small poodle.

Bramble was looking bedraggled and was shivering dramatically. He gave a sneeze just to make sure everyone was aware he warranted sympathy. Clara was endeavouring not to laugh at her brother as he emerged from the water.

"We best get you home," she said, hiding her smile.

Tommy clicked his tongue at her.

An hour later they were both settled in a train carriage on their way to London. Tommy had dried off sufficiently at home and changed into clean clothes, but he had not managed to get warmth back into his body as yet. He still kept shivering every now and then.

Annie had been beside herself at the sight of him, but he had concocted a story about a child falling into the pond and needing rescuing, which had mollified her somewhat. She had sent Brilliant Chang off to bed with a cup of beef tea and strict instructions to rest. He was not going to be allowed out of her sight and that suited Clara just fine.

They had promised not to be late back from London. Clara had no intention of spending the penultimate day of the year chasing around the streets of the Capital after a poet. She would do her best for Chang, but that was it.

London was sitting under a dull, grey sky. There was no winter sun breaking through the clouds to cheer the residents. People wandered around huddled in coats, hats, and scarves, waiting for whatever the weather cared to throw at them next. There was a hint of snow in the air, but mostly there was the smog which was thickening as Clara and Tommy left the train. With so many fires burning heartily in London to warm the residents, the London smog was almost never gone, and it made everywhere seem murky, as if walking into a thick, dark grey fog.

Clara was reminded of why she did not much care for London in the winter.

They asked for directions to the address they had been given at the station and then hopped onto a bus. Several stops later, they arrived in a nice residential row of houses, each with green gardens set behind tall iron fences. The road itself was wide and carriages clatters along, taking those who lived here to various appointments and engagements. Clara located Ariadne Griffiths' address in the centre of the street and approached the front door.

The property proved to be split into three substantial flats. A smart board nailed to the wall by the door listed the names of those who resided there. There were buttons for each of the flats, so you could ring up the person you wanted. Clara studied the buttons for a moment, then decided it would be better to present herself to Miss Griffiths in person. She tried the front door and found it was unlocked.

In a neat foyer, they could see a door labelled Flat A and which presumably led down to the basement flat. There was another door marked Flat B, but they were interested in Flat C, which was up a flight of stairs.

There was no one around to see them go up, and no one to ask who they were.

Flat C occupied the majority of the first floor. As they reached the landing, they could hear music playing. Tommy tipped his head to listen.

"I know that tune," he said, starting to whistle it.

Clara glared at him to stop.

"No whistling, we had an agreement."

"That was before the war!"

"What has changed?"

Tommy looked deflated.

"Fine."

There was a door to their left and Clara knocked on it, hoping the music would not overwhelm the sound. They waited a while and it seemed likely they had not been heard. Then the record suddenly came to a stop.

Clara glanced at her brother, saying with her eyes to be ready and follow her lead. There was no knowing what a woman who would lead Brilliant Chang to believe he was cursed would be like. As it happened, a man opened the door. He was young and well-groomed, you might not go so far as to say he was handsome, but he had a charm that came from a sense of self-confidence. He studied them.

"Yes?"

"We are looking for Miss Griffiths," Clara said.

"Isn't everyone?" the young man snorted. "Are you something to do with her family?"

Clara was reluctant to say too much about her association with Chang to this gentleman she had only just met. She asked a question instead.

"Do you mean Miss Griffiths is not here? Or do you mean that lots of people have come asking for her lately?"

The young man gave her a bemused look, processed her words, then answered.

"The former, I think. No one has seen Ariadne since Christmas Eve."

"You do not seem terribly worried," Tommy remarked.

"Oh, I never worry about a thing," the young man chuckled. "What a pointless exercise! Besides, I am sure she will turn up eventually. She usually does. Do you want to come in and have some coffee? It is terribly strong stuff, but I rather needed it after one too many late nights this week. The festive season is quite a challenge, is it not?"

The young man did not wait to hear their response but wandered away down a corridor and appeared to assume they would follow. Tommy shrugged his shoulders at Clara, and then entered the flat, closing the door politely behind them. The music had been restarted and they followed the sound to a large living room, decorated with a seemingly random assortment of modern and antique furniture. A very streamlined sofa in black leather was set beside a Victorian armchair, while a modern gramophone was propped open atop an antique table that looked straight out of Jane Austen's day. The gentleman who had invited them in had started to dance to the music, shimmying across a black and white rug and narrowly missing a low table where a coffee pot stood.

"Help yourselves," he waved at the coffee.

Clara was not keen on the dark beverage. It left a harsh aftertaste in her mouth, but Tommy was happy to have a cup. It might help take the chill out of his bones.

"Who, precisely, are you?" Clara asked the dancing young man.

"Roderick Jones," he announced. "Ariadne's cousin. We share this flat together."

"That is somewhat unconventional," Clara added, thinking that many parents would be most alarmed if two single cousins of the respective sexes were flat sharing.

"Darling, we are delightfully unconventional here! It is what makes things so charming!" Roderick grinned. "But if you are wondering if that implies some romantic intrigue between myself and Ariadne, I can assure you, you are barking up the wrong tree."

Roderick crashed down on the sofa as the record stopped playing. He appeared exhausted from his dancing.

"It is the sort of thing people think," Tommy said. "A man and woman living together."

"Ah, but only if they are inclined towards one another in such a way would that be a problem," Roderick grinned.

"And you are not inclined towards…" Tommy was careful with his next question. "You perhaps are not so interested in female company."

"Darling, I love female company!" Roderick rocked with laughter and leaned forward, resting his arms on his knees. "I might be somewhat flamboyant in my demeanour but do not take that to mean anything! No, I was actually referring to Ariadne. You see, my cousin has chosen to abstain from all men. She made a vow when she was sixteen. Considers us ghastly creatures and much prefers to be single."

Clara exchanged a look with Tommy, because this information did not tally with what Chang had told them.

"We have a cousin with similar inclinations," Tommy said, being just as careful with his words. "She prefers to be in the company of her own sex."

"You are referring to Sapphists," Roderick said casually. "We have quite a few in our circle here in London. A number of the ladies in the literary clique are supposed to be of that nature, though I fancy in quite a few cases it is more that they feel it is the fashionable thing to be. Besides, it keeps unnecessary marriage proposals at bay."

"What of your cousin?" Clara asked.

"Oh, I don't think so," Roderick said. "I am not sure she is inclined towards anyone, really. Something of a cold fish is dear Ariadne. But we live here together comfortably."

"If that is the case, then, what about her pregnancy?" Clara said.

This broke the spell over Roderick, and he suddenly paid them close attention.

"Pregnancy?" he parroted.

"Isn't Ariadne pregnant?" Clara said.

Roderick's eyes now widened in astonishment.

"She never told me!" he declared. "Well, I never! I always thought she would spurn intimate associations with a man! I have more than one friend who have offered her their company and been sent packing."

Clara was confused. The way Chang had described things, it had seemed that Miss Griffiths had been several months along in her pregnancy and would have been showing, especially if she was fashion conscious and followed the current styles. They left no room to hide anything. But if that was the case, Roderick ought to have realised, unless he was so utterly oblivious to the world around him, he had not even spotted his cousin was pregnant.

"You do not seem very worried about Ariadne," Tommy remarked to Roderick.

The young man shrugged.

"We are free birds. We come and go as we please. We do not feel the need to tell one another what we are doing or where we are going. We share this house as a stopping point, that is all."

"What if she is in trouble?" Clara said, feeling that even such casual flat mates ought to have some regard for each other and pause when one had gone absent without saying a word.

"I suppose she might be," Roderick said without seeming troubled by the idea.

"Christmas Eve is six days ago," Clara added. "Has she ever been missing for that length of time before?"

"I couldn't tell you," Roderick flashed her another smile. "I really don't take note. She is probably just staying with a friend."

"And what if she is not?" Clara asked him darkly.

Roderick's smile faltered.

Chapter Five

"The plot thickens, as they say," Tommy remarked when Roderick had disappeared to grab a pen and paper at the behest of Clara. She wanted the names and addresses of all of Ariadne's friends in the city. They would begin looking for her among them and if that failed, they would broaden their search. "Do you suppose she meant to disappear?"

"That seems unlikely," Clara replied. "What would be the point when she had Chang on the ropes."

"Maybe one of Chang's associates decided to get rid of her."

"Out of consideration for Chang?" Clara was amused by the idea. "I doubt he has associates who care that much, besides, would you take a chance and get rid of the woman potentially carrying Chang's child when he might suddenly start to feel fatherly? People like Chang are fickle and don't like others making decisions for them."

"Good point. Why take the risk when Chang might change his mind and take to the idea after all," Tommy sighed. "Still leaves us with a peculiar mystery. You realise Ariadne went missing before Chang came to us."

"I had noted that, yes," Clara said, trying not to sound annoyed he had felt the need to point out something so obvious. "Which also implies Chang was genuinely unaware she was missing. He would not have poured his heart out to me otherwise."

"And then there is all this curse business. If Ariadne is gone, the curse ought to be broken."

Clara gave him a look.

"I mean, in Chang's mind," Tommy said hastily. "He ought not to still think himself cursed if the person behind it has vanished."

Roderick was returning with a sheet of paper. It had quite a lot of writing on it.

"I have been as comprehensive as I could," he said passing Clara the sheet. "And this is Ariadne's address book. I stumbled over it when I was looking for paper. Unfortunately, most of the names are just initials, so I only can tell you who a handful are. We had only a few friends in common."

Clara took the address book and flicked it open at random. As Roderick had stated, addresses were listed under unhelpful sets if initials such as M. S. Ariadne would know what they meant, but that did not assist Clara, how was she to know which of these sets of initials referred to a friend or Ariadne's hatmaker?

"Don't suppose you recall anything happening in the days before Christmas Eve, old man?" Tommy asked Roderick. "Perhaps Ariadne seemed upset about something?"

Roderick paused to consider the question.

"We did not exactly talk and bare our souls to one another," he said. "But there might have been something. It would have been a couple of days before Christmas Eve. Ariadne was sitting in this room and had clearly been crying. I asked her what the matter was, as seemed appropriate, she refused to talk about whatever it was, but she did mutter something about men being so unreliable and quick to break their word. I could not say what she was referring to."

Clara would hazard a guess she was referring to Brilliant Chang and his refusal to acknowledge his responsibility towards her.

"Have you ever heard of Brilliant Chang?" she said aloud.

Roderick blinked fast.

"Hasn't everyone who moves in certain circles in London? He is a criminal type, but attractive with it. All the ladies – and some gents – want him at their parties to add some fashionable danger to the event. I have always felt it was prudent to keep my distance from him."

Roderick did not sound entirely convincing, but Clara did not see that as sinister. He had probably spent time in Chang's company and was trying to distance himself now there was trouble in the offing. She changed direction.

"Do you know where Ariadne was on Christmas Eve?"

"I do, as it happens, because we went together. The Bumptons' Christmas party. One of our few mutual acquaintances. I left around ten, as I had other people to call on and wish festive cheer to, but Ariadne was still there when I went and as far as I know, she intended to be there all night."

"We start with the Bumptons, then," Clara nodded.

"I do hope we find her," Roderick said as he showed them towards the front door. "We might be like ships that pass in the night, but I would hate to think something had happened to her."

Roderick frowned, beginning to realise that his failure to note his cousin was missing sooner might have jeopardised her safe recovery. A pang of shame filled him. How could he have failed to notice she was gone?

"One last thing," Clara said. "Take a look around Ariadne's bedroom and see if anything significant is missing. There might be nothing, but if you do discover anything, let me know."

She handed him one of her business cards.

"I have been past her bedroom so many times the last few days. I have to go past it to reach mine," Roderick explained. "Her door is always open, she never fussed about things like that. All her clothes and things are still there, right down to her shoes cast all over the floor."

"That tells us she did not mean to leave," Tommy explained to him. "Take another look, all the same."

Roderick nodded, shame-faced at his failure.

"I hope you find her safe and sound, I really do."

They left him to mope and consider his shortcomings as a cousin and caring flatmate, and stood on the pavement outside the flats, working out how to reach the Bumptons' residence.

"Do you think Ariadne is dead?" Tommy said bluntly.

The thought had been stirring in his mind for a while. People who disappeared suddenly and were not heard from for days were quite often dead. He was somewhat of a pessimist in regard to such cases.

"I prefer to consider her alive," Clara replied. "Since we do not know why she disappeared, we can hardly speculate on the potential consequences of her vanishing."

She had been studying a map of London she had brought with her.

"The Bumptons live only a couple of miles away. Ariadne could easily walk there and back," she now began to lead the way to the Bumptons' home.

Tommy followed quietly for a while, pulling up the

collar of his coat against the cold wind that was bringing a hint of snow to the city. The streets were clear for the time being, a white Christmas had not occurred, but the possibility of a white-out before the end of the year seemed to be growing more and more likely.

"I hope she is not stuck outside in this weather," Tommy remarked, thinking of the cold biting into his bones. "You know, in a shed or outhouse."

"You make Ariadne sound like a cat that has got itself shut in somewhere."

"You know what I mean. If someone has taken her and is holding her against her will, I just hope it is somewhere in the warm and not some dingy outbuilding with nothing to keep her comfortable."

Tommy gave a shudder as he considered this idea more thoroughly. He had spent plenty of time stuck out in the cold during the war, when winter in the trenches was a grim prospect without the spectre of fighting looming over you as well. He sympathised with anyone who found themselves without a warm place to get out of the cold in the winter.

Clara was trying not to think too hard about what might have happened to Ariadne, at least not until she had more facts to consider. Getting caught up in a state of despair over the girl and becoming morose about her condition or whether she was suffering or not was hardly productive. She needed to be clear-headed and to focus on the task at hand.

Tommy continued to make odd comments about the weather and Ariadne's misfortune all the way to the Bumptons. He only fell silent when they were stood on the doorstep of the house, awaiting a response to Clara's sharp knock. Clara glanced at her brother and noted he was looking very worried.

"You are taking this hard," she said to him.

"I have this bad feeling, Clara," Tommy shrugged.

"I can't explain it. It makes me think something awful has befallen Ariadne and her poor unborn child."

"Feelings are just that, feelings," Clara consoled him.

"What about instincts? And hunches? You have those all the time."

"Those are different. They are more like educated guesses," Clara replied, though it was not the best answer. "Until we know more, we cannot think the worst. It will do nothing to assist us. We may find that Ariadne is here at the Bumptons' home, having been struck down by a bad cold so she had to stay over. I doubt she even thought of alerting Roderick to her predicament."

This suggestion brightened Tommy's mood temporarily and he was much more like his usual self when a butler opened the door to them. The servant was the tall, gloomy sort that takes up butlering because they seem built for the part. He had mastered the art of staring down his nose at unexpected guests. Clara could sense the sneer before he even spoke.

"Yes?"

"Clara and Tommy Fitzgerald," Clara declared, giving him no room to comment by talking swiftly. "Here to see the Bumptons."

"You are expected?" the butler asked, clearly implying they were not.

"We have come concerning Ariadne," Clara pressed on, rather hoping the butler would suddenly say something along the lines of – 'at last, someone has come for her!' Instead, he frowned.

"You mean Miss Griffiths," he said. "I shall ask my employers if they care to see you."

The butler shut the door in their faces.

"Cheerful fellow," Tommy remarked.

Clara was disappointed that the butler had not reacted as she had hoped to Ariadne's name. She tried to mask her emotion, to avoid confirming Tommy's 'feelings' or suggesting she was having some of her own.

"Butlers are employed for the express reason they are cheerless and surly," she said to her brother. "I have yet to meet one of any other demeanour. I believe they are taught it all at butlering school."

Tommy snorted with amusement and for just an instant they were distracted from everything. The butler returned to the door and seemed to have an expression of mild surprise on his face.

"Mrs Bumpton asks for you to come to the drawing room," he said, sounding deeply astonished by this turn of events. He had been looking forward to turning the pair away. He cared little for the regular Bumpton guests and even less for those he did not recognise immediately. New nuisances, to his way of thinking. However, the mention of Ariadne's name had had such an effect on his mistress that he had hastened back to the front door to let the Fitzgeralds in.

He showed them to a smart drawing room with blue wallpaper and the sort of antique furniture one has to inherit to own. Mrs Bumpton was a small middle-aged woman, sitting on one of the sofas with a cat perched just beside her. She was wearing a quite ordinary morning dress and had a blanket over her knees, despite a nice fire burning in the hearth grate. She had gone grey young, and her colourless hair meant she seemed older than her years. Her face was still holding onto the smoothness of youth, but she was fast turning that corner from youngish to old. She gazed at them with worried blue eyes.

"I wasn't expecting anyone today," she mumbled, motioning to the blanket over her knees and her humble attire. "I feel the cold dreadfully and I have been rather under the weather over Christmas."

Her hasty explanation seemed a little forced and

Clara realised she was embarrassed to be found in such a state. She was the sort of woman who put a lot of store in her appearance and Clara was sure had it not been for the mention of Ariadne's name, she would have automatically turned them away.

"I apologise for disturbing you like this," Clara began, the butler was eyeing them up still, waiting for instructions.

Mrs Bumpton suddenly realised he was still present and dismissed him.

"I imagine you would not have come to see me if it were not important," Mrs Bumpton said, dry-mouthed. "I do not know either of you."

"Clara and Tommy Fitzgerald," Clara explained. "We are brother and sister, and we work as private detectives."

Mrs Bumpton's face drained of colour and their declaration clearly did not make her feel better.

"You can call me Mindy," Mrs Bumpton said. "Everyone does. Formality is so old-fashioned and cold, don't you think?"

She had rambled to distract herself, but her thoughts all too quickly turned back to what was really on her mind.

"Why are you here about Ariadne?"

There was no easy way to say what she needed to, but Clara had a hunch Mindy Bumpton would not be entirely surprised by the news. She had the appearance of someone who already had their suspicions.

"Ariadne is missing," Clara answered. "We are looking for her."

Mindy Bumpton shut her eyes and let out a shaky breath.

"I knew it," she said, hands clasping tight to the blanket on her lap. "I just knew it. When she failed to come to us for Christmas dinner my heart sank, and I started to fear the worst. Ariadne would never have just ignored us. If she could not come, she would have told us."

Mindy swallowed hard on her emotions.

"How serious is it?" she asked.

Chapter Six

Clara felt it was prudent to limit how much she revealed to Mindy Bumpton about her friend's recent activities – at least until she knew how much Ariadne had already told her. She preferred to have Mindy tell her as much as she knew first without Clara assisting too much. She therefore kept things simple.

"Ariadne does not appear to have returned home Christmas Eve. We have spoken with her cousin, Roderick."

"What a waste of flesh that man is," Mindy tutted at the mention of Roderick. "I don't suppose he had even noticed she was missing."

"No, you are right about that," Clara confirmed. "He is very concerned now he is aware."

"Fine thing that amounts to," Mindy huffed. "You wonder sometimes why certain people were put on this earth. If everything happens for some divine purpose, I would like to know what God was thinking when he created Roderick."

"It is safe to say you have little time for him."

Tommy observed.

"You are quite correct. I am amenable to most people in this world, but not to Roderick. He drives me to distraction. However, I always thought Ariadne was perfectly safe living with him. He showed about as much interest in her as he might in a rock."

Mindy paused, considering the situation further.

"She disappeared on her way home from our party?"

"It appears that way," Clara said. "What time did she leave your home?"

Mindy winced at the question, because by the time Ariadne had been due to leave everyone had been rather tipsy, and time was a relative concept.

"I suppose it was some time after midnight," she said. "Probably around three in the morning. I know I crawled into bed around half three and Ariadne had left not long before that. We expected her back at two o'clock for Christmas Day dinner. I was concerned and did try ringing her flat, but I received no answer."

"Did she walk home with anyone?" Clara asked. "Or perhaps she hailed a hansom cab?"

"For such a short walk?" Mindy was bemused by the suggestion. "No, Ariadne always walked and seeing as she was the last of my guests to leave, she walked home alone."

"Three in the morning is not the nicest time to be wandering around London by yourself," Tommy remarked.

"Oh, these streets are very safe, and Ariadne did not have far to go to. You must have noted how close our address is to her flat?"

Mindy waved off his concerns. Tommy glanced at his sister. However safe you might suppose your local streets to be, there was always the possibility of someone with evil intent lurking about it. It would seem that was precisely what had occurred to Ariadne. For all they knew, she could have been abducted by a lunatic who had dispatched her and hidden her body. This might have nothing to do with her associations with Brilliant Chang.

"How was Ariadne that night?" Clara asked, knowing that pestering Mindy about whether it was wise to allow her young guest to walk home alone late at night was not going to achieve anything.

"She was…" Mindy hesitated. "I suppose she was distracted. She had a lot on her mind."

Clara waited to see if she would elaborate upon that. Mindy glanced between them, not sure what to say.

"Look, who are you two? I have never met you before and if you want me to speak freely to you about Ariadne, I think I ought to know just how you are connected with her."

It was a fair question.

"We are private detectives, hired to discover what has occurred to Ariadne by a concerned party," Clara said, adapting the truth to suit the situation.

"Who might this 'concerned party' be?" Mindy asked cautiously.

"I am not able to reveal who I am working for. It would invade my client's privacy. Suffice it to say they are most concerned for Ariadne's wellbeing."

Well, Brilliant Chang was certainly that, but perhaps not in the way the statement implied. Clara fancied that he would be quite relieved if Ariadne turned up dead by coincidence.

"I cannot think who that might be," Mindy said. "But, seeing as no one else appears interested in her disappearance. I suppose you will have to do. At least you are bothering to talk to me about it. I tried to inform the police of my anxieties for Ariadne, after I could not get in touch with her, but they responded that as none of her close family – meaning Roderick – had reported her missing, they could do nothing. My concerns as a friend were not heeded."

"I am sorry to hear that," Clara said, thinking that Inspector Park-Coombs would not be so careless.

"I imagine they could simply not be bothered about it, what with it being Christmas and all. I suppose they assume she was just another partygoer who had drunk too much and gotten lost, and will turn up soon enough," Mindy looked defeated.

"Did you not try to contact Roderick when Ariadne could not be reached?" Tommy said.

"Have you tried contacting him? The man is barely ever home and when he is the odds of him answering either his telephone or doorbell are slim. You have met him, I take it?"

"We went to his flat first," Clara explained, before adding. "He is not our client."

"I hardly imagined he would be," Mindy raised an eyebrow at the notion. "He is not the sort to consider hiring private detectives. In any case, you already mentioned he had failed to appreciate his cousin's absence."

"I just thought it would be best to be clear," Clara replied.

"Well, all I can say is you were lucky he saw you. Perhaps he just has a sixth sense for when I try to ring him or summon him to his front door. I have attempted to reach him concerning Ariadne, naturally, but my efforts have been in vain. I doubt he spent much of the Christmas week in his own flat, anyway."

Mindy became solemn, feeling a sense of failure that her own endeavours to find Ariadne had been so wanting. She had not put the energy into looking for her that she should have. She had been worried, yes, but there had been the Christmas Day dinner to distract her attention, followed by an evening drinks party and then on Boxing Day they had gone to her husband's family for a meal. She had spent the next day recovering from it all, and the next few days catching up with old friends who were in the city for the festivities. She had been so busy that Ariadne had rather slipped her mind at times. Mindy felt this said very little for their friendship.

"Now we have explained our role in this search for your friend, perhaps we could go back to the night she vanished?" Clara dragged her from her doldrums. "You seemed about to elaborate on how she was behaving on Christmas Eve?"

Mindy pulled her thoughts together.

"What I was going to say was I wondered if you were aware of her situation?"

"Do you mean her pregnancy?" Clara asked.

Mindy blinked and cleared her throat.

"Unfortunately, yes, I do mean that. I see you are well informed."

"Roderick was not aware his cousin was pregnant," Clara added.

Mindy looked up to her ceiling in exasperation and seemed to be casting a glance at God for creating such a hopeless human being.

"Roderick is oblivious to most things in life," she sighed. "Ariadne was most certainly pregnant. She was showing for anyone who had the eyes to look."

"Had she discussed her baby with you?" Clara asked.

"I had attempted to broach the topic," Mindy explained. "Ariadne was cagey about it. I had not thought her the sort of girl to get herself in trouble, and that combined with her reluctance to talk made me wonder if the situation had been somewhat against her will."

"You wondered if she had been raped?" Clara was blunt because hedging about such topics was good for no one. There was too much quiet conspiracy about such things, which made them taboo to discuss and thus aided the culprit while causing more suffering for the victim.

"I did," Mindy said at last. "Ariadne was not a girl to cast herself at every man she saw. Some of the women and girls in my social circles I would quite expect to turn up pregnant, but not Ariadne."

"She had not mentioned any male friend she had been spending time with?" Tommy asked.

Mindy shook her head.

"You must understand that Ariadne was not attracted to passion in that regard. She was absorbed in her work and nothing else much mattered. I had endeavoured to encourage her with certain male acquaintances I thought would be a good match. But she just seemed to bore them all."

"She must have mentioned something about the pregnancy," Clara pressed her. "Such a thing is impossible to keep utterly secret from a close friend."

"And yet, that is what she did," Mindy responded. "Ariadne is very good at silence. If she does not care to discuss a given topic, she simply will not."

"Let's go back to Christmas Eve," Clara said, seeing the pregnancy was something of a dead end. "You mentioned she seemed distracted?"

"Yes, she did not care to join in with the games I had arranged, and she was more aloof than usual. You have to understand, Ariadne is not precisely the life of a party, but she would normally involve herself to a degree," Mindy explained. "That night she seemed to want to remain apart from everyone. I felt there was a shadow hanging over her. I should have asked her more, I should have insisted she speak to me, but how could I?"

"It is not your fault," Clara assured her. "If Ariadne did not want to talk about it, you could not have made her."

"When she left to go home, you had no concerns for her apart from her seeming a little more quiet than usual?" Tommy asked.

"I had no reason to suppose there was anything much the matter," Mindy said. "I certainly did not suppose she would disappear."

Mindy paused. She had had a lot of time to think about what could have occurred to her friend, usually in the dark, early hours when she found herself lying in bed unable to sleep. Some of those thoughts had been so disturbing she had barely dared to consider them.

"It has crossed my mind since that she might have..." Mindy gulped, and tears brimmed in her eyes. "Women who find themselves inconvenienced in such a way as Ariadne did, sometimes do irrational things. Perhaps I misread her that night and she went away to... to..."

The words failed her, and she hung her head. If she did not speak her fears, then perhaps they would remain unfounded.

"Did Ariadne strike you as someone who might choose suicide as a way out of her problems?" Clara finished the thought Mindy had hardly dared to allow into her mind.

"I don't know anymore. If you had asked me before Christmas Eve, I should have said no, never. She had so much to live for. I perhaps have painted her as somewhat dull and lifeless, but that was not my intention. Ariadne had drive and passion, just not for the things we usually think of when discussing such topics. She might not have had a lot of interest in romance or parties, but when it came to her poetry, she was something else," Mindy became wistful at the memory. "She came alive when we discussed her work, or when there was a literary or artistic engagement ahead of us. Then she was vital and magical. When you saw her like that, well, you would never think she could consider death as a solution to her woes."

"You have spoken about her a lot in the past tense,"

Tommy pointed out. "You have already given up on her being found alive."

"No!" Mindy declared, but his statement had hit home. She cringed. "Yes. Yes, I have already given up on her. Isn't that terrible? But no word has reached us, no demands from a kidnapper or a message to say where she is if she had just decided to escape the world a while. I do not know what else to think."

"We are going to do everything in our power to find her," Clara said, realising she was speaking the truth.

Brilliant Chang had not asked her to locate Ariadne, he had wanted them to find a way out of his curse and his commitments, but it seemed important now that someone made the effort to determine what had happened to the woman, and Clara would gladly do that while Chang was footing her bills.

"One last thing, do you know a man named Brilliant Chang?"

"That is rather like asking me if I know who the King is," Mindy snorted. "Of course I know Brilliant Chang. He has been to my home more than once."

"He is a dangerous criminal," Tommy pointed out, still amazed at the way Chang had inserted himself into certain respectable circles.

"I always found him most gentlemanly," Mindy replied. "He was much more pleasant company than some of the English nobility I have had the misfortune to entertain."

"Did he associate with Ariadne?" Clara asked.

Mindy narrowed her eyes. She was not stupid, and she saw that Clara was suggesting a connection between her two guests.

"I do not recall him spending time with Ariadne in particular," she said. "Do you think he is responsible for her disappearance?"

"No," Clara said firmly because that was one thing she was sure of. "I am just working out who to speak to next."

"I cannot see Brilliant Chang having anything of use to tell you," Mindy declared. "I doubt he exchanged more than a handful of words with Ariadne. As delightful a man as he is, he is not inclined towards poetry. More is the pity, for he has the sort of money that could arrange for a private print run of Ariadne's work. She has been turned down by so many publishers and cannot justify footing the cost herself for such a thing. Her parents are skinflints when it comes to her allowance. She has to be constantly careful."

"Was there anyone who Ariadne might have confided her problems to?" Clara asked.

"Other than me?"

Mindy looked hurt at the suggestion.

"People sometimes do not want to confide in their closest friends because they fear they might lose their friendship as a result of their confession," Clara hastened to add. "Sometimes people feel better able to confide in someone impartial."

Mindy was not impressed, but she did allow the thought to take hold and to consider it. Finally, she spoke.

"I can only think of one person. I do not care for him myself."

Chapter Seven

Annie took another cup of tea up to Brilliant Chang. He might be her least favourite house guest, but she would be damned if she would allow his health to dwindle on her watch. Curse or no curse, she was certain she could find a cure.

Chang had proven a surprisingly amenable patient. He had not stirred from the bed once he had been settled into it and had made no murmurs about the cups of tea and bowls of soup and stew Annie regularly brought him. He simply consumed them, though not with great vigour and he genuinely seemed to be suffering from a lack of appetite.

For Annie, this was a sure sign he was very unwell. In her opinion, the loss of appetite in a person was likely a symptom of something terminal and she would do all in her power to restore Chang's desire to eat in an effort to save his life.

Aside from slowly eating or drinking whatever she brought to him, Chang spent most of his time lying back on the pillows and looking out the window to his right. Annie had met Chang only briefly on the various occasions he had crossed swords with Clara. On each of those times he had seemed energetic and driven, not this depressed, quiet man who seemed uninterested in anything.

"More tea," she informed him as she put the cup beside him. "I brought some biscuits with it this time too. They are homemade. I rarely buy biscuits from a shop, except for those terrible Garibaldi biscuits which are a particular favourite of Tommy's."

Annie was finding Chang's silent acceptance of the situation somewhat irritating. She wanted to talk to him, even if it was just an argument over her tea making skills. Only then would she feel he had not completely given up on life. As it was, he seemed to be considering death as a reasonable prospect and was preparing himself for it.

"Squashed fly biscuits we used to call them as children," she added.

Chang had not turned his head away from the window, he was effectively looking away from her and she was not sure he even cared she was there. Annie was not going to stand for such nonsense. If there was one thing she was good at, it was getting a reaction from people. They might not appreciate her efforts, but if it jerked them out of their doldrums, all to the good.

She sat down firmly on the end of the bed, rocking it slightly, which caused Chang to twitch his lip in annoyance. It was a promising start, Annie considered.

"You are just going to lay there and mope?" she asked him.

Chang reluctantly glanced her way and replied.

"What else is there to do?"

"Get on with things, that is what there is to do," Annie told him. "The trouble with men, especially men who have people doing things for them all the time, is they get locked up into their own heads. When you have floors to mop and shelves to dust, and chickens to feed, you cannot mope."

Chang made a low noise under his breath. It was somewhat like a growl.

"It might not make you feel any better, cleaning and cooking and doing all the chores necessary to keep life moving, but it gets you out of your head and at least you are not lying in a bed waiting to die."

"You were the one who insisted I go to bed," Chang reminded her.

"I never meant for you to end up like this," Annie waved a hand at him. "I thought you would rest a while and then be back ready to resolve this problem. Instead, you have given up."

"Maybe it is time I gave up," Chang said softly.

Annie poked his knee beneath the blankets. Chang jumped in surprise.

"Ow!"

"None of that! No one gives up in my presence."

"You have sharp fingers!"

Annie shrugged her shoulders at him.

"Why do you even care whether I have given up or not?" Chang demanded of her. "We are not friends. You can barely stand my presence."

"That is not the point," Annie answered. "Clara left me in charge, and I will not allow you to die under my care. I shall have you cured, curse or no curse."

"Precisely how do you intend to achieve that?" Chang asked cynically.

"Sheer determination and persistence," Annie answered him, daring him to challenge her words. "I am going to begin by having a doctor come and give you a full check over."

"I already told you…"

"Your doctors saw you, I know. But all doctors are not equal and maybe they were reluctant to tell you the truth."

"They preferred to tell me they had no idea what was wrong?" Chang barked.

"Maybe, if the truth was not something you would care to hear."

Chang grumbled to himself and turned his head away.

"I am going to ask over Dr Cutt. He is a very reliable doctor. I trust his opinion, but if he cannot say what is wrong, well, I have other plans in mind."

"I dread to think," Chang puttered. "Will it involve more of that ghastly beef tea you tried to force down me."

"Beef tea is restorative, and everyone knows that things that are good for you never taste nice," Annie said sternly. "You are under my care now Chang. You opted to be, after all, and so you must lump it."

"I came to Clara for help," Chang sneered.

"And you supposed I would not interfere once the situation was explained to me?" Annie raised an eyebrow at him. "You knew full well by coming to our house you placed yourself in all our hands."

Chang, who had known such a thing would occur and reluctantly recalled a recent moment in time when he had welcomed the idea of being under Annie's attentive care, kept his mouth shut.

"We are all in this together," Annie said stoically. "Whether we like it or not, of course."

Chang quietly groaned to himself.

"Are you leaving me alone now?" he asked.

Annie remained rooted to his bed, her mind elsewhere.

"Why would it be so terrible if you were to be a father?" she asked abruptly. "That is the thing I have been trying to get my head around since you arrived here. All you had to do was acknowledge the woman and agree to support her – which is not any skin off your nose with the fortune you have accrued – and this matter would be resolved."

"I am not adverse to being a father," Chang retorted in a low voice. "I am adverse to being used."

"You say you had nothing to do with this woman, or at least you do not remember having anything to do with her, and yet the evidence seems clear."

"Evidence? That she is pregnant?" Chang snorted. "Who knows who fathered that irksome bump. It could have been anyone and she thinks I shall pay for her mistake, just because I found myself in the same room as her one time. If the child was genuinely mine, I would respect my responsibilities."

"Surely, considering your lifestyle, this situation has cropped up before?" Annie elaborated.

"My lifestyle?"

There was a grin on Chang's face now.

"Precisely, what do you think my lifestyle is, Annie?"

Annie cleared her throat nervously; she was crossing into territory she was far from familiar with.

"Well, I was assuming... how I imagined things...," Annie glared sternly at the wardrobe opposite her in the room as if it was personally responsible for the situation she found herself suddenly in. "What I am trying to say is that I imagined you to have had many women in your life."

"In what way?" Chang pushed her. "I have met many women at dinner and luncheon, at various garden parties and gala events. I do not believe merely sitting beside me would result in pregnancy, though I have heard such rumours."

Annie huffed, disliking being teased by the crook, though secretly pleased he had brightened up and was paying enough attention to want to torment her.

"I was referring to other sorts of encounters. Private ones."

"I do occasionally having meetings alone with

women in regard to business arrangements. I find women can be very reliable business partners, under the right circumstances, but again, sitting opposite me at a desk seems hardly likely…"

"Brilliant Chang, stop being obtuse! You know perfectly well what I mean!"

"Do I?" Chang smiled, enjoying seeing Annie so infuriated.

"I refer to encounters with ladies in the bedroom department."

"I don't recall ever meeting with a lady in the bedroom section of a department store," Chang feigned misunderstanding. "I do frequent Harrods a lot, but that particular department has never interested me."

"For heaven's sake!" Annie gasped. "I mean women you have slept with, Chang, and I shall not be made to say anything cruder than that, so you can stop with your mischief!"

Chang was satisfied. Behind her angry expression, so was Annie. Chang was no longer the forlorn, depressed patient she had been pandering to all morning.

"I knew you had a low opinion of me, in my regards to female relations," Chang acted hurt.

"I have a low opinion of you because you operate as a criminal," Annie shrugged. "It was hardly made lower by considering you also to be a man with certain interests. I might not care to talk about such things, but I am not naïve. I know that men who do not have wives, do not necessarily live celibate lives. It is the consequences of those situations that is troubling. The child brought into this world through a casual act of passion."

"Such disregard," Chang tutted under his breath. "I shall try not to be terribly hurt."

"Are you saying you are not a man inclined towards

women?" Annie decided to take a jab herself.

Chang startled at her saying such a thing. He had not considered Annie so aware of the intricacies of the world, he was also annoyed.

"No, Annie, I am not inclined into perverse habits, though I know men who are. I prefer to avoid their company."

Annie tilted her head playfully.

"I have never been worried by such men. It seems to me that nature has a curious need for diversity. If you were such a man…"

"That is enough," Chang said, stabbed enough by the comments and now being stirred to anger. "You want to know if the possibility of a child of my own making has ever cropped up before, and the simple answer is, no. I have always been very careful. Yes, I have certain female friends who have spent considerable time in my private company, but we take precautions. Besides, I make a point of only associating with married ladies who, if something occurred, would be suitably taken care of."

"That is somewhat cynical."

"Yet, terribly practical. There may be some well-to-do heirs running around with Chinese blood in their veins, but I have never been told of them and no irate husband has ever come knocking on my door."

They both knew the odds of any sane man crashing into Chang's world because he questioned the origins of one of his children was extremely slim.

"You perhaps understand now why this situation with Ariadne is so… strange. She is not even the sort of woman I am attracted to."

"You really remember nothing about it?" Annie asked, trying to imagine having no memory of an event someone said she had been involved in. It was hard to conjure up the notion.

"Nothing, as I explained to Clara. Of course, I have

tried to pull a memory from the depths of my mind, but nothing stirs. I should add, Annie, that I have never before been in the situation to have lost my memory of events either. In my line of work, that would be particularly dangerous."

Annie could see his point. Chang endeavoured to control every aspect of his life in an effort to keep himself safe. Such a man did not take the risk of losing his memories due to excessive drinking or deliberate indulgence in drugs.

"Someone did this to me," Chang concluded for her. "I do not know if there was any real intimacy with Ariadne, but if it occurred it was while I was under the influence of something and thus, I cannot be held responsible for my actions."

"It is a peculiar situation, to suggest a man was forced against his will by a woman," Annie mused.

"If that is what occurred," Chang looked aggrieved at the thought he had allowed his guard down and made himself so vulnerable that night so many months ago. He did not like being a victim, it dented his ego.

"Whatever happened, we are left with this curse business," Annie moved the subject along. "But I am certain that is fixable. I know some women who dabble in the old traditions and could advise us."

"Witches, Annie?"

"You may call them that if you must, but they prefer to consider themselves holders of the old ways. Wise women, so to speak. Sometimes the modern world does not have all the answers."

"I suppose," Chang smiled. "We Chinese have quite a bit of magic and tradition in our heritage. I did consider consulting a Chinese medicine man, but I was not sure Chinese magic would mix with English curses."

Annie was not sure if he was teasing her again. She decided not to rise to the bait, if that was what it was.

"We shall begin with Dr Cutt, who can determine what physical causes might be ailing you and how to treat them. That is the logical thing to do, and Clara would want us to go down that route first. However, it will not hurt to do a bit of traditional stuff to ward off any malign influences. If only it were summer, I should have plenty of sage in the garden, instead I shall have to raid my dry supplies and hope there is enough to burn."

"Burn?" Chang asked a touch nervously.

"Burning sage is a sure way to ward off evil influences, and to cleanse a house, oh and to keep ghosts at bay," Annie replied. "It will do no harm to try, will it?"

"I suppose not," Chang said, starting to wonder at what he might have to endure to relieve himself of his curse. "Are you sure about this?"

"Positive," Annie promised him. "My mother and granny used to do it all the time."

"Were they much plagued by evil influences and ghosts?"

"No, because it worked," Annie rose and stared at the undrunk cup of tea, now cold. "I best make you another one."

She was at the door when Chang spoke softly and caught her attention. She turned.

"I would not mind being a father," he said. "To answer your previous question. It would not be so bad, at all."

Chapter Eight

The person Mindy Bumpton did not care for was named Alfie Gloucester. She muttered something about the possibility he ought to be 'Sir' Alfie Gloucester, but she was not sure if his father had died yet and passed on the title. Her disregard for the Gloucester family was plain. Clara had been tempted to ask what had caused it, but she sensed a deep, long-standing feud with a complicated back story that she simply did not have the time to listen to.

Mindy had not been terribly forthcoming about Ariadne's friendship with the man, either. She muttered something about them moving in the same literary circles and that was it. She did however say that if there was anyone who might have been willing to hide Ariadne away from everyone, it was most likely Alfie.

The address she gave them was several roads away and after assessing the distance, Clara determined they would need to catch a bus or hail a cab to get them there within a reasonable time.

"I am beginning to think we may need to spend

longer in London," Clara remarked to her brother. "This matter is going to take a while to figure out."

"We could just report back to Chang that Ariadne has disappeared and that might satisfy him," Tommy suggested.

"Chang is not so easily appeased," Clara replied. "And I don't think I can let things be. Not without knowing Ariadne is safe and sound."

"No, I thought you would say that," Tommy smiled at her. "I should add I completely agree. I just thought I should make the suggestion."

"At least it is not too tiresome to travel back and forth to Brighton and keep everyone updated," Clara sighed. "I wonder if train tickets would be cheaper than a hotel?"

Mulling over the question of arrangements for an extended stay in London, they finally hailed a hansom and were escorted to the salubrious surroundings of Piccadilly Gardens, one of the older areas of London and home to more than one lord and lady.

Deposited outside Alfie Gloucester's home, they found themselves looking at a pair of stately gates, leading into a large garden still coated in the morning's frost. Beyond was a mansion in the Georgian style. There was no better way to describe it. The number of windows defied counting, and it was anyone's guess how many rooms were within. It made Mindy Bumpton's own home, though substantial, seem small. Perhaps that was part of the reason she could not stand Alfie Gloucester.

The gates were unlocked, and they let themselves through, seeing no one as they made their way along a gravel drive towards the house. Tommy pointed to one of the large downstairs windows, which must have been eight feet tall and stretched nearly down to the ground. There was a substantial Christmas tree visible through it, decorated in cream-coloured ornaments.

"Never seen one so big in a private home before," he said. "Even the Bumptons only had a small six-foot tree in the drawing room."

There was also an ornate wreath on the front door, with matching shades of ribbon.

"I think it is safe to say Mr Gloucester likes Christmas," Clara said as she lifted the knocker and rapped on the front door.

They were greeted by a butler, though not of the surly kind that the Bumptons employed. He actually smiled at them.

"Good morning. How may I assist you?"

"Is Sir Gloucester in?" Clara said, deciding it was prudent to add the title just in case.

"Are you referring to Master Alfred or his father?" the butler politely enquired.

"Alfred," Clara confirmed. "We were told he was Sir Gloucester these days."

"Not as yet," the butler said, still with that helpful smile on his face. "His father continues to thrive, and long may it last. Master Alfie has not arisen from bed as yet, but I shall see if he is inclined towards visitors. Who shall I say is calling?"

"Please could you state we are Clara and Tommy Fitzgerald, sent to make enquiries concerning Ariadne Griffiths who has not been seen since Christmas Eve. You understand the urgency of all that?"

"I do indeed," the butler nodded, his smile fading to a look of concern. "Miss Griffiths visits quite often. I do hope she is all right. I shall inform my master at once."

The butler showed them through to the drawing room, which proved to be the room with the vast Christmas tree in the window. It was not the only sign of the festive spirit in the room, there were garlands along the mantelpiece of the fireplace, and upon the tops of the windows. Two large wooden nutcrackers, painted in vivid hues, stood guard either side of the fireplace.

Clara had already noted garlands wrapped around the banister of the staircase as they entered the hall, and a large display of winter flowers upon a central table. She had no doubt that the rest of the public rooms in the house were decorated in a similar fashion.

Tommy headed towards the Christmas tree, enamoured with its size and glory.

"Quite a change to have a butler who is jovial," he remarked as he studied the tree, wondering if the glittering ornaments were truly made of silver and gold. He had a suspicion they were.

"I suppose there must be some who break the mould," Clara replied.

She glanced around the room thoughtfully.

"I rather fancy Mr Gloucester is of a similar ilk. I cannot think many bachelors would take this amount of effort to decorate for Christmas. Alfie Gloucester must be a gentleman of big heart."

"My dear, what a delightful comment!"

Clara and Tommy both spun around at the sound of the voice and saw a gentleman stood in the door of the drawing room. He was mid-thirties, somewhat thin but with a gracefulness to his slender form that avoided him seeming spindly. He wore a long green silk dressing gown, beautifully embroidered with designs that seemed to emulate peacock feathers. He smiled at them broadly.

"Do you like my tree?"

"I do," Tommy declared. "It is something else."

"I feel if one must celebrate Christmas, one must do so in style," Alfie Gloucester nodded.

"You are not keen on Christmas?" Clara asked in surprise.

"It is not a season that greatly appeals to me, no," Alfie admitted. "It is time to consider family responsibilities, which is always a bore, and yet another family dinner will come around where my father will demand to know when I am to marry, and I shall make inadequate excuses followed by a grim argument that we will both fume over for the next twelve months. No, I am not keen on the season, but I do rather like the jolliness of the decorations, and they cheer me up no end. A compensation, I fancy."

Gloucester wandered into the room and deposited himself on a sofa. His smile had gone, and a serious expression had come over his face.

"My butler said you are concerned about Ariadne?" he frowned. "I was not aware she was missing."

"We came to London to speak to her," Clara explained, sitting on the sofa opposite him. "That was when we discovered she has not been seen by her cousin since Christmas Eve. As far as we are aware, none of her friends have seen her since then."

"Roderick," Alfie groaned. "A man oblivious to life in general. I am not surprised he failed to notice Ariadne's absence. I doubt he has been sober much this last week."

"No one seems to have a high opinion of Roderick," Tommy remarked, heading back over from the tree. "Then again, we have only really spoken to Mrs Bumpton."

"Ah, there is a woman whose high opinion is rarely bestowed on anyone," Gloucester said. "I suppose she had a sour look on her face when she mentioned my name?"

"She did murmur something along the lines that you two do not get along," Clara shrugged, feeling there was no point in being dishonest. "She also said you were close to Ariadne."

"She is correct on both points," Alfie agreed. "When it comes to our personal association, Mindy and I simply clash too much. It is a personality issue, nothing more. She finds me flamboyant, decadent and, she might say, a little too big for my boots. I find her annoyingly narrow-minded and prone to judging her associates by their marital status. She finds it most vexing that she has failed to marry me off to one of her friends as yet.

"In contrast, Ariadne and I are souls of a kindred spirit. We share the same literary tastes and an inkling for poetry, though in that regard I am woefully lazy, while she is wonderfully productive. I am acting as editor for her book. She values my input, and I am prepared to tell her when something is not quite right. Unlike her fawning friends such as Mindy Bumpton who will only ever say her work is perfect. No artist can improve when they are not offered constructive criticism."

"When did you last see Ariadne?" Clara asked.

"Christmas Eve, in the afternoon," Gloucester said. "We had afternoon tea together. I was not invited to the evening at the Bumptons' home, which suited me fine as I had to catch the train and head to the family estate in Shropshire to endure Christmas with my family."

"How long were you away?" Clara asked.

"I suffered until Boxing Day and then spirited myself back home. It was utterly unbearable, but what can one do?"

"We wondered if Ariadne might have come to you on Christmas Eve, or rather, the early hours of Christmas Day."

"She would have found the house empty," Gloucester shook his head. "I sent the servants off to their own homes for Christmas. They appreciate the time with their families. Do you have reason to think she came here seeking me?"

Gloucester looked distressed at the thought Ariadne might have come to his home for help only to find he was gone.

"It was just a thought," Clara said. "But she would have known you would be away."

"Yes," Gloucester said. "Yes, she did know. It was why we met for afternoon tea. She wished me a safe trip and I wished her a happy Christmas."

The reality of the situation was starting to sink into Gloucester. Until that moment, he had not really had a chance to consider Ariadne as missing. It had washed over him and failed to hit home. Now he was contemplating all the possible reasons for her disappearance and his stomach sank.

"Ariadne has never simply disappeared before," he said. "Do you think she has been hurt?"

"It is not an easy one to judge," Tommy said. He was leaning on the back of the sofa Clara had settled herself on. "She may have vanished on purpose. We understand she was under some trying circumstances."

"That is a very polite way of inferring she was up the duff," Gloucester remarked. "Mindy told you?"

"We knew before then," Clara replied. "It was the reason we came down to London to see her. The gentleman who she claims is the father is concerned about the validity of the accusation."

"He thinks she is lying?" Gloucester said in horror. "The fiend! Ariadne is not a liar!"

"Do you know who she said was the father of her child?" Tommy asked him.

Gloucester had been about to work himself up into righteous fury, now he deflated.

"No," he admitted. "She would not tell me and that was in itself quite troubling. We had no secrets, and I should have thought she would have confided in me."

"Mindy Bumpton is equally in the dark," Tommy added. "Roderick had not even noticed."

"That hardly surprises me. I doubt Roderick would notice his hand before his face, unless it slapped him,"

Gloucester groaned. "I was hurt she would not tell me. I thought, of anyone, I would be the person she would tell who the father was. Apparently, I was mistaken. The secret was very important to her, that I can tell you."

"This strange mystery becomes more and more peculiar," Clara sighed. "Ariadne's disappearance seems to have no logic."

"Are you sure the man who she claims is the father is not behind her vanishing?" Gloucester asked urgently. "Maybe he was desperate to avoid the scandal?"

"He would not have hired us to look into the truth of the matter if that was the case," Clara pointed out. "Besides, there is much more to this story than meets the eye. I am becoming concerned Ariadne was caught up in something she should not have been and had no way out."

"Except to disappear?" Gloucester finished the sentence, though Clara had not precisely meant that. "Ariadne seemed tired and depressed lately. I thought it was logical under the circumstances. She had not mentioned anything to her parents and was determined to avoid going home for Christmas. If she was in such trouble, she could have confided in me!"

"Do not beat yourself up about it, old man," Tommy said. "She must have felt it was impossible to tell you."

"Would she have thrown herself into the Thames?" Gloucester asked the question of himself rather than anyone else. "No, no, she would never do that."

"Is there anything else you could tell us about Ariadne that might be useful?" Clara said. "I know it is rather asking a lot, but if you recall any upset Ariadne had had recently or some concern, it could be helpful."

Gloucester was too lost in his own thoughts to know what to say. He shook his head.

"I am sorry, nothing springs to mind."

"What about places she might go to hide from everyone? Maybe a distant relative or friend?" Tommy asked.

"I rather fancy I am that 'friend'," Gloucester said. "I am somewhat aloof from the world, and she could have hidden here in safety. I don't know of anyone else who the same could be said about. I feel rather useless about it all. Maybe, if I had been here…"

"It is not your fault," Clara reassured him.

"What will you do now?" Gloucester asked her.

"Retrace Ariadne's steps," Clara replied. "It is all we can do. Maybe we shall find some clue along the way as to what happened."

"This is very bad, isn't it?" Gloucester said. "That we have had no word, no mention… it is a bad sign."

Clara did not know what she could say to make things better. It was a bad sign that no word had come about Ariadne, but what use was there in fretting about that?

Chapter Nine

Gloucester was not prepared to leave the matter of Ariadne's disappearance in the hands of Clara and Tommy alone. He wanted to be involved. He felt a weight of guilt that he had not been there for Ariadne when she needed him, even though he could not have known that something was going to happen. He was constantly going over in his mind the last few weeks. Had there been a sign of something serious afoot? Perhaps he should have pressed Ariadne harder on the matter of her mysterious pregnancy?

In any case, he refused to be left out of the investigation and insisted he must accompany the Fitzgeralds. Though Clara was reluctant for the interference of Gloucester, she was swayed by the fact Gloucester owned a car (two, in fact, both just a year old) and could therefore supply them with effective free transport. Hiring hansom cabs or catching buses, was not only inconvenient but costly and so the promise of a car was very welcome.

There seemed no real harm in allowing Gloucester

to accompany them, anyway.

In a short time, they were back outside the Bumptons' home and beginning the task of retracing Ariadne's last steps.

Gloucester grimaced at the sight of the house.

"Things really that bad between you and the Bumptons?" Tommy asked at the sight of his expression.

"Enough that I would deeply prefer not to encounter her," Gloucester replied. "It is strange sometimes the enemies we make without even trying. I have never aimed to be awkward or disagreeable to the woman, yet she considers me a terrible example of manhood."

"I think that says more about Mrs Bumpton than it does you," Tommy replied.

"Perhaps, but it still makes life complicated when we are both friends with Ariadne."

The mention of Ariadne's name brought Gloucester back to the reality of the situation with a bump. Clara had moved off ahead of them and was already looking for clues about Ariadne's disappearance. Gloucester and Tommy hastened to catch up.

"It is a ten-minute walk from the Bumptons' residence to Ariadne's flat," Clara said, thinking of their brisk stroll earlier that morning. "However, Ariadne was pregnant and perhaps worse for wear after the party. The walk could have taken her considerably longer."

They walked up the street, grand house after grand house passing by them on their left.

"Plenty of basement areas for someone to hide in," Tommy remarked, poking his head over a set of iron railings, and looking down into one of the gloomy excavated pits that created a small courtyard for the basement level of the houses. It was below street level and reached by a short staircase.

Such areas were full of shadows at the best of times, but in the early hours of the morning they would be a perfect place for someone to lurk unseen.

"The flaw in your logic is the time," Clara said to her brother. "It was the early hours of Christmas morning, perhaps one of the toughest days of the year for servants. The staff would have been up early preparing Christmas breakfast, to be swiftly followed by organising the Christmas feast. With so much to do, they would have been out of their beds much sooner than normal and the kitchens of these houses look directly into the area."

Clara pointed down as they went past another area. As it happened, there was a scullery maid working at the sink right before the basement window.

"Even if no one was looking out at just that moment, the sound of a scuffle, perhaps a scream, would have alerted them. No assailant would place himself in such a risky, easily observable position."

"I had not considered that," Tommy confessed.

"Annie is always telling me how much work it takes to do Christmas dinner," Clara smiled at him. "She likes to mention how the servants in the big houses have to get up before three to make sure everything is prepared. If the master of the house wants to take breakfast at seven, ahead of going to church, followed by a large dinner, the servants near enough have to work through the night."

"Ah, but supposing the family went away for Christmas?" Gloucester suggested. "Like I did. That would leave the house empty."

"Then, if the assailant knew the house would be empty, he could risk hiding in the basement area," Clara agreed. "That would suggest someone who plotted the abduction of Ariadne, rather than some lunatic just taking a chance."

As they passed all the houses, they glanced in windows to see if the families were at home. There were familiar signs of life that indicated people were in residence. As they reached the end of the street, they also discovered that the basement areas of these houses did not have a staircase leading to road level. That ruled them out as hiding places for a kidnapper.

"You know, three in the morning on Christmas Eve is quite a busy time," Gloucester remarked. "Lots of people are bumbling home from parties."

"You mean there could have been witnesses about?" Tommy asked.

"Well, it is possible. People have just stumbled home and are taking something for their overindulgence before heading to bed. Aspirin and dyspepsia powders were nearly out of stock in the local pharmacies, my butler tells me."

They had crossed a road, leaving behind the affluent homes of the Bumptons and their neighbours, and coming into streets where the houses were divided into two or three apartments. The residents were still rich, but not to the point they could indulge in the luxury of a large house and servants.

Clara was watching out for any alleyways between the properties were someone could have hidden themselves. She was disappointed to find the houses nestled against one another like birds on a branch. She was starting to have difficulty seeing where precisely someone would hide to sneak up upon Ariadne.

Gloucester scuffed his shoe against a wall to dislodge some mud that was marring the toe. He was about to say something when a car roared past and straight through a deep puddle. Water went up in a wave and splattered down on Gloucester. He looked baffled by the turn of events, as if he could not comprehend how such a thing could occur to him.

"Bad luck!" Tommy said, cringing at the sight of him and feeling a touch bad he had not alerted him to the impending catastrophe the second he had noticed the car. Tommy had darted to one side away from the puddle when he realised how fast the vehicle was coming, but then he also spent a lot more time walking along roadways where the risk of being drenched by passing traffic was higher. Gloucester did not spend a lot of time out of his own car and tended to avoid these sorts of mishaps by chance.

"That rotter!" Gloucester declared when his voice returned to him.

"People are utterly careless," Tommy came over and tapped the man's coat, discovering it was drenched right up to the shoulder.

Gloucester's hair was also soaked, and water ran in drips down his face. He looked astonished that such a thing could happen to him and utterly confused as to what to do next.

"We need to get you dry," Tommy stated the obvious.

"Just straight through the puddle. No thought for me! No thought!" Gloucester was still trying to comprehend what had happened.

"I say, do you need help?"

Gloucester and Tommy looked up at the voice, which came from the front door of the house they were stood outside. At the top of the stairs that led to the door stood a gentleman in his forties. He looked like he should work in something involving numbers and a good deal of paperwork. The term 'academic' would not go amiss when used in relation to him. He was looking at them with a frown of concern.

"My friend has been soaked by that reckless driver," Tommy said.

"I know, I saw everything out of my window," the helpful gentleman replied. "Please, do come and sit by my fire to dry off. I know exactly who owns that dreadful vehicle and they have no regard for anyone."

Gloucester was only too grateful for the invite and started up the stairs. Tommy looked behind him to see what his sister was up to. Clara had crouched down by the puddle.

"Clara?" Tommy called to her.

She rose up at once and turned to him.

"We need to get Gloucester dry before he catches a chill," she said.

"We do," Tommy concurred, then glanced at her out of the corner of his eye. "What were you up to?"

"Later," Clara replied, a slight smile on her face.

Tommy knew that smile. It suggested she had learned something. He wanted to know more but decided now was not the time to ask. They followed Gloucester up into the house.

"Jude Stanford," their host introduced himself, showing them through a door that led into a spacious apartment.

Stanford's accommodation comprised the left half of the large house, spanning over three floors. Across the entrance hall he had two neighbours, one who lived in an apartment on the ground floor, and the other who resided in a similar set of rooms on the first floor. All of the residences came from titled backgrounds and used their smaller apartments as boltholes when they were in London.

Stanford's home demonstrated that he was a keen enthusiast for everything medieval, particularly arms and armour. Swords and shields were mounted on his walls and a full suit of armour stood on guard next to the spiral staircase that connected the floors of his apartment.

"Sit by the fire," Stanford motioned for Gloucester to take a leather armchair next to a well stoked fire.

He helped the man to take his coat off, Gloucester

seeming to have gone into a strange slump at the shock of it all.

"Luckily, it seems your coat took the worst of it," Stanford observed. "I shall get a towel for your hair."

He disappeared up the spiral staircase, his feet clattering as he ran. Gloucester stared at the fire, dazed by the ordeal.

"Well, what did that puddle tell you?" Tommy asked his sister, now they were alone.

She motioned for him to come with her to the window, which he did, then she drew something from her pocket and showed it to him. It was a small gold brooch in the shape of an A, with pearls inlaid to define the letter.

"I spotted it sparkling in the puddle in the split-second before that car roared through," Clara explained. "It caught a glint of the sun. I thought the car might have crushed it or caused it to be thrown into a nearby drain and be lost for good. Luckily, it was still there when I went to investigate."

"A for Ariadne?" Tommy suggested.

"Possibly," Clara nodded. "We shall ask Gloucester when he is feeling recovered. It could indicate that Ariadne was here at some point that night if it is hers."

They heard footsteps returning and so went back to the fireplace. Clara pocketed the brooch again and they were sitting on a sofa when Stanford returned with towels for Gloucester.

"Here we go, do you feel warmer?" he fussed over his guest, handing Gloucester towels. "I should make some hot tea for us all?"

He hurried off again. Gloucester was beginning to wake from his momentary distraction. He dried his hair and face with a towel.

"That was a rather unexpected turn of events," he said. "People ought not to own a car if they do not take a care when driving it."

"Alfie, I spotted this in the puddle. Might it have belonged to Ariadne?" Clara took the brooch from her pocket and showed it to him.

Gloucester stared at the glimmering ornament. It was a little stained from the mud of the puddle, but it was otherwise unharmed by its time in the water. The look on Gloucester's face told them he recognised the brooch. He had gone pale, and his jaw had dropped. Clara folded her fingers over the brooch and returned it to her pocket. Gloucester lifted his eyes to hers.

"Ariadne's," he said. "She always wore it either clipped to a scarf at her neck, or on the lapel of her coat. In the summer, she would pin it to her dress. Her mother gave it to her."

"She was stood outside this house at some point on Christmas Eve," Clara surmised. "If she had lost the brooch before the Bumptons' party, the absence would surely have been mentioned. Mindy said nothing about it, which leads me to think she lost it on her way home."

"Maybe she was abducted from this very spot?" Gloucester said, wide-eyed, then a new, terrible thought struck him. "Could our 'helper' be responsible? It was right outside his home!"

"Mr Stanford seems to have no reason for doing such a thing," Tommy frowned.

"He could be one of those dreadful fiends who snatches young women to do awful things to them!" Gloucester said in horror. "She could be a prisoner in this very house!"

"I think that is a leap," Clara said, trying to calm him. She had not expected the brooch to cause such a reaction.

"He has her!" Gloucester rose up, the shock of being drenched had rather affected his rational senses. "She is here! I can sense it!"

"Gloucester, don't be ridiculous!" Tommy stood, trying to get him to sit down.

"I am not being ridiculous!" Gloucester retorted. "Ariadne was walking this way when she disappeared. She walked past this very house."

He pointed a finger at the floor with a jerky downwards movement to emphasise his statement.

"She vanished right here, and we have her brooch from the puddle outside to prove it. And who happened to be looking out of his window today just at the same spot where Ariadne went missing, but this strange Stanford fellow!"

"You are taking disparate pieces of information and attempting to link them together," Clara said to him. "None of which makes sense."

"It makes very good sense if you listen to what I am saying!" Gloucester said, infuriated they would not hear him out. "I say we call the police and search this place from top to bottom!"

Poor Jude Stanford was returning with a tray of tea things. He saw Gloucester stood up, ranting and raving, and looked rather anxious about the person he had let into his home.

"What is the matter?" he asked, coming towards them with the tea tray. He was holding it rather as a shield against anything untoward occurring.

"You, sir!" Gloucester pointed a finger at him. "You have kidnapped Ariadne and I demand you tell me where she is!"

Stanford gaped at him, transfixed by the bizarre accusation.

Then he let go of the tea tray and everything fell to the floor with a terrible smash.

Chapter Ten

Dr Cutt levered himself upright from examining Brilliant Chang in his bed. The good doctor was an octogenarian, whose back had become rather stiff these last years, and this meant certain manoeuvres had to be taken with consideration. He adjusted his glasses on his nose and smiled brightly at the patient.

"Precisely what tests have been undertaken so far?"

Chang, who had not lost his look of astonishment since the aged man entered his room, stared at him.

"I beg your pardon?"

"What tests have previous doctors had you take?" Dr Cutt repeated himself.

"Oh, they stabbed needles into me," Chang grimaced. "Took blood, I suppose."

"Did you ever see the results of these blood tests?" Dr Cutt asked.

"They informed me there was nothing wrong with them," Chang replied.

Dr Cutt nodded. Annie, who was standing quietly to one side, thought it was a somewhat knowing nod.

"I should like to repeat those tests," he said. "Along

with a few of my own."

Chang was not impressed.

"My doctors charge me a small fortune for the privilege of taking my blood. I am satisfied with their results."

"Are you?" Dr Cutt asked him in amusement. "Because it rather seems to me that your doctors have let you down Mr Chang. On the face of things, you are a fit and vital young man, yet clearly something is causing this debilitation. I intend to discover the cause."

Chang winced, because in his mind he was thinking of the curse. He was not prepared to say as much aloud, however.

"I suggest you continue to rest," Dr Cutt spoke. "Drink plenty of tea and eat fortifying meals. I am sure Annie shall supply them both in abundance."

Dr Cutt smiled at Annie who returned his look with satisfaction.

"Now, that blood test," the doctor started to open his medical bag to withdraw a large syringe.

"I already said…" Chang began to protest.

Dr Cutt met his eyes and something in his gaze cut off Chang's argument mid-sentence. There was a determination and strength in Dr Cutt's eyes that made you both trust him and fear to resist him. Chang, who was not used to being cowed by people, shut his mouth, presented an arm, and turned his head away from the sight of his blood being drawn.

"All things have an answer," Dr Cutt talked as he went about his work. "Sometimes we just need to find the right question first."

"You are implying my doctors, men from Harley Street no less, men who serve lords and ladies and even royalty, are not as clever as you," Chang said through gritted teeth, glaring at the curtains hanging by the window.

He felt the sting of the needle and clenched his teeth harder. Chang hated pain of any sort and worked hard to avoid it. He was highly sensitive to even the slightest injury. That was just one reason he avoided such traditional Chinese medicines as acupuncture, even though it had been suggested to him as a means of curing his sickness. He had decided to keep that as a last resort – a very, last resort. The thought of something piercing him with fine needles while he was naked gave him such a tremor of vulnerability and fear he did not like to even consider it.

When it came to a choice between baring his soul to Clara, or submitting to acupuncture, he had considered Clara the lesser of two evils. Which was saying a great deal about his phobia around needles.

Dr Cutt drew his blood sample and carefully concealed his syringe in his medical bag, to avoid disturbing the patient further.

"I shall have some results for you soon enough," he told Chang.

Chang nodded miserably, defeated yet again. He was fed up with doctors, with feeling unwell and with having no energy to go about his business as he usually would. He did not even have the gumption to mutter something to the doctor about medical men being vampires for their patient's blood.

"Am I dying?" he asked, morbidly.

"I very much doubt it," Dr Cutt replied. "But you never know."

He said this with good cheer. Chang was not impressed and would have barked back at the doctor, except Annie had come over.

"I shall make you a cup of tea before you go, Dr Cutt," she intervened, knowing all too well that Chang's tolerance for the good humour of the doctor would be extremely limited. "We know you will do your best for us."

Chang glowered at her. Annie ignored him and escorted the doctor downstairs.

In the warm and cosy kitchen, there was a smell of cake slowly baking in the oven. Bramble and Pip, the Fitzgeralds' dogs were attentively watching the oven, in hopes the cake would miraculously jump out and into their mouths. Annie herded them off to their big basket in the corner to make way for the doctor.

"Explain to me again how you happen to have a gentleman of the Far East in your guest room?" Dr Cutt said as he took a chair by the kitchen table. He was intrigued by the arrangement. There was always something interesting happening at the Fitzgeralds' residence.

"He is Clara's nemesis. They have crossed swords more than once," Annie explained. "They first met when there was that drama with a corrupt policeman in the Brighton Constabulary."

"I recall the affair. A young constable was knocked down and left for dead."

"Yes, by Chang's car. Whether Chang was driving it or not, he certainly was behind the assault."

"Ah, then he is hardly a friend to you all?"

"Hardly," Annie agreed. "But he came to us asking for help and you know Clara, she refuses no one."

"He must be in a very dire situation to come to his enemy for assistance. I take it Clara would like to see him in prison?"

"She would like that very much and has tried her best to achieve it, but he has eluded her constantly," Annie warmed the teapot and popped in some loose leaves. "Still, in a strange way he respects her for her downright honesty and felt she was the only one he could trust in this matter."

"That says a good deal for Clara's honourable nature, that even such a man as Chang considers her trustworthy and would turn to her in a time of need."

"I think it says he is desperate," Annie shrugged. "Have you any idea what is wrong with him?"

"I have a few suspicions, but nothing firm until I have run further tests. The blood may very well reveal all. The question is, if I can find the answer, why cannot his doctors?"

Dr Cutt had that knowing expression on his face again.

"You are thinking they do know what is wrong, but they did not want to reveal the answer to Chang because it is never wise to be the bearer of bad news when your employer is a criminal gang leader?"

"You are very insightful Annie," Dr Cutt said jovially. "Fortunately, I shall have no such qualms. Chang is just another patient to me, and I shall treat him the same as any other, with kindness, patience, good manners, and pure honesty."

Annie brought the filled teapot over and poured out a cup for each of them.

"Dr Cutt, have you ever come across a patient who was affected by a… curse," Annie asked uncertainly.

Dr Cutt was helping himself to sugar. He was a man who believed nothing could ever be too sweet and claimed his longevity and good health was due to the medicinal benefits of sugar.

"I have heard many afflictions termed curses," he said, not appreciating what Annie meant.

"But what of someone being made ill because of a curse?" Annie said, finding it very difficult to voice her thoughts. "My grandmother believed she could put the Evil Eye on people and very often those she said she had cursed became unwell."

"The human mind is a very curious thing, Annie," Dr Cutt explained gently. "People can convince themselves they are unwell, for sure. They start to suppose a cough, or a headache is something more than just a nuisance we all endure from time to time. A person gets the notion they have been cursed and then any niggle they suffer is a consequence of that. It does not mean the curse is real. It just demonstrates the power of the human mind."

"Then, you do not believe in curses?" Annie asked.

Dr Cutt frowned at her.

"What is all this talk about, Annie?"

Annie sucked in her lower lip and considered whether to say anything further or not. Reluctantly, seeing as she had begun this process in the first place, she answered him.

"Brilliant Chang thinks he has been cursed and that is why no doctor can find the cause for his condition."

Dr Cutt did not look amazed or surprised, he took the news as if Annie had been referring to something mundane, such as the change in the weather.

"When medical science offers no answers, people fall back on older ideas. For much of history medicine has been heavily steeped in magic and superstition because doctors were so very limited as to what they could do for a patient," the doctor explained. "Only in the last few decades have great leaps been made in the understanding of the human body and why things go wrong. I recall from my days as a young doctor, when I was employed at a larger practice, that the senior doctor informed a woman that her baby had been born with a hare lip because she must have been thinking about hares during the pregnancy. It was preposterous, but that is how things were."

"Then, my grandmother did not really curse people with the Evil Eye?" Annie asked carefully.

"Now, that is a complicated question," Dr Cutt smiled at her. "Because it requires us to consider the nature of a curse. Does a curse have to be an actual thing if just by believing in it a person can suffer greatly? Most curses are not specific, such as informing someone their hair will all drop out, they are just general bad luck, and people can put great power into such things."

"I see," Annie said. "It is not really magic, just the power of belief in magic?"

"Something along those lines," Dr Cutt agreed. "I do not believe Brilliant Chang is cursed. However, if he believes it, it is likely to hold back his recuperation process. Just worrying about the possibility will be draining for him and has the potential to make him unwell."

"Which means a curse does not have to be real to cause someone bother?"

"Exactly Annie," Dr Cutt thought for a moment. "Think about Tommy when he came home from the war in a wheelchair. All the medical men told him there was nothing wrong with his legs, but he could not walk."

"There was something going on in his head," Annie nodded. "Shellshock."

"Shellshock is one of the most mysterious and disturbing phenomena I have come across in my medical career. A man can have suffered no actual physical injury and yet be severely, acutely affected by this condition of the mind to the point he seems deranged or suffers severe incapacitation. I fear we do not appreciate both the power and the sensitivity of the brain. It is both a marvellous instrument, and something incredibly vulnerable."

Annie thought about this. It did make a certain sense, but there was a part of her, an instinctual, emotional part that could not quite let go of the idea of a curse. She almost felt that if she neglected the possibility of Chang being cursed, she would make matters worse. Like ignoring a symptom that proved very important to determining what was wrong with a person.

If she forgot about the curse, told herself it was

nonsense, would she be letting Chang down?

"You can't quite let it go, can you?" Dr Cutt had read her mind.

Annie met his gaze.

"I should be able to, but I fear doing so."

"That is perfectly normal, Annie," Dr Cutt assured her. "But, for Chang's sake, try to convince him this curse business is nothing to fear. Do not belittle his concerns but find a way to make him see that he is not cursed."

"How will I do that?" Annie asked, thinking she had been tasked with the impossible.

"I am sure you will figure something out," Dr Cutt said, rising from his chair. "Now, I have a lot of tests to run to determine what really is wrong with our friend. Thank you for the tea, Annie."

Dr Cutt looked a bit stiff on his first couple of paces away from the table, but then he started to move and seemed to have regained his sprightliness. He put his hat on his head as Annie saw him out of the front door and wished her well in a cheerful manner.

Annie closed the door behind him and was thoughtful for a while. She rather fancied Dr Cutt was right and this curse was just a product of their fears. Or maybe, the curse only held power if you believed in it? Annie mused over this idea. If that were the case, then it could be broken if she convinced Chang the curse no longer had a hold over him.

How was she to do that?

Annie headed back to the kitchen. Bramble and Pip had resumed their positions before the oven. Annie glanced at the clock. Another ten minutes and she would need to get the cake out, but there was time before then to try something.

She headed into her pantry and rummaged around right at the back, drawing the interest of the dogs. In a wooden box tucked in a dark corner there were some old, dried herbs. These were bunches that had hung around for a little too long and which she had deemed unsuitable for cooking but did not quite feel able to throw away. Annie was glad she had kept them now.

She pulled out a bundle of sage leaves that looked to have been nibbled at by a mouse. Retrieving some matches next, she headed back upstairs. Chang glanced at her as she entered the bedroom.

"Sage," Annie told him, then, standing in the middle of the room, she struck a match and held it to the leaves.

The dried sage caught faster than she had expected and started to smoke furiously.

"Smokes out bad spirits," Annie coughed.

"Smokes out us!" Chang replied.

As the room filled with clouds of smoke, Annie regretted her plan.

Chapter Eleven

Jude Stanford stared at the smashed crockery at his feet. He was not sure if he was more gobsmacked at the accusation or at the fact he had dropped the entire tea service in shock. It had been his mother's tea service and he was rather fond of it.

"Let me help you, Mr Stanford," Clara jumped to his aid. "Mr Gloucester, sit down at once and stop shrieking at people."

Her sharp comment towards Gloucester cowed him and he sat down at once. Clara dropped to her knees and started rescuing the pieces of the tea set from the carpet, carefully piling them onto the tray.

"Do you have some glue, Mr Stanford? We can put these back together in a jiffy if you do. I know a trick that means the cracks will be virtually invisible."

Stanford blinked at her, then knelt down and started to collect up a broken saucer. The rug beneath their feet was damp with hot tea.

"I'll fetch a cloth," Tommy said, heading past the others to where he assumed the kitchen was. It was an excuse to take a look around as well – just in case

Gloucester's accusations were not so far off the mark.

"Did you accuse me of abducting a young lady?" Stanford was gradually recovering from his shock and asked this of Gloucester.

Gloucester looked at Clara before he answered. She gave him a warning nod – you can speak, but don't go too far again.

"I did," Gloucester answered. "I accused you of kidnapping my friend Ariadne Griffiths."

"Never heard of her," Stanford said. "And I do not go around kidnapping young ladies, in general. I am offended you would suggest such a thing."

Gloucester kept his mouth shut, though he plainly wanted to say more.

They had arranged the broken crockery on the tray and Stanford now lifted it up with a sigh. Tommy was returning with a large cloth to mop up the spillage.

"We shall wash and dry the cups and then repair them," Clara consoled Stanford. "We shall all help."

She cast another pointed look at Gloucester who was sulking and pretended he did not hear her.

In the kitchen, they washed and dried the broken cups and saucers. The teapot had survived with just a chip to its sturdy spout. They washed and dried that too.

"We need to make sure the broken portion of the ceramic is fully dry," Clara pointed out the porous surfaces where the crockery had cracked. "We shall just pop them in the oven for a while."

Stanford watched her in a quietly dejected manner. He had not expected such an ordeal when he had endeavoured to help Gloucester.

"I am sorry about all this," Clara told him. "Mr Gloucester is rather overwrought at the moment."

"Because his friend is missing?" Stanford guessed. "Why did he suppose I had anything to do with it?"

"Your house happens to be on the route Ariadne

took to reach home on Christmas Eve," Clara explained. "She probably passed your house. We found this outside, in the puddle that car kindly swirled up."

Clara drew out the brooch and showed it to him.

"It belongs to Ariadne, according to Gloucester."

"So, he thinks she disappeared outside my house?" Stanford was beginning to understand. "But why accuse me?"

"You happened to be the nearest person at the time," Clara shrugged. "That is the long and short of it. Gloucester is not thinking rationally."

Stanford gazed at the brooch a while longer.

"Christmas Eve?" he said, mulling over what she had just told him. "I was home on Christmas Eve. I had a terrible cold and could not sleep. I spent most of the night in the armchair by the window, trying to distract myself."

Clara was listening keenly.

"Do you think you saw Ariadne that night?" Clara asked

Stanford frowned.

"My memory is a touch blurred from that evening. I was feverish and I drifted into short dozes once in a while. I don't want to tell you something that was just a dream or a misremembrance."

Clara understood. He did not want to set Gloucester on another person by mischance. False accusations were never good.

"Give me a little while to think," he said.

They carried the dry pieces of crockery back through to the front room where there was a table by the window that would provide them with sufficient natural light to work on piecing them back together. Tommy had soaked up most of the tea from the rug and asked where Stanford would like him to put the sodden cloth. When he was informed to place it in the upstairs bathtub, he took this as a good excuse to check the upper floors for signs of Ariadne and departed swiftly.

Gloucester had had time to sit by the fire and mellow. He stared at the flames a while longer, then he sighed and rose to come over to the table by the window. Gruffly, he began his apology to Stanford.

"I was impulsive and rash," he said. "Accusing you was foolish and without reason."

He could not quite look Stanford in the eyes. The other man listened carefully and then nodded his head.

"This young lady explained the situation to me," Stanford replied. "By the way, I do not believe we ever properly introduced ourselves?"

In the commotion of Gloucester accusing Stanford of abduction they had failed to tell their host their names. Clara rectified the situation as swiftly as she could, explaining who she and Tommy were and how they came to be there with Gloucester.

"Gosh, detectives looking for the young lady," Stanford said, duly impressed. "Is she very important?"

"All people are important to someone," Clara smiled at him. "Do you have that glue?"

Stanford thought for a moment, then went to a cabinet and opened a drawer, removing a pot of glue with a screw lid. He fudged around in the drawer again and pulled out a brush to be used with it.

"The trick to gluing crockery back together seamlessly is to not overuse the glue," Clara said. "People always use too much and then it either squeezes out or creates a very slight gap between the two edges which makes the crack noticeable. A bare minimum of glue is necessary."

Clara demonstrated how little glue was required and stuck together the halves of a saucer. She took great care and when she was done, the seam was virtually invisible.

"I have mended a lot of broken crockery in my

time," she informed the gentlemen, recalling a time when Tommy was first back from the war and took out his frustration and unvented anger on the teacups. More than one had been flung at a wall and smashed to pieces. Clara had learned how to make running repairs to keep the cost of replacing them to a minimum.

Stanford took up the brush and began on a cup. After a moment, Gloucester decided he should assist as a means of making an apology. He took the brush off Stanford and set to work on the chipped spout of the teapot.

"Could you perhaps describe Ariadne to me?" Stanford said as they worked. "I recall seeing more than one lady walk past my window that night. Christmas Eve is always busy with people coming and going."

"Ariadne has fair hair and is slightly built," Gloucester explained. "Though, she would have been wearing a bulky coat."

He was not quite prepared to mention she was pregnant. It would raise the awkward question of whether she was married or not and it might cause Stanford to ponder on Gloucester's relationship with her.

"She would have been going past your window around three," Clara added.

Stanford pulled a face.

"Time was somewhat irrelevant to me that night. I saw more than one fair haired girl walk past."

"Ariadne is quite tall," Gloucester added. "And she has a bit of a stoop, a compensation, I fear, for her height. She has recently been wearing a distinctive red hat, close cut to the head and with a green feather in the band."

This detail sparked something in Stanford. He paused in the process of replacing a teacup handle, his thoughts drifting away.

"I remember a girl in a red hat," he said. "I almost thought she was a dream because I must have just been rousing from one of my short dozes when I saw her. Her hat seemed quite remarkable, because she walked beneath the streetlamp outside my window, and it was extremely vivid in the light. Of course, it did not look a true red, but you could tell it was a very colourful hat and there was indeed a feather in the band."

"She walked past your window?" Clara asked.

"Not exactly," Stanford said. "She was going to walk past, but a car pulled up alongside her and she stopped. The driver rolled down the window and he was speaking to her. I couldn't hear what they said, and I was not really listening. They talked for a few minutes and the girl drew closer to the car. Then she suddenly became angry and yanked at the scarf around her neck, causing it to pull off. She flung her hands in the air and seemed furious."

"Ariadne can be dramatic at times," Gloucester admitted slightly sheepishly.

"Perhaps that was the moment she lost this?" Clara said, holding out the brooch once more.

"She seemed quite upset, but the driver must have spoken to her, and she calmed down," Stanford continued. "A few moments later, she went around the car and climbed into the passenger seat, then the car drove off."

This was significant.

"Ariadne got into a car?" Clara repeated, thinking that this opened up a whole new gamut of possibilities. Searching around the nearby streets was starting to look rather pointless. In a car, the kidnapper could have taken Ariadne far away.

"She must have known who was driving that car," Gloucester said. "Ariadne would never just get into any car. Not without good reason. She was naturally cautious."

"The thing is," Stanford continued gingerly, "I recognised the car. I suppose that was why I never gave it much thought."

"You know who owns the car?" Clara asked swiftly.

"I do," Stanford nodded. "It happens to be the same fellow who drove through that puddle and drenched Mr Gloucester a short time ago."

Gloucester started at this information, thinking that he had stood mere inches from the vehicle that had whisked away Ariadne. Tommy was at that point returning from his exploration of the upstairs. Obviously, he had not found anything suspicious. His extended absence had also not been noted by Stanford, who was now absorbed in both repairing the crockery and explaining what he saw on Christmas Eve.

"What is this about a car?" Tommy asked, coming up behind them.

"He saw Ariadne getting into a car the night she vanished," Gloucester explained sharply. "Whose car was it? Tell me the name of this fiend!"

"Before we jump to another conclusion," Clara intervened, "it is important we remember that just because Ariadne climbed into this car does not mean the person driving it is a kidnapper."

Gloucester scowled at her, rather keen to 'jump to conclusions,' but he conceded she had a point and kept his mouth shut.

"The fellow who owns that car is named Benjamin Fitzroy," Stanford explained. "He lives in Berkeley Square and has a fiancée in Lincoln Avenue. The quickest route between the two is down this road, hence why I see him often going back and forth. He is somewhat arrogant and rather oafish, but he never struck me as being dangerous."

"Is he titled?" Gloucester asked, forgetting he was meant to be holding his tongue. "Titled gentlemen think they can get away with anything."

He was tactlessly forgetting that he had a title too.

"I don't know much about the family. He is a younger brother to someone, that is as much as I can offer. I do not move in those circles."

"A younger brother," Gloucester looked smug, as if this explained everything.

"We shall need to go speak to him," Clara concluded. "He can tell us where Ariadne went next."

"Obviously he has her!" Gloucester snapped, startling poor Mr Stanford who had been somewhat unnerved by events.

He nearly dropped the repaired cup he was holding.

"Gloucester, I already said…"

"Fine, fine," Gloucester grumbled. "But she has been missing for days, he could have done anything with her."

A hush fell over them because they all knew the longer a person was missing without a word of where they might be, the worse things usually were.

"Apart from his fancy car and disregard for pedestrians, can you tell me much else about Mr Fitzroy?" Clara asked Stanford.

Stanford considered for a moment, then shook his head apologetically.

"Ariadne never mentioned him to you, Gloucester?" Clara turned to the other man now.

"No," he said. "Before you ask, I have no personal association with any man named Fitzroy. I am aware there were Fitzroys involved in the Navy, quite high up in the Admiralty. But this fellow is not someone I have happened to meet."

"He might be part of the Bumptons' circle," Tommy suggested.

"The Bumptons have all sorts of 'friends'," Gloucester huffed. "Nothing would surprise me.

Cavorting with kidnappers!"

Clara did not bother to correct him this time, she knew when she was wasting her energy. She finished sticking together the last cup and looked at their handiwork. The tea set had a slightly battered look to it, not all the cracks lined up perfectly where Stanford and Gloucester had been in charge of them, but they were all back together. Whether they could be used for tea consumption ever again was another matter, and Clara would not like to chance her arm.

"Mr Stanford, thank you for your help and once again, we are most sorry to have disrupted your day so badly," she said.

Stanford glanced at his tea things forlornly and Gloucester felt a pang of guilty remorse. He had rather jumped upon the man and scared the life out of him.

"I believe this is a Windsor tea set?" he said. "I have a strong feeling the exact same set resides in a cupboard in my house. It was a gift to my parents on their wedding day from the family servants. It has never been used, as far as I know. I shall send it along to you at once, Mr Stanford, as an apology."

Stanford would have been more moved had Gloucester not needed to explain how an inferior, mass-produced tea set had ended up in his possession. Fortunately, Stanford was well-mannered.

"Thank you, Mr Gloucester and I do hope you find your friend."

"We will," Gloucester said brightly, though it was forced. "We will, Mr Stanford."

Chapter Twelve

Gloucester was agitated as they returned to his car. Clara was regretting allowing him to come along. He had no tact and blurted out things. He had demonstrated all this with Stanford, and she was not convinced he would be any better around Fitzroy. He already seemed convinced that this Fitzroy was responsible for causing some great harm to Ariadne and was beside himself. Clara was expecting the conversation with Fitzroy to be challenging with Gloucester present.

Seeing how Fitzroy's car had passed them going away from Berkeley Square, they assumed he was headed for the home of his lady friend. They headed to Lincoln Avenue in the hopes they would spy his car and deduce which house he was visiting.

They were in luck, for they had barely turned into Lincoln Avenue when they spied the distinctive car that had doused poor Gloucester in muddy water barely an hour ago. He glared at it, and it was plain he was not just furious with Fitzroy over Ariadne – he was holding a grudge about getting soaked.

The car was parked before a white-stone townhouse. Gloucester pulled up behind it and stormed out of his car. He marched over to the offending vehicle and glowered at it, as if the inanimate object could be ashamed of its actions.

Clara ignored him, hoping he would be distracted long enough by the car to enable her to speak to Fitzroy first and avoid too much of a scene. The whole situation was complicated and curious. What was Fitzroy doing picking up a pregnant woman late at night when he had a fiancée? And why had Ariadne been so angry with him? As the last person to see Ariadne that night, as far as they knew, Fitzroy was now a prime suspect. If the police had bothered to become involved, he would likely be already headed to the police station for questioning. Well, depending on how fearsome the detectives at Scotland Yard were. Some policemen became rather shy and bashful around those with money or influence.

Clara had never been called shy or bashful, and she had no intention of earning such appellations now. She rang the doorbell of the house before which the car was parked and waited. Tommy was just behind her, watching Gloucester over his shoulder.

"He is trying to peel the paint from that car with his gaze alone," he remarked. "I do suppose he realises it is just an object and not responsible for running through that puddle?"

Clara was willing the door to open before Gloucester lost interest in his task. She was relieved when a maid opened the door and asked her what her business was.

"I am trying to locate Mr Benjamin Fitzroy," Clara explained. "It is very urgent and concerns the disappearance of a lady called Ariadne Griffiths. I must speak to him at once."

The maid looked puzzled by all this talk. Clara

could see the majority of what she had just said would fail to be relayed to the lady of the house and Fitzroy. She tried a different approach.

"Sir Gloucester is here to see him," she said. "He is rather angry, because Mr Fitzroy drenched him with his car an hour ago."

The maid reacted to the use of a title as Clara had expected. Her eyes widened and she looked most alarmed. She asked them to wait a moment while she hastened to take their message to her mistress.

Gloucester, by this point, was done with glaring at the car and was joining them on the front steps.

"Use my name if they won't let you in," he said.

Tommy grinned at him.

"Already have, old boy."

It was not many more moments before the door opened again, but this time it was not the maid behind it, but a gentleman with a frosty expression on his face. He was about their age, with a playboy slouch to his manner and style of dress. He had a rather hard face, to Clara's way of thinking, and could not be called attractive. Though it might have been the deep, grudging frown on his brow that was making this impression upon her.

"Who is bandying noble names about willy-nilly?" he demanded. "Just to get our attention. I shall not have it! Trying to suggest there was a lord on the doorstep upset with me!"

"Ahem," Gloucester coughed haughtily and drew the young man's attention. "No one is bandying names about willy-nilly or otherwise."

There was something in the voice of a lord's son that could not be imitated. It was something about having a sense of value, of self-worth that was nothing to do with who you were, but rather who your family were. Just the tone of Gloucester's voice impressed on everyone that he was who he said he was.

The colour drained from the man at the door's face.

"I am presuming you are Mr Benjamin Fitzroy?" Clara asked him.

"I am," Benjamin Fitzroy gulped. "Did I really drench you when I ran through that puddle?"

He had addressed his question to Gloucester.

"You ruined my new coat," Gloucester grumbled. "I doubt it shall ever be the same. Not to mention my shoes."

Gloucester lifted a foot and showed the water damage to his fine leather shoes.

"You are a disgrace, sir, and ought not to be allowed to drive!"

Fitzroy was looking stunned and frightened. Clara decided to move things along before Fitzroy became paralysed with fear over what he had done. After all, the puddle incident was only a coincidental part of why they were there.

"We need to come in, Mr Fitzroy. We have lots to discuss," she said to him.

"Who are you?" Fitzroy demanded, still finding room for his arrogance when it came to her. Clara was clearly no lady.

"Sir Gloucester's legal representation," Clara lied.

Fitzroy was not taken in.

"You are a woman," he sneered.

"So is Ariadne Griffiths," Clara said darkly. "A friend of Sir Gloucester's, who is missing and has been missing since she was last seen getting into your car."

"If you have harmed a hair on her head..." Gloucester waggled a fist at Fitzroy. "I shall use all my connections to see you hang for it!"

Fitzroy was becoming overwhelmed by all this information. He glanced between them and was lost for words.

"I think we ought to come inside," Clara suggested.

Fitzroy slowly realised this was not a bad idea, after

all. He shuffled back from the door and stood to one side to let them through. Then, once they were in the hall and the door was shut, he found himself stuck in indecision. This was not his home, and he was not sure where to take them to have a private conversation, but what he did know for sure was that he was not going to allow his fiancée to meet these people.

After battling with this internal crisis, Fitzroy plumped for showing them into the ground floor library, which was rather underused and not a place they were likely to be disturbed. He broadly motioned for them to take seats at the long reading table, while he preferred to stand.

The room had no fire burning and was chilly. Gloucester refused to be seated and started to prowl around looking at the book titles on the shelves. Fitzroy paced and watched him anxiously. Clara found she was not only glad Gloucester had been present to get them through the door, but she was relieved that he seemed to have learned his lesson and was restraining himself. Clara turned to Fitzroy.

"Mr Fitzroy, on Christmas Eve you picked up Ariadne Griffiths in your car," she stated.

Fitzroy glanced at her.

"I did," he said, still anxious about Gloucester's presence. "She was walking home late at night, and she looked exhausted. I was being a gentleman."

"But you drove off in the opposite direction to where she lived," Tommy pointed out, recalling what Stanford had said.

Fitzroy hesitated, just long enough to make it plain he was formulating a lie.

"I had an errand to run. I dropped her off afterwards."

"An errand at three in the morning?" Clara said in disbelief before suddenly changing tack. "Why was Ariadne so angry with you?"

"What?" Fitzroy bleated, looking horrified they knew so much about his activities. "You are mistaken."

"You were witnessed," Clara said calmly. "Ariadne was seen shouting at you and tugging off her scarf. In the process she dropped this."

Clara showed him the brooch that was proving to be quite a crucial piece of evidence. Fitzroy stared at it.

"That is Ariadne's favourite brooch."

"It is," Gloucester rumbled from where he was on the other side of the room. "Care to tell me what made her so irate she risked losing it?"

Fitzroy took a deep breath, but he had no intention of revealing himself to these people even if one was a lord – well, not quite a lord yet, but Gloucester had bumped himself up in rank for the sake of getting Fitzroy's attention.

"We had a disagreement, and Ariadne was a touch drunk."

"Ariadne was not a heavy drinker," Gloucester barked.

"No, but she could get tipsy," Fitzroy replied. "And it was Christmas Eve."

Clara intervened before Gloucester lost them the advantage they had gained.

"Are you saying, Mr Fitzroy, that after you completed your errand, you took Ariadne straight home to her flat?"

"I am," Fitzroy said firmly.

"Then, it seems you are the very last person to have seen her," Clara continued. "For she disappeared that night and no one has seen her since. Not her cousin, not her dear friend Mindy Bumpton, who she was supposed to spend Christmas Day with. If I was a policeman, I would find it very suspicious that you were the last to see her."

"Now, hang on," Fitzroy said fast, "I have never

caused any harm to Ariadne. She made it home, safe and sound."

"Then where did she go afterwards?" Tommy asked. "Did she give you any indication she was going to go out again?"

"I thought she was going to bed," Fitzroy shrugged. "I cannot help that she took herself out afterwards. I cannot fathom why she would want to."

"Precisely what is your relationship with Ariadne?" Clara asked next.

"What does that mean?" Fitzroy replied sharply.

"I think you know what I mean," Clara answered. "I am curious how you knew Ariadne. You have a fiancée, after all, and you were presumably heading home from seeing her on Christmas Eve when you saw Miss Griffiths."

"She was an acquaintance," Fitzroy answered, a little too fast. "Nothing more."

"It rather sounded as if she was more than just an acquaintance," Tommy added. "You had to pull over on the wrong side of the street to talk to her, and she clearly had a lot to say to you. Besides, we have it on good authority Ariadne would not get into a car with someone she was not well acquainted with."

Gloucester had a reproving look on his face, and his eyes were burning into Fitzroy. It was becoming harder and harder to dance around the truth.

"I suppose you could call us friends," he said. "We had played cards together. Talked about poetry. That night, I saw her and recognised her. It was cold, wet, and dark. Not a night to be walking home alone, and so I pulled over and offered her a lift. Ariadne was not in a great mood, and I said something innocuous about her looking unsteady on her feet and she snapped at me. Said if I was calling her drunk, I should just come out and say it. After a few moments she calmed down and agreed to get in the car. I completed my errand

and took her home. That is the end of it."

"You did know she was pregnant?" Tommy asked.

"Of course, it was obvious," Fitzroy shrugged. "It had nothing to do with me, however."

Fitzroy looked shifty and Clara was not convinced by a word he said. Unfortunately, they had nothing to prove he was lying. Not at that moment, at least.

"Where was this errand?" she asked.

Fitzroy had not been expecting such a change in direction and took a moment to regroup.

"Ah, it was back in Berkeley Square. I was dropping off a present."

"You live in Berkeley Square?" Tommy enquired.

"Yes," Fitzroy nodded. "I have a nice townhouse."

"Then, why would you drive all the way to Berkeley Square to complete your errand, and then turn around and drive all the way back to Ariadne's flat, before going back again to Berkeley Square?"

Fitzroy was stumbled by his question. It was logical, of course. Why had he made such a complicated trip? He could have turned around immediately and driven Ariadne home, and then returned to Berkeley Square, completed his errand and gone to bed, saving him time and petrol.

"Doesn't really make sense, does it?" Tommy said.

Fitzroy was looking more and more alarmed at his predicament. There was something he was not telling them, that was for sure.

"Look, we can settle all this quite quickly," Clara smiled at him, offering him a reprieve. "If you tell us who you were running the errand to, then we just can go and speak to them and confirm you had Ariadne in the car at that point. It won't confirm you took her home, but it will prove you are telling the truth and that is a start."

"I cannot involve anyone else," Fitzroy said swiftly.

"Why not?" Gloucester demanded. "You were only

dropping off a present, according to what you said. Why would anyone be troubled by confirming such a thing?"

"Well, the person is very private," Fitzroy fumbled.

"Is it someone you would prefer that your fiancée know nothing about?" Tommy suggested.

"No, no," Fitzroy forced a laugh. "I have no secrets from her."

"Then you can tell us, and this matter will be one step closer to being resolved," Clara explained to him politely.

At this point Fitzroy clamped down. He refused to say anymore. He was not going to be bullied into revealing what he did not want revealed. He shook his head and held up his hands to indicate he was done.

"I have nothing more to say," he declared.

"What if the police came to visit you?" Clara asked.

"Call them, if you care to," Fitzroy folded his arms across his chest. "I have nothing more to say."

He dared them to contradict him. They were at a stalemate.

"You see? You have nothing," Fitzroy said in triumph. "Nothing at all!"

Chapter Thirteen

Having nearly killed Brilliant Chang due to sage smoke inhalation, it had been necessary for Annie to shuffle him downstairs, where he gasped and gagged by the back door she had propped open to allow the cold air to blow in.

"Was that supposed… to help?" Chang wheezed at her.

"My sage was perhaps a little old," Annie shrugged. "But I can assure you there are now no spirits or evil influences in that room."

"But nor am I!" Chang snapped. "And now I am freezing cold, to boot!"

He was visibly shivering, though making no effort to remove himself from the doorway. It was as if he did not have the energy to move away. Annie had to make the decision for him and hustled him to a chair by the kitchen table, before shutting the back door firmly.

"I'll make more tea," she said, because this was a default for Annie.

Chang glowered at her as she moved about the

kitchen.

"I was trying to help," she complained. "It was old magic to dispel a curse. You are the one who believes in the curse, after all. Clara would have none of this."

Annie found that despite Chang's reputation she was not feeling intimidated by his gaze. She was actually quite calm. Perhaps it was because she was in her own kitchen, going about her usual routine for making tea. Or perhaps it was because she had seen Chang lying in a bed, looking as if the world was ending, and wearing a borrowed pair of Tommy's pyjamas that were too long in the legs and sleeves for him. She had used safety pins to fasten the cuffs back so his hands could emerge.

From behind her, Chang gave a long sigh, and she turned to see what was wrong. He no longer looked angry, instead he looked miserable again. Annie paused and watched him for a moment.

"What is it?" she asked him.

Chang shrugged his shoulders.

"You said that burning sage will remove evil influences, but I don't feel any better for it. I feel just the same."

Annie set the kettle to boil and came over to the table and sat down.

"Sage is just a starting point," she consoled him. "There are other means."

"How are curses lifted?" Chang asked.

Annie realised that if Clara were there right now, she would be furious about this conversation. To encourage Chang's belief in a curse was unthinkable to her. To Annie, it was as logical a possibility as any other. Besides, whether there was a curse or not, the believing in it was doing Chang no good whatsoever.

"There are a variety of ways," Annie said, though she was largely making that up as she was not altogether confident of such things. "Most often, people either do the thing the person who cursed them wanted, or somehow make amends with them to have the curse lifted."

Chang cringed.

"I can't do that. I am not going to be forced to be that woman's stooge. Not by a curse, not by anything. It would destroy my reputation if people learned Brilliant Chang had given into a woman due to a curse!"

Annie could see his point, but she was out of her depth now. She sucked in her lower lip.

"There is someone who might know," she said. "An old friend. I haven't seen her in years, not since my parents' passing. She was a family friend when we had the farm and knew all the old ways."

"How do we get in touch with her?" Chang demanded.

Annie considered.

"She is not on the telephone, but if I were to ring up the Hove Post Office, they could send a message to her and ask her to come to see us. It will take time."

"Do it," Chang said. "Please."

He sounded desperate. It was unsettling. Annie headed to the telephone in the hallway and did as she had said, ringing the Hove Post Office and arranging for a message to be delivered as soon as possible. All they could do after that was wait and see if the lady bothered to come.

She returned to Chang as the kettle started to whistle.

"You must not be despondent," she remarked to him. "We shall sort this all out."

"I have never been sick before," Chang said forlornly. "Not like this. I have seen men grow ill and just... wither away."

"Now, hush, that is not talk that will help you," Annie rebuked him. "No surer way is there to stay sick than to give up. It is time you resolved yourself to fight this."

"How?" Chang growled at her. "How can I fight a curse?"

"I don't know," Annie answered. "That is what we have to find out, but I know this, giving up will not find a cure. Giving up does not help anything."

Chang did not want to admit she was right. He sulked and glared at the table.

"Talk to me," Annie said. "Maybe we can find something in this mess that gives us a clue to break the curse."

"You said I had to give in to the woman," Chang sneered.

"I said that was the only way I knew how to break a curse, but there are bound to be other ways. Besides, you have said yourself that something happened at that party. You do not remember a thing after a certain time."

"I am sure I was drugged," Chang agreed. "I never lose my memory, even when I drink. I am cautious, always. Alertness is vital for my survival."

"Well, if that is the case and you were drugged, how did it happen?"

Chang glowered at her.

"It must have been in my drink."

Annie met his fierce gaze with her own stubborn one.

"Are you telling me, a cautious man like you was not watching his drinks being poured?"

Chang, who had not expected this insight from Annie, was chastened. Sheepishly he dropped his gaze and focused on the table once more.

"You are right. Normally I watch my drinks being poured."

"What was different about that night?" Annie asked. "What caused you to drop your guard?"

Chang went back in his mind to that day and to the fateful party.

"I did watch all my drinks being prepared. I was at the Bumptons' home. Mrs Mindy Bumpton is a terrible snob who thinks she is better than she is, but she has an exceptional chef and moves in quite interesting literary circles."

"You do not strike me as a book man," Annie raised an eyebrow at him.

"Do you suppose I am uneducated?" Chang responded with anger. "I like books. I like to read. They are a simple pleasure one can enjoy alone and safely behind a locked door. I can appreciate the written word. A good book takes me away from reality for a time. I am self-educated. I had to be. My learning was because of books."

Chang, to Annie's surprise, was hurt.

"I am sorry," she said, meaning it, because Annie was a gentle soul. "I just meant I could not imagine you having the time. I shouldn't have said that."

Chang relaxed.

"Well, I suppose there are a lot of things about me most people would not realise or expect. I have dreams, Annie, of what I shall do after all this."

"After?"

"I cannot be the head of a criminal organisation forever," Chang grinned at her. "I shall get old. I shall lose my edge. Younger men will want my power. I maintain my position partly because I am respected by my subordinates and partly because I am always ready for an attempt against me. I have to be always on guard. It is tiring, but right now I can manage. As you get older, you do not want such effort. You want to be able to enjoy the life you have made for yourself."

"You mean, one day you want to retire?" Annie said, finding the concept absurd. The idea you could retire from being a criminal mastermind made no sense. "Is that even possible?"

"I shall make it possible," Chang replied. "That is why I am looking into beginning my own publishing company. It shall be a legitimate business, everything above board. Respectable, even. I want the finest literary minds to be fighting over me and whether I shall publish their latest works."

"A legitimate business, built with the money from your criminal dealings," Annie said.

"There is an irony there, but once it is established there will be nothing to tie back to my criminal days. It shall be my retirement. I shall move away from London. I thought Stratford sounded appealing, and there I shall pursue my publishing desires, and no one will know I was ever anything other than a quiet, old man from the Orient who likes English books."

Annie thought about this a moment.

"It is a nice dream," she said. "Surely that makes Ariadne Griffiths useful to you?"

"Her poems yes, as a person, no," Chang replied. "Honestly, I can barely tell you anything about the woman from that evening at the Bumptons' home. She existed, at the corner of my vision, but she never approached me. She could have been a shadow, for all the attention I paid her."

"Which brings us back to how you were drugged," Annie said. "If you watched all your drinks prepared, how could it have occurred."

"I have considered the matter and there is only one thing that stands out in my mind," Chang explained. "During the course of the evening, I was chatting to a young lady whose name was Olivia. She was pretty and rather loud, and also very drunk. I had hoped to extract myself from her company, but she proved rather awkward to escape. During the course of our conversation, if that is what one can call it, she knocked my hand and spilled my drink. Apologising profusely, she offered me hers in exchange, which was fresh and untouched by her. It happened to be the same drink as I had been consuming and so I accepted."

"A very subtle way to get a laced drink into your hand," Annie nodded. "You know that means this Olivia person was involved in this scheme somehow."

"Yes, I had realised that," Chang concurred snidely. "Trust me, I have considered searching for her and demanding to know what she was playing at, but I decided there was no point. She was working for Ariadne, clearly. I should have been more cautious, of course. I never suspected and that was my mistake."

"It was a perfectly innocent seeming arrangement. A little accident that can happen," Annie consoled him.

"And it has led me to this," Chang indicated himself, the pyjamas, the curse and being stuck in Clara's home. "Not long after I consumed that drink, my memory becomes a blank."

"You can remember nothing at all except waking up on the floor of a bedroom?"

"Nothing," Chang promised. "Trust me, I have dredged my mind for something, anything that might hint at what occurred. A sound, maybe, an image. There is no clue for me there."

Annie was thoughtful for a while, finding the whole scenario rather perplexing. She could not understand why Ariadne had gone to such trouble. What did she hope to gain? Money? Then she was a fool, for anyone could have told her Chang was not someone who gave away money willingly. She had also placed herself in the path of a very dangerous man. He could have had her killed for all she knew. She was lucky that Chang was more gentlemanly than most criminals and was inclined to resolve matters without bloodshed.

"Why did she do it?" Annie voiced the question. "Why did she take such risks?"

Chang shook his head.

"I do not know," he admitted. "I suppose, she had to drug me to ensure the seduction, because I would not have looked at her otherwise. She is not a particularly beautiful woman, nor does she have a particularly dazzling personality. As I said, during that entire party I barely noticed her."

"She could not guarantee she would become pregnant either," Annie persisted. "And if she did not, then she had gone to all that trouble for nothing."

"If she was looking to blackmail me, she went to a lot of trouble."

Annie was frowning, deep in thought.

"I wonder if Ariadne was the sort of girl to think up such a scheme alone," she mused. "Gosh, I sound like Clara! I don't suppose your doctors told you what drug it was you were given?"

"I did not go to them about it," Chang said. "Quite frankly, I was rather humiliated by my lapse, and I preferred to tell as few people as possible. I would rather no one knew."

"It is most peculiar," Annie recalled the teapot and what must now be very stewed tea. She retrieved it as she went over all the information Chang had mentioned. "Do you think you would have published Ariadne's poems, had this not occurred?"

"I don't know. They are not to my liking. Are you saying she did this to get me to publish her poetry?"

"Oh no," Annie said, knowing how preposterous that sounded. "I was just thinking that Ariadne rather cut off her nose to spite her face, if indeed she had hoped you might publish her poems. By raising your anger, she has left herself without that as an option and, so far, she has no money, either."

"I think of her stood in my office, the look of determination on her face, but just a hint of fear and how she bellowed at me for taking advantage of her. Taking advantage of her!"

Chang's anger was back.

"She had the nerve..." he banged a fist on the table and rattled the teacups.

Annie pretended not to notice and poured tea.

"Whatever her intentions, Clara will sort it all out and things will go back to normal," Annie heard what she was saying and felt awkward. Going back to normal for Chang was returning to a life of criminality. He had a finger in many illegal pies and however smartly he dressed, however politely he spoke, he was a killer and a man of corruption. Annie must not forget that, though it was easy to begin to when sitting quietly chatting with the man. She resolved herself to being tougher.

"Why have we had no word from Clara?" Chang demanded.

"Because she is busy," Annie answered. "And rushing to a telephone every half hour to update us is a waste of her time."

Chang growled to himself

"I am not a patient man," he muttered.

Annie put the teapot down loudly.

"Right now, Mr Chang, patience is the one thing you need to master."

Chapter Fourteen

It was plain Fitzroy was not going to back down from his stance of silence. It was also infuriating. Gloucester looked fit to explode and for once, Clara was inclined to let him. Let a lord's son throw his weight around and maybe Fitzroy would break his silence.

"This is ridiculous!" Gloucester blustered. "You have to tell us the truth!"

"I have," Fitzroy stated flatly. "I took Ariadne home and that is that. If she left again, I am hardly to blame."

"I do not believe you," Gloucester pointed a finger at him. "There is this preposterous errand nonsense for a start."

"It is not nonsense. It is the truth. Can't a man be careless about his driving and double-back on himself unnecessarily? It was late, it was Christmas Eve, and I was not really thinking straight."

"That I believe," Clara told him. "The rest is questionable."

Fitzroy was going to say something back, but he then happened to turn his head and glanced towards the door. He clammed up as he spotted that the door was open and leaning against the door frame was his fiancée.

Clara followed his gaze and saw a tall, handsome woman observing them with cold, calm eyes. She had not made a sound and had clearly been intent on secretly watching them. Fitzroy winced, but it was Gloucester who spoke first.

"I say, Elaine DeVaughn? Is that you?"

The woman in the doorway cast her eyes in his direction.

"Alfie," she said. "Why, I have not seen you since I was ten, I think."

"You were a girl with braids," Gloucester nodded. "I did not realise you were living here."

"I keep myself to myself," Elaine shrugged. "I am not interested in those pretentious parties everyone throws. Besides, I only come down for the winter. Winter in the countryside is terribly depressing. At least in London there is some life."

Fitzroy's composure was fracturing. He was perturbed his fiancée was familiar with Gloucester, on first-name terms, no less.

"I thought you would be with your family at Christmas?" Elaine asked Gloucester.

"I was," he replied. "But I can only endure father for so long."

"I remember your father. Rather a pedantic sort and prone to going on and on about the same thing time and time again."

"Yes, currently he is hounding me to marry," Gloucester smiled morosely.

"I never pegged you for the marrying sort," Elaine replied.

Gloucester chuckled.

"I think that is what father fears too. But here you are on the brink of marrying this gentleman."

If there was an edge to the way Gloucester

pronounced 'gentleman' it was subtle enough to go unnoticed. Elaine walked into the room, taking long languid strides, and looking quietly confident. Clara thought she outmatched her intended husband quite dramatically.

"Fitzroy is a good fellow," Elaine said, though her defence of her husband-to-be seemed slow, as if she did not really care. "Why are you haranguing him?"

"It is just a misunderstanding," Fitzroy said fast. "I drove through a puddle and splashed him with water."

"Drenched," Gloucester said with careful pronunciation. "But that is just a part of the matter at hand. Your future husband appears to be the last person…"

"This has nothing to do with Elaine and there is no cause to be troubling her," Fitzroy interrupted. "I have told you all I can, and now you should go. I shall pay for a new coat if that will satisfy you, Gloucester."

Fitzroy thought his fiancée would meekly respect what he had said and leave him to his business. He was terribly wrong in that regard. Elaine DeVaughn raised an eyebrow and pointedly turned to Clara, who she perceived as a woman after her own heart.

"I would like to know what this is all about. Clearly it is not just some nonsense concerning a puddle, though I am most sympathetic Gloucester and I have told Fitzroy before to be more careful of such things," her aside to Gloucester was a smooth attempt to mollify him, but her attention was swiftly back on Clara. "Tell me what this is about."

"My dear…" Fitzroy began.

Elaine shot up a hand to silence him and he obeyed. What fight he had shown to Clara and the others, he could not show to his wife-to-be.

"We are searching for a young lady who has gone missing," Clara explained, keeping things simple. "Your husband appears to have been the last person to have seen her."

"Really?" Elaine said, a strange smile on her face. "How odd. Who is this young lady?"

Fitzroy started to babble, desperate to prevent the discussion continuing. He was not going to succeed. Clara spoke over him.

"Her name is Ariadne Griffiths."

The strange smile became something more akin to a grimace on Elaine's face.

"Oh, but I should have known!"

"My dear, it is not what you think!" Fitzroy bleated.

"There is something else here," Tommy spoke over him. "Isn't there?"

Elaine gave a soft sigh. Fitzroy was trying to conjure up some words for her and soundly failing.

"Prior to our association, Fitzroy was involved with Ariadne Griffiths," she said. "Indeed, some of my friends thought he might still be involved with her after we had become engaged."

"You were close to Ariadne?" Gloucester said in astonishment. "She never mentioned you to me!"

"You never struck me as the jealous type, Gloucester," Elaine eyed him up. "At least, not over a woman."

"Ariadne is a close friend. At least… I thought we were close, but now I see she was keeping quite a few secrets from me," Gloucester shook his head. "Why would you put up with a fellow who is courting another woman behind your back, Elaine?"

Elaine was unmoved by his shock.

"I am not much for jealousy," she remarked. "And Fitzroy suits me, but I did make it plain that I would not have any two-timing nonsense. I place value on my reputation, and I shall not be seen as one of these women whose husband is darting off with all and sundry behind her back."

"That was not how it was," Fitzroy said urgently,

because he had heard the sinister bite to her tone. "I had broken things off with Ariadne long before we got together."

"Then why did you pick her up in your car on Christmas Eve," Clara demanded, finding all this beating around the bush tiresome.

"Because she looked cold and tired!" Fitzroy said angrily. "I was just being a gentleman!"

"You promised not to associate with her," Elaine said to him.

"It was late, and dark," Fitzroy bleated.

"I do not care. You broke a promise to me. How am I to know you did not spend the night with her? You were not here with me after all. I assumed you were in your own bed, now I find myself wondering."

"It was not like that," Fitzroy insisted. "I dropped her at home."

"After your mysterious errand," Tommy mentioned, not about to let Fitzroy get away with things easily.

Fitzroy groaned as Elaine's eyes widened.

"What errand?" she demanded.

"Just a Christmas present to drop off," Fitzroy insisted. "I mentioned it before I left here."

"No, you did not," Elaine told him sternly. "And who drops off Christmas presents in the early hours of Christmas morning when everyone ought to be abed?"

"It was a last-minute thing," Fitzroy kept flogging a dead horse.

"Perhaps, if you told us who you ran this errand to, we might have a better time believing you," Clara pointed out.

Fitzroy shook his head.

"Who was it?" Elaine joined in. "I shall know where you were trailing off to late at night."

"With Ariadne in the car with him," Gloucester could not resist.

Fitzroy had the four of them plunging metaphorical daggers into him, but he would not give in. He shook his head once more.

"You have no right to hound me," he said. "Wherever Ariadne has disappeared to. It is nothing to do with me."

"For someone who clearly cared enough about Ariadne to give her a lift in his car, you seem wholly unconcerned she is now missing," Tommy noted.

Fitzroy glanced at him; his mouth flopped open but there was nothing he could say.

"I would like to suppose you would have more concern if I went missing," Elaine remarked, hands on her hips in indignation.

"You wanted me to have nothing to do with Ariadne!" Fitzroy gurgled. "And that is why I was not going to get involved with this disappearing business."

"Rather cold-hearted," Clara said. "Considering Ariadne is with child too."

She had known the reaction this information would get from Elaine, which was precisely why she had wedged it into the conversation, somewhat bluntly, it had to be said.

"Ariadne was pregnant?"

"Elaine, the child is not mine!" Fitzroy said quickly. "I was never intimate with her. I swore that to you, and I stand by it."

Elaine was glaring at him.

"I always knew you were callous and self-absorbed, Fitzroy," she said. "I suppose I thought I could improve you a little and I could overlook a lot of your faults, but to think a woman you allegedly once cared about is missing, and pregnant with it, and you give not a jot about the matter, beggars belief."

Fitzroy's head was spinning. He had tried to twist and turn to be perfect to everyone in the room, trying to do as his wife said and yet somehow incurring her wrath, nonetheless. He was so utterly confused by it all, he was terrified to open his mouth again. But one thing was for sure, he was not going to let them drag anymore information from him.

"I am done with this," he informed them. "I have done nothing wrong, and you cannot harangue me like this."

He took a step back from the library table, waiting to see if someone would physically stop him. He seemed convinced they would, but when no one budged he took his chance and headed for the door.

"Don't bother about apologising Elaine," he snapped as he left. "This time, I shall not accept it. You can break the engagement off at your leisure."

He tried to regroup some of his dignity as he departed. Elaine watched him without a flicker of deep concern. She turned back to the others once they had heard the front door slam.

"I rather fancy you have saved me from a grave mistake," she said, though she still seemed rather unmoved by everything. "I ought to have realised how flighty he was, but I liked to suppose he would be different after the marriage."

"Why were you marrying him?" Gloucester demanded. "You are worth so much more."

Elaine smiled at him.

"Oh, I know that, but rather like you are not the marrying kind, nor am I. But the parents were insistent I find someone and if I left it much longer there was a real risk they would choose someone for me. I thought I could live with Fitzroy. Obviously, I was wrong."

Everyone was gloomy after that. They had achieved little in their search for Ariadne and the day was fast drawing on. It would not be long before Clara and Tommy had to catch their train if they wished to be back in Brighton that night.

"Ariadne is really missing?" Elaine broke the

silence.

"Yes," Gloucester answered her. "Since Christmas Eve. We are very worried."

Elaine nodded at him and there was at last a hint of a person behind her façade of cool, calmness. She reached out and touched his arm, offering him solace as best she could.

"Why would Fitzroy cause her to disappear?" she said.

"We are not sure he did," Clara spoke. "But, as the last person to see her, he has to come under close attention. Ariadne argued with him before she got into his car."

"She was probably not best pleased with him. He broke things off with her to charm me," Elaine explained without a hint of remorse. "I believe she was rather hurt."

"Ariadne never mentioned she was seeing anyone," Gloucester was still struggling to fathom why the friend he thought told him everything had kept this a secret.

"How do you know Fitzroy offered her a lift?" Elaine continued.

"He was seen pulling over to the pavement and talking to her and then she got into his car," Clara elaborated. "He then drove off in the direction of Berkeley Square, which is curious because Ariadne's flat was in the other direction."

"I imagine he had an excuse to explain that?" Elaine asked. "Ah, the errand story you were pressing him about. He said he was running an errand and took Ariadne with him. Only, it makes no sense that he took her all the way to Berkeley Square, then drove her back to her flat, then turned around and headed to Berkeley Square again."

"Precisely, there is no logic to it," Tommy concurred. "If he was just wanting to get Ariadne home out of the cold, why not turn around immediately and take her home? It would have taken a few minutes, that is all."

"Maybe he never took her back to her flat. Maybe she went with him to Berkeley Square and stayed there," Elaine said darkly. "I always fancied he had not fully finished with her. He swore he had, but there was something always drawing him back, I sensed it."

"If she stayed at Berkeley Square, then where is she now?" Gloucester asked the obvious.

Elaine was thoughtful as she considered the question.

"I want to know if Fitzroy is involved in her disappearance or not," she said. "You will get nothing from him, I fear. When he is determined to keep a secret, he is dogged about it. We must go about things in another direction."

"What are you thinking?" Gloucester asked her.

"If Ariadne went back to Berkeley Square, then perhaps there is something she left behind there. Or some clue as to what happened next. Something you could present to Fitzroy to force him to tell the truth, or even go to the police with."

"All very well, but how would we find such a clue?" Tommy said.

Elaine smiled.

"I have a key to his house. I shall lend it to you and then I shall ask Fitzroy to return here to discuss our future. I have already made up my mind, but he is not to know that. You can search his home while he is here."

Clara might have argued about breaking and entering, if a woman's life was not potentially in danger. Gloucester frowned at Elaine.

"Why are you doing this?" he asked.

Elaine tilted her head at him as she replied.

"I want to know if the man I nearly married is a

kidnapper, or worse. I would like to understand just how shocking my judgement is, for future reference."

Chapter Fifteen

"We have a couple of hours before we need to catch our train," Tommy said, marking the time by a large church clock they spotted as Gloucester drove them in a roundabout route to Berkeley Square to avoid Fitzroy catching sight of them.

"We shall make it," Clara promised him.

"I can take you to the train station by car," Gloucester assured them both. "It will save you a lot of time."

Elaine had telephoned to Fitzroy while they were at her house. She had asked him to return at once, they had to talk. The others, she promised him, had left, and would not interfere. It took some convincing to get Fitzroy to dismount from his high horse, but he had had time to simmer down and was aware that his engagement to Elaine came with some significant financial advantages. It was why he had been prepared to put up with all the restrictions she had placed upon him. He eventually decided it was worth his time to try to salvage things.

When the telephone call was concluded, Elaine

turned to the others.

"He is on his way over," she said, and handed them her key. "I shall aim to detain him for a good couple of hours. I can ask him to dine with me and that shall prevent him leaving too soon."

She had wished them off, advised them not to use the straight route to Berkeley Square in case Fitzroy saw them (Clara considered this obvious, but said nothing) and then hustled them out the front door. She was plainly done with them as well.

Now here they were, driving cautiously into Berkeley Square from the opposite side to which Fitzroy would leave, hoping he had already departed. There was no sign of his car and they all relaxed.

Gloucester pulled up outside Fitzroy's house and hesitated for just a moment.

"Is this illegal?" he asked, starting to wonder what he was getting himself into.

"It is not breaking and entering, because we have the key and were given permission by Fitzroy's fiancée," Tommy reassured him.

"But, does that count?" Gloucester said, still uneasy. "I cannot end up in a courtroom for common housebreaking. My father would go spare."

"It is enough of a grey area to probably not be completely illegal," Clara remarked. "Elaine asked us to do this, after all, and gave us the key."

Gloucester was not entirely convinced that would prevent them from being arrested if Fitzroy caught wind of all this.

"You can wait here," Clara told him. "We shall go inside and see if there is any sign Ariadne was here recently."

With the mention of Ariadne's name, Gloucester rallied. He remembered why he was doing this, and his nerves calmed.

"No, I shall come. You will not know if something

belonged to Ariadne or not unless I am there to identify it."

All resolved to the task, they headed towards the front door and tried the key. They entered without a problem and stood in the quiet hall, getting their bearings. Elaine had mentioned that Fitzroy did not employ a full staff for his property. He had a steward who managed his day-to-day existence, ate his meals out and had his washing sent to a lady who cleaned it and returned it once a week. The steward was away visiting family over the Christmas period and so the house was completely empty. Elaine was sure the lack of a servant to pick up after Fitzroy, and the promise of a good dinner for free, would overcome any objections her fiancé might have to returning to her home. It seemed she had been completely correct.

"We might as well begin on the ground floor and work room to room," Clara suggested, heading towards a doorway on their right that led into a drawing room.

It was quite obvious that Fitzroy's steward was away. Fitzroy had no concept how to clean up after himself and scattered about the room were discarded glasses and cups, coats, scarves, pairs of shoes, and plates covered with the debris of hastily constructed meals. There was a faint odour of stale food hanging in the room, along with cigarette smoke. It made Clara itch to open a window, but she knew that was not a good idea. They had to slip in and out of this house like ghosts.

The shutters at the windows were drawn closed and latched. It seemed probable they had not been opened since the steward had departed. Fitzroy apparently had no qualms over wandering about in the dark.

"I have to say, this man makes a worse mess than Roderick," Tommy said, picking up the edge of a blanket that had been discarded on a sofa and looking beneath. "This room is a disgrace."

Gloucester was moving about with great care, trying to be sure he did not stand on something unexpected and disagreeable. Clara wanted to flick on a light and illuminate the room, but it was better to rely on the grey light coming in around the edges of the shutters. She paced the room slowly and methodically. Nothing that could be obviously linked to Ariadne caught her eye.

They moved on to a dining room, shuttered just like the drawing room. More plates clustered upon the table, covered with greasy residue from long discarded meals. A soft scurrying noise near Tommy's foot told him that the resident mice were enjoying the absence of the steward and were having their own Christmas celebrations.

The dining room offered no clues other than confirming Fitzroy was slovenly when left to his own devices. They moved on again, however, the next room was clearly rarely used and was collecting a thin layer of dust after a week of neglect. The remaining room was a library which had to have been installed by a previous occupant. It was immaculate because Fitzroy never entered it.

They moved up to the first floor, Gloucester sagging with despondency. He had been so sure there would be an obvious sign of Ariadne's presence in the drawing room, now he was wondering if they had it all wrong. Maybe Fitzroy had taken her home as he had said and had nothing to do with her disappearance.

They discovered Fitzroy's bedroom, which was a heap of bedding and dirty clothing. It reeked of stale alcohol and Tommy pointed out where a decanter of port had been knocked over and emptied itself onto the floor. The decanter had been hastily replaced, but the soaked rug had not been removed.

Clara found herself frowning as she gazed about the

room. She sensed something in the jumble, something more than sheer untidiness. She touched one of the bed curtains and realised it had been partly torn from its rings. There were goose down feathers nestling on the floor, just a handful as if someone had emptied a pillow of its contents and then stuffed them back in. The more she scanned the room, the more she felt sure there were hints of something occurring here other than sleep.

"I think there was a struggle in this room," Clara said to the two men.

"A struggle?" Gloucester said, surprised.

"We have the spilled decanter that was neglected long enough to pour out most of its contents onto the floor. Someone would only ignore that if they were distracted by something else. We have a torn bed curtain as if someone yanked on it hard, perhaps as they fell. And we have these feathers which indicate someone was messing about with the pillows, perhaps they threw them at someone else?"

"They could also be signs of Fitzroy stumbling in here incredibly drunk," Tommy suggested.

"True," Clara admitted. "But, considering the circumstances of us being here, I think we ought to consider it a possibility that something else happened in this room."

"Ariadne was here?" Gloucester paled at the thought. He now saw the signs of a struggle Clara had noted and his mind was inferring too many unhappy possibilities from them. "What has he done with her?"

"Firstly, we must be careful about jumping to conclusions," Clara headed him off before he could become carried away. "Secondly, we should take a good look at this room to see if there is any sign of Ariadne's presence."

They resumed the search, though they all felt a little overwhelmed by the task. The room was so untidy, so dishevelled, that it seemed hopeless to find anything among the chaos. As it happened, it was only when they had concluded the room was a dead end for clues, that they found what they were looking for. Clara had been searching under the bed, which was a haven for discarded shoes and lurking spiders. As she removed herself, she dragged away the blanket on the bed by accident, as she went to restore it, she saw there was a scarf lying on the mattress. It had been beneath the blanket and hidden from view. She reached out for it.

Quite clearly it was a woman's scarf and its presence in the bed suggested that a lady had been up here. Since Elaine was not inclined to keep company with her husband-to-be in such a way before their marriage, the obvious conclusion was that an unknown woman had been in Fitzroy's bedroom recently. Elaine would not be happy.

"Gloucester, does this scarf look familiar?" she held the article out to him.

Gloucester took it and fumbled the silk of the material.

"I am nearly certain it is Ariadne's," he said bitterly.

"Then, it seems we have proof Fitzroy brought Ariadne back to his house," Tommy said. "But where is she?"

Clara was feeling increasingly uneasy about the scene before them. The signs of a struggle raised dark thoughts in her mind. There were no signs of blood, but there were ways to be rid of a person without shedding it. Had Fitzroy felt compromised by Ariadne somehow and decided to do away with her? Or had she continued the argument begun on the pavement once they were here, in his bedroom, and it had gotten out of hand?

"Ariadne must be in this house," Gloucester said a touch desperately.

He darted out of the room and began racing around looking for her, expecting to find a locked door behind which she was just sitting and waiting to be rescued.

"Keep an eye on him," Clara nodded to her brother. "I am going to look around for an explanation for this riddle."

Tommy nodded to her and darted after Gloucester, who had found all the room doors unlocked and had resorted to opening wardrobes and climbing under beds to find his missing friend.

Clara wandered across the upstairs landing and entered a room that was set aside as a study, of sorts. Fitzroy was not a man for letter writing or for business in general, but he could not ignore the correspondence he received, nor avoid having to deal with the day-to-day fundamentals of running one's life. His steward only had time to do so much, and Fitzroy preferred to deal with such things as his tailor's bill, or an irate notice from his favourite club concerning his late membership fees, himself.

The study was one of the neatest rooms in the house, other than those that were unused. Clara went to a large writing desk and started looking through what was there. She discovered that Fitzroy was a secret collector of risqué cigarette cards, the sort where a voluptuous lady without clothing contorted herself into novel positions for the interest of the viewer. He had a whole album filled with them, and several loose ones that were clearly in the process of being glued in. Clara doubted he would be taking this with him when married Elaine.

She opened drawers and looked through his bills, noting a great number of them were overdue. Some were the second or third notice concerning an outstanding sum of money. It all suggested that Fitzroy was struggling financially. That would explain why he was considering marrying Elaine. It was obviously a loveless match of convenience. For Elaine it would stop her parents asking questions and also be an annoyance to them that she had married someone like Fitzroy. For Fitzroy it was a means to secure his financial future and ensure he had a roof over his head.

The more Clara explored through his papers, the plainer it became that Fitzroy gambled too much, drank too much, and spent too much. He was in dire straits and some of the people he owed money to were not particularly pleasant.

Clara found several threatening letters shoved at the back of one drawer. Their contents were not for delicate eyes and went into excruciating detail about what would happen to Fitzroy if money was not forthcoming. She could imagine him sitting here, trembling as he read the letter, and then somehow pulling himself together and heading off to see Elaine. She was his one hope, after all.

Nothing, however, explained the matter of Ariadne's disappearance. What precisely had gone on between them? Had the two old lovers argued about him casting her over for Elaine and things had gotten out of hand? Could it be that simple?

Such things happened all the time, but that still left some big questions behind, such as why Ariadne had connected herself to Brilliant Chang in the first place.

Clara continued to sort through the letters, hoping for a clue and then suddenly it was in her hand. Another letter, from someone who identified themselves as Bruno. The words were blunt and gave her a hint of a connection at last.

Bruno was offering Fitzroy a chance at redemption, a way to pay off all his bills and keep all his fingers and toes intact. Bruno wanted Brilliant Chang out of the picture, and he had an idea how it could be achieved. First, he needed to get Chang away from his inner circle where he was most protected, then he needed to weaken him and leave him vulnerable. He had this idea that would play on Chang's slightly superstitious nature. It was audacious, but the only way he could think of getting Chang sufficiently distracted to make him drop his guard.

He was outlining the plan to drug Chang and then make him think he had slept with an unknown woman. As Clara read, it all became obvious what he was attempting, and it had worked.

Clara blinked as she realised something. Bruno wanted Chang away from London, he wanted him somewhere he could be got to, and Chang was now in Brighton, in Clara's home.

Clara gulped. They had to get back to Brighton at once.

Chapter Sixteen

Chang had insisted on demonstrating to Annie how to cook a traditional Chinese dish, though he was somewhat hampered by the limits of Annie's pantry. After raiding what he could from the very English ingredients, he determined he could make an approximation of a Chinese dish, using spices and Worcestershire sauce to add the flavour. It would not be exactly right, but the very fact the ingredients were all the ones Annie used on a regular basis at least made her more amenable to the idea.

She was also being agreeable because it was good to see Chang with a little energy once more. After their deep discussion about the matter of Ariadne, they had moved onto other topics of a more innocuous nature. Sooner or later, cooking was bound to come up. When Chang asked if Annie had ever eaten a dish from the Orient, he had known the exact answer he would receive, and it was a touch of spiteful glee that he said he would cook her something to demonstrate his birth country's cuisine.

Annie had done her best not to sneer at the notion

and then embraced the inevitable as long as it meant Chang was not thinking about his curse.

He set about locating pans for the process, selecting a heavy frying pan Annie was rather fond of. She hoped the procedure of cooking 'something foreign' in it would not ruin it forever. Chang had instructed her to slice the vegetables he had selected as thinly as possible, wafer thin, if she could. Annie had done her best but was concerned that the selection of carrots, beans, and cabbage she had sliced had been irredeemable damaged by this attention.

"Do you have rice?" Chang asked her.

"Of course, I have rice," Annie tutted. "Who does not? I like to make kedgeree on a Sunday. I also have pudding rice for making…"

Chang had a look of complete horror on his face.

"Kedgeree is a defilement of rice," he informed her. "I shall not even begin on the English delight for rice pudding."

Annie folded her arms across her chest, deeply offended. It was dangerous territory for Chang to stumble into, even if he was being given leeway because of his condition.

"Get the rice and I shall show you how we fry it with egg," Chang went on, happily.

"Fry it?" Annie gawked. "It will be all hard!"

"You cook it first," Chang snorted, as if this was obvious.

Muttering to herself, Annie went to fetch the rice from a back corner of the pantry. She was returning with it when the front doorbell rang. Annie wondered if it might be Dr Cutt returned with news and placed down the bag of rice to answer it. Chang was happily heating butter in the frying pan and humming to himself, clearly content.

"Well, at least that is something," Annie puttered to herself as she went to the door and opened it.

The doorstep was empty, no sign of anyone about.

"Kids," Annie grumbled. "As if I have all day to waste answering the door to no one."

She stepped into the front garden and peered about to see if she could spy any of her neighbours' children hiding somewhere and chuckling at luring her to the door unnecessarily. She could see no one about and with the dusk fast falling, and temperatures dropping it seemed ridiculous for children to be playing such larks. Shaking her head at the youth of today, Annie was setting foot back in the house when she heard a scream from her kitchen.

Annie's first instinct was to run and discover what Chang had done, assuming he had mishandled her range and burnt himself. Her common sense kicked in fast enough to stop her as she realised she could hear two voices in her kitchen. Both now yelling and screeching.

Annie had no idea what was occurring, but there were two things she did know – first, she had a criminal leader in her house, and he was the sort of person trouble followed, and, second, that a fire poker was a very handy weapon.

She dashed into the front parlour and grabbed up the nearest poker, (for good measure she took the coal shovel as well) then she dashed for the kitchen.

The scene she came upon took a moment to work out. There was a big, burly man brandishing a knife, but he was also clutching a hand to his face where the cheek was badly reddened, and he had trouble opening one of his eyes.

Chang, still dressed in borrowed pyjamas, was wielding Annie's favourite frying pan as a weapon, and was shrieking in Chinese at the intruder. Whether it was something offensive he yelled or a war cry, Annie had no clue, but she was concerned for her frying pan.

The two men were squaring off in the middle of the

room. The big burly man was trying to get past the frying pan and slice open Chang. Despite his condition, Chang was proving too adept for him and was keeping him at bay. The problem was the situation had rapidly turned into a stalemate and it was not obvious which direction it would go next.

Annie glanced at her kitchen floor and noticed her carefully sliced vegetables were scattered across the tiles. Something snapped inside her. Her kitchen was her sanctuary, her temple, and this fiend had violated it coming in and brandishing his knife. After that revelation, her temper was unstoppable.

She came alongside Chang and moved so fast neither of them noticed her until it was too late. She was silent in her fury, charging at the thug with her poker aiming to crack him over the head. She had underestimated how tall he was and instead of his head she landed a sound blow on his shoulder.

He yelled out, his hand dropping from his face and his attention flicking to her. It was all the distraction Chang needed and he swung the frying pan, hitting the assailant square in the head and causing him to stumble sideways dramatically.

Remarkably, he remained conscious, though a little dazed.

Annie came at him again, now wielding the coal shovel in her other hand and giving him a good crack to the temple. The man fell with a grunt, hitting his head on the edge of the butler sink as he went down. Annie winced, expecting to see her sink chipped, but it proved more substantial than she had feared.

The burly man lay on the floor and groaned softly.

Chang had a look of utter rage on his face. His teeth were bared, his lips pulled back in an awful grimace. His eyes seemed to have expanded beyond ten times their normal size and he trembled with pent up aggression. Annie gently removed the frying pan from his grasp and returned it to the stove.

This emergency dealt with, she turned her attention to Chang who seemed unsure whether to continue to rage at the unconscious thug or faint. She pulled out a chair and pushed him down into it. Chang was streaming with sweat, and she had no doubt when the excitement of the moment wore off, he would be exhausted and frail again. She was about to make a cup of tea for him, when she remembered the assailant resting on her kitchen floor.

"I shall have to call the police," she said.

"No police," Chang said, his teeth still gritted as if they had seized up that way.

"Then what do I do with him?" Annie said in her practical fashion, waving a hand at the thug. "He can't remain on the kitchen floor. When he wakes up, he will be out for both our heads."

Chang was starting to calm down and take in the situation. There was just a hint of fear in his eyes.

"He came for me," Chang said. "He was going to kill me."

"I guess he followed you down here," Annie sighed. "Do you think this is all connected with the business with Ariadne?"

"Either that or someone suspected I was weakened and when I came here, away from my usual security arrangements, they saw their chance. Assassination attempts are not exactly unusual for me."

Annie stared at him sadly.

"Well, that is a pretty tragic state of affairs," she sighed. "But I am still calling the police. I will not be happy unless this man is in a police cell and unable to get into my kitchen again."

At the mention of the room, she glanced around its walls to reassure herself that nothing else had been damaged in the skirmish. She was satisfied that her kitchen was untouched, aside from the mess with the vegetables.

"Inspector Park-Coombs has nothing to arrest you for," Annie said. "In that regard you are safe from him. If you want, you can go back upstairs, and I shall pretend you are not here."

Chang had more dignity than to hide away from a police inspector and allow Annie to lie about his whereabouts. He said nothing and she nodded her head.

"That is what I thought."

She went to the hall and rang the police station, asking Inspector Park-Coombs to come at once as an intruder with a knife had caused her some bother. Then, having alarmed the desk sergeant no end, she returned to the kitchen and knelt by the attacker.

"His face is burnt."

"When he burst in the door, I reacted by throwing the melted butter in his face. It was just starting to bubble nicely," Chang explained, giving a forlorn look to the mess on the floor where his ingredients for the meal now resided. "I am sorry your bottle of Worcestershire Sauce has fallen and broken."

"Better than your head being broken," Annie answered, pragmatic as always. "I just want to check on the chickens, in case he disturbed them when he crossed the yard."

Annie hastened outside to check that her beloved chickens were safely shut in the henhouse as she had left them a short while ago. A quick peek inside assured her they were all present and unaffected by the disturbance.

She returned inside to find Chang toying with the knife she had used to chop the vegetables. The sinister look he was giving the man on the floor suggested his intentions.

"No, Chang," she said firmly. "The police are on their way."

"Only one way to be sure he cannot attack me again," Chang said fiercely.

"That way means we can get no information from him," Annie told him firmly. "Don't you want to know who sent him? Or if he was working alone? You kill him, we shall get nothing."

"He won't talk," Chang shook his head. "I know his kind. Nothing will persuade him to speak."

"Perhaps you are right, or perhaps being in a police cell might knock his confidence a fraction. Either way, I shall not let you kill him," with that, Annie stood in front of the man as a physical barrier.

"What is to say I don't just dispatch you to get to him?" Chang said nastily.

Annie folded her arms and stared at him, defying him to try it. She had called his bluff and Chang backed down. It helped he was feeling terribly ill again, and he was not sure he could even rise from the chair, let alone struggle with Annie.

His resolve faded and his shoulders slump as the last dregs of fight spilled from him. He looked frail again and Annie felt sorry for him.

"We still have the rice," she said as a way to cheer him. "Why don't I get it cooking and then you can show me how you fry it?"

It was a gesture of peace and Chang accepted.

"I should help you clear up this mess."

"Stay sitting there," Annie commanded, not quite sure if he was referring to the vegetables on the floor or the thug. "I don't need you collapsing on me."

"I am not going to collapse," Chang snapped.

"I am not taking any chances."

Annie filled a large pan with water from the pump and began to heat it on the range. While it was coming to the boil, she checked on their intruder. He was breathing, thankfully. The wounds to his head were unpleasant and could have led to a far worse outcome.

The knife he had been carrying had fallen to the floor beside him. She picked it up carefully and placed it on the draining board. Then she loosened the man's collar and tried to make him as comfortable as was possible.

"You are being far kinder to him than he would have been to us," Chang grumbled.

"What is your point?" Annie demanded of him.

Chang was silenced. Things were not going the way he had anticipated when he came to Clara's home. He was beginning to fear things were spiralling out of his control and for a man like Chang that was terrifying. His very life depended on him being in charge of every detail of his existence. It was exhausting, no doubt about that, but it kept him alive.

Now, he felt as though his brain was in a fog and he could not keep his thoughts straight. His clarity was gone, along with his focus. It scared him more than he cared to admit to himself. Every instinct in his body was telling him to kill the thug and be done with him. In any other situation he would have done just that and sent a message that Brilliant Chang is a survivor, and no assassin will take him down. But something about Annie's presence was making his usual methods impossible. He was still confused at how he could have allowed her to summon the police. Why was he waiting here for them? Was he so sick, he did not have the energy to resist anymore? The energy to battle on?

He dropped his head in his hands, feeling like his life was over and as if he did not even have the strength to care.

"Cheer up," Annie instructed him.

He lifted his head and saw she was stood closer to him. He had not even heard her move.

"This is all just temporary," Annie told him. "Remember that."

"What if it isn't?" Chang asked.

"If you are not dead, then everything else is just

temporary," Annie told him. "Death is the only permanent thing we have to look forward to. This is just a blip."

"You are not cheering me up," Chang griped.

"I didn't intend to. I just want you to stop moping and remember you are Brilliant Chang."

Chang would have replied, but the doorbell rang, and Annie wandered off to answer it. He eyed the thug on the floor, the knife still tempting him. Then he heard the door open and Annie's voice.

"Hello Inspector, you best come this way at once."

Chapter Seventeen

Clara and Tommy caught their train just in time. Gloucester had wanted them to stay longer. He was anxious about the signs of a struggle in Fitzroy's house and wanted to confront the man further about Ariadne's disappearance. Clara convinced him that they had very little that would force Fitzroy to speak, and it would be best if they held on until she could make some more enquiries.

Gloucester was not happy about this idea, but she repeatedly reminded him that if they sprang too soon, they would get nothing from Fitzroy, and he may even start to claim they were harassing him and call the police. It was important to remember they had trespassed in his home to retrieve this information and the only way they could avoid getting into trouble for that was if they could prove Fitzroy was involved in Ariadne going missing. Right at that moment, they could not. All they had was a scarf that Gloucester had dubiously identified as Ariadne's, and the second they brought that up they would reveal they had been inside Fitzroy's house.

Gloucester waved them off forlornly, after they assured him they would be back the next day. Clara hoped the man had enough sense to go home and stay there. But if he suddenly decided to confront Fitzroy, there was not a lot she could do about it. She needed to get home and make sure that Annie was safe.

The train seemed to take an eternity, but they arrived at last and hurried to catch the last omnibus to get them home. When they arrived on their doorstep, they were alarmed to see a police constable stood outside.

"Not to worry, Miss Fitzgerald," the constable said brightly as Clara raced over. "We are just waiting for the ambulance."

Needless to say, this did not reassure Clara one bit.

"Who needs an ambulance?" she demanded.

"Oh, some fella who broke into your kitchen," the constable said cheerfully.

Clara's shoulders sagged with relief. As long as it was not Annie who was hurt, she could relax. Tommy was itching to get indoors and see that his wife was all right.

"I need to get past!" he told the constable urgently.

As if he had only just realised he was in their way, the constable looked startled and moved to one side. Clara followed Tommy, acutely aware that a number of her neighbours had suddenly found chores to attend to in their gardens and were watching what was going on at her house with grave curiosity. Not that it was unheard of for Clara to have policemen on her doorstep. For that matter, it would not be the first time she had had an intruder unconscious in her house.

She hurried past the constable and to the kitchen, where she found Inspector Park-Coombs sat at the table, calmly slurping a cup of tea. Annie was sat opposite him, trying to convince him to eat a third helping of homemade fruit cake. Lying prone behind them, seemingly unnoticed, was a large, stout man who had clearly suffered head injuries recently.

Clara took in the scene, feeling she was viewing something in a madhouse.

"There is a man unconscious on my kitchen floor," she said.

"Yes," Park-Coombs nodded at her. "That is why we are waiting for an ambulance."

"Drinking tea and eating cake?" Clara said, aghast.

"What else were we to do?" Park-Coombs shrugged. "We have done our best for the fellow and need to keep an eye that he does not wake up and try to run or cause more trouble."

"By the look of those blows to his head, he won't be waking up in a hurry," Tommy frowned.

"I clobbered him with a poker and the coal shovel, then he fell and hit the sink," Annie explained. "I summoned Inspector Park-Coombs at once and he agrees it is clearly self-defence. He was carrying a knife and burst into the kitchen."

Clara gave her a look that implied she wanted to know the full story but was not sure how much the inspector knew. Annie nodded at her.

"He knows about Chang," she said. "I had to explain why a man would burst into our kitchen wielding a knife."

"Wait, this thug crashed in here, waving a knife around and you hit him with a poker?" Tommy was trying to catch up with what she had just said.

"Well, what else was I to do?" Annie asked. "Chang had already thrown melted butter in his face, but that was not going to stop him for long."

"Melted butter not being renowned for its use as a combat weapon," Clara said drily.

"Chang was showing me how to cook Chinese food," Annie elaborated unnecessarily. "Actually, in that regard I am rather relieved we were interrupted."

"Where is Chang now?" Tommy asked as clearly the man was not in the kitchen.

"He was exhausted from it all," Annie explained. "I thought he was going to collapse. After the inspector arrived and had spoken to him, I made sure he went back up to bed. I imagine he is asleep now."

"Annie has told me how you come to have a criminal lodger," Park-Coombs leaned back in his chair as he looked at Clara. "It is a curious tale."

"You know what I am like, Inspector. Someone asks me to help them, and I cannot resist. Chang was desperate. He had to be to come to me for help."

"Someone came after him," Park-Coombs reminded her. "I don't like the idea that you are housing a man who has assassins after him."

Clara did not say so, but she was not happy about the idea either, but what choice did she have?

"He needs my help and that is that," she sighed. "In any case, it looks as though his assassin is out of action for a while."

"Any luck with Ariadne?" Annie asked.

"There is another mystery," Clara replied. "Ariadne disappeared on Christmas Eve, and no one seems to know what became of her, though we suspect one person we spoke to has more knowledge than he is letting on. He is also connected to Chang."

Clara produced the letter from 'Bruno.' She had shown it to Tommy in the train but had thought it best to keep it quiet from Gloucester for the time being. She placed it on the table before the inspector.

"This Bruno is gunning for Chang," Park-Coombs read the letter.

"He certainly is," Clara agreed. "I hoped Chang might be able to tell us more about him."

"You think he is connected to Ariadne?" Annie said,

thoughtfully perusing the letter.

"I am starting to think that is probably the case," Clara nodded. "As is the person who received this letter."

"Chang believes he was drugged at the party where Ariadne supposedly seduced him. He cannot remember a thing and there was another woman involved. Her name was Olivia, and she seems the most likely person to have passed him the drugged drink," Annie revealed her own information.

"He didn't mention her second name?" Clara asked.

Annie shook her head.

"But he did say the party occurred at a house belonging to Mr and Mrs Bumpton. Perhaps they will recall Olivia?"

Both Clara and Tommy jerked their heads up at the name.

"That would be the home of Mrs Mindy Bumpton," Clara said, a smile forming on her face. "Who told us this morning that she knew nothing about how her dearest friend Ariadne became pregnant."

"She lied," Annie said. "She had to have known because the incident took place in her house, in one of her bedrooms."

"Sounds like she is involved in all this too," Park-Coombs rumbled. "What a complicated business."

"We will go back to London tomorrow morning and see if we can rattle out some more information," Clara nodded. "In the meantime…"

She waved a hand to the man on her floor.

"Where is that ambulance?" Park-Coombs checked his pocket watch.

Tommy drifted over to the man on the floor and felt his neck for a pulse. It was a relief to find it pumping strongly. He would prefer if his wife had not managed to kill a man in her kitchen, even if it was in self-defence.

As if Park-Coombs had talked up the vehicle, the clanging of a bell indicated the ambulance was arriving. Clara was relieved they would soon have the injured man safely on his way to hospital.

The ambulance driver and his assistant entered the house with a stretcher and discussed how best to get the heavy-set man onto it. He was considerably bigger than either of them and they were wondering if they could lift him.

Annie, always the consummate hostess, made sure they had a cup of tea and a slice of cake before they had to undertake their task. The slowness of the whole affair was driving Clara to distraction, and she had to get out of the way. She headed upstairs to check on Chang and to see what further information he could provide her with.

She knocked on his bedroom door lightly and heard him call for her to enter. She found him sitting up in bed, but without a light on so the room was in darkness. Just the trickle of light from the moon outside allowed her to see him. She flicked on the light and Chang winced at the sudden brightness.

"Are the police gone yet?" he asked solemnly.

"Not until the ambulance men have removed the thug on my kitchen floor, and that could take a while as Annie is currently feeding them tea and cake."

"She cannot resist, can she?" Chang said, though without his usual snideness.

He seemed very depressed, which was a somewhat alarming sight. Clara moved further into the room and handed him the letter.

"Annie told me what happened earlier. I found this while I was searching a house in London."

Chang took the letter and read it slowly.

"I don't know who this Bruno is," he said. "But I can see what he has planned for me."

"I think he might be connected to Ariadne," Clara paused as she had to impart the next piece of information. "Ariadne has vanished. She has been missing several days and at this stage I cannot say if she is alive or dead."

Clara was disappointed to see that Chang's face lit up at the news. She had hoped for better, but she supposed she could not really expect much, not from a man like Chang.

"This is good news. If she is dead, the curse will be broken," Chang smiled to himself, but a second later his face fell. "Except, I feel just as ill as before. Worse, indeed, after my skirmish earlier."

He rubbed at his face, feeling the weight of exhaustion drifting over him.

"I am going to try to find Ariadne," Clara told him. "We need to know what has become of her. I think all this muddle is connected to Bruno and his plans to make you vulnerable to attack."

"And it worked," Chang nodded. "Look how I have stumbled straight into his trap. No doubt that is his man downstairs."

"It could be Bruno himself."

Chang shook his head.

"A man like that, who wants to take over my empire, has people working for him. He does not do things like that himself."

"Do you know a man called Benjamin Fitzroy?" Clara asked next.

Chang gave himself a moment to consider the name.

"He sounds vaguely familiar."

"He may be responsible for the disappearance of Ariadne."

"Then I owe the man my thanks," Chang snorted.

"It was also in his home I found this letter," Clara added.

Chang's amusement diminished.

"I am going back to London tomorrow to investigate further," Clara said. "I was hoping you might be able to give me a hint where to look for this Bruno fellow."

Chang chuckled.

"I doubt it would be wise for you to find him," he said.

"It was not particularly wise me finding you, but that is the way my cases have gone," Clara reminded him.

Chang was not amused by the remark, especially as he was frustrated at being stuck in Clara's house, in her spare bedroom wearing her brother's pyjamas. He turned his attention to the letter again, trying to see something within it that would offer him a clue to who Bruno might be.

"He could be one of your associates," Clara suggested. "Someone already working for you."

Chang was about to sneer and say something mean, but then he realised she had a very good point.

"He certainly knows a good deal about me, about how to press my buttons," he admitted miserably.

"Exactly. He knew how to get you away from London."

"A man in my line of business, Clara, has a lot of enemies," Chang sighed. "And most are within his own organisation. It is certainly depressing, but just how things are. Maybe this man is someone who works for me, maybe he is not."

"I shall keep looking," Clara said, feeling the need to give him some hope. "Ariadne is the key to all this. If we can find her, we may get some answers."

"I have to admit, though I am angered at my situation, I am impressed by the skill with which I have been manipulated," Chang mused. "It is an impressive work of deception."

"That is one way to look at it," Clara nodded.

Outside the house, they heard the ambulance bell ringing again and it seemed at long last the driver and his assistant had eaten their cake, drunk their tea, and determined how they could carry the heavy man out to the vehicle.

"Maybe the man you put in hospital will provide some answers," Clara nodded her head towards the window and the direction of the ambulance.

"If he is a hardened brute, I doubt it," Chang sniffed.

"I like to remain optimistic," Clara told him. "Pessimism is rather like giving up before you begin."

"I am just stating the truth," Chang grumbled.

"The truth comes in many forms," Clara replied. "Well, I am going to leave you to rest. Annie no doubt has meal plans for you."

Chang pulled a face. Clara retrieved the Bruno letter from his unresisting grasp.

"Think about this name and try to come up with a suspect for me," she said.

Chang muttered something under his breath about doing her work for her and feeling he had already given her more than enough information. Clara was not going to argue with him. She was headed for the door when his voice called across the room.

"Your friend Annie," he said, "she is mean with a fire poker. I never thought she was the bloodthirsty type."

Clara glanced back and saw Chang had a genuine look of shock and mild alarm on his face at the memory.

"You don't mess with the Fitzgeralds," Clara laughed.

Chapter Eighteen

The following day, Clara and Tommy were back on the train to London with fresh questions for a number of people. They telephoned Gloucester in advance to let him know they were coming, and he was waiting for them at the station with his car. It was something of a relief to discover he had listened to Clara and stayed at home the previous night, though there was no doubting he had been desperate to get out and demand the truth from Fitzroy. He looked to Clara eagerly as she appeared from the station, hoping they were about to interview Fitzroy again and break his silence.

Clara had to somewhat disappoint him.

"We are going to see the Bumptons first," she told him.

"The Bumptons?"

"Mindy Bumpton lied to me yesterday," Clara elaborated.

She did not have to say more, this was enough to have Gloucester putting his car into gear and racing off.

"Lied," he said to himself, elated that his old enemy

had disgraced herself in such a fashion and was now going to be interrogated.

"At the very least, she was rather unobservant," Clara said, attempting to rein him in. She had been a bit too hasty with her words and saw how he was getting excited.

"Lied," Gloucester repeated to himself in satisfaction.

They arrived a short time later outside the home of the Bumptons. Clara suggested Gloucester would be best waiting in the car for them to deal with everything. Gloucester was having none of it.

"I have come this far," he said, "I deserve answers too."

There was no persuading him otherwise and Clara had to accept he would be joining them. She just hoped his presence would not cause Mindy Bumpton to clam up.

They knocked on the door and made the usual enquiries of the butler, explaining who they needed to see and asking if she was in. He did his part and left them lingering on the doorstep in the cold while he went to see if Mindy was in the mood for guests. Clara did not expect her to refuse, though Gloucester being with them was awkward. She had wanted to avoid giving his name, but after stating the Fitzgeralds were there to see Mrs Bumpton, the butler had looked rather pointedly at Gloucester, and it had been impossible to avoid introducing him.

They waited and waited. It seemed to be taking an age to get Mindy's opinion on whether to let them in or not. A fine drizzle started to fall, as if to remind them they were being forced to wait on someone's doorstep.

"I am sorry," Gloucester said when the length of time they had stood outside was clearly beyond what was necessary and seemed to suggest some deep discussions going on inside about what to do with them. "I should have stayed in the car. I did not think she detested me this much, however."

He was just finished speaking when the front door opened. They expected the butler, they did not expect Mindy Bumpton. She looked between them, her brows forming an angry line and then she made up her mind.

"You best all come in."

She had added the 'all' to make it plain Gloucester was going to be tolerated, though, in fairness, it would be difficult for a lady of Mindy Bumpton's position in society to completely refuse to allow a lord's son into her home. Under different circumstances, she would have tried, however.

They were shown into a different room from the one they had first met Mindy in. This was a snug of intimate proportions tucked away from the main household and presumably a place Mindy felt they would be free from prying ears.

"I take it this is about Ariadne?" Mindy said nervously. "Have you news?"

"Not as yet," Clara replied. "But this is about her and, more specifically, about how you lied to me the last time we spoke."

"Lied?" Mindy said, attempting astonishment and not quite achieving it.

"You informed me that Brilliant Chang had no connection to Ariadne, that they had never associated. I now know that to be a lie. Admittedly, Chang did not choose Ariadne's company willingly but a combination of a drugged drink and someone making sure he came up to one of your bedrooms achieved the same result," Clara said calmly, ignoring the fact Gloucester's eyes were now boggling as he heard this revelation. "You knew full well how Ariadne came to be pregnant, or rather, how she claimed she had become pregnant. She set up Chang and you assisted her."

"Now, now, that is quite the statement," Mindy said, trying to laugh off the talk. "I am not sure what you are talking about?"

"If we must play games, so be it," Clara sighed. "Though time is of the essence if we wish to find Ariadne in good health. Brilliant Chang is quite sure he was served a drugged drink at a party at your house. He recalls the women who slipped him the glass was named Olivia, perhaps you recall her?"

Mindy kept her mouth firmly shut. Losing her patience, Clara pressed on.

"Chang does not remember anything after that until he woke up in one of your bedrooms, undressed and apparently having consorted with Ariadne, though he has no memory of it."

"Fine excuse!" Mindy snorted.

Clara jumped on the comment.

"Then, you admit that Chang was here and that he and Ariadne were up in one of your bedrooms?"

Mindy, not a master of deceit, realised she had stumbled. She put one hand out to balance herself against the back of a chair.

"All I meant was, it is the sort of thing men do to try to avoid responsibility. In any case, I mentioned to you I thought Ariadne had been raped and, if so, Chang is clearly trying to avoid taking the blame…"

"Really, Mrs Bumpton!" Tommy had had enough of her double-talk. "You denigrate every man in this house and beyond with your talk! Chang might be many things, but I do know he has the sense to be respectful of the ladies he associates with, especially when he is a guest at a house party."

Mindy was losing a little of her colour. She had heard the way he talked about Chang. She cleared her throat nervously.

"You seem to know Chang rather well," she said.

"He is an associate," Clara explained. "And he wants

to know where Ariadne is too, because he wants this matter cleared up and to determine who conspired against him. Honestly, Mrs Bumpton, he is displeased with you for helping with this farce."

"I did not," Mindy bleated.

"Then how did Ariadne get the use of one of your bedrooms?" Clara pointed out. "And why lie to me and say she had not associated with Chang, that he had no interest in her?"

Mindy did not know what to say. She clung to the back of the chair for dear life, trying to think of some answer that did not make it seem as if she had conspired against Chang. Finally, she found an ounce of resilience in her soul.

"Whatever Chang says, I have nothing to do with Ariadne going missing. She used me. I see that now. I recall that there was mention of someone feeling unwell and could they lie down in one of my spare bedrooms. I agreed, naturally."

"Mindy!" Gloucester scoffed. "Do you really suppose we believe that? For a start, when did Ariadne become capable of concocting such elaborate schemes? She is not the sort to even think something like that up!"

"Oh, she is not as innocent as you like to think, Gloucester," Mindy sniffed haughtily.

"I know Ariadne," Gloucester countered. "She was not behind this scheme. What purpose would it have for her, anyway?"

"Money," Mindy said, forgetting she was not supposed to know about Ariadne's plot. "She wanted money."

"There are far easier ways of gaining money than drugging a dangerous criminal and then blackmailing him," Clara pointed out. "In any case, we have to consider Benjamin Fitzroy's role in all this."

"Fitzroy?" Mindy seemed genuinely alarmed by the

name and had to sit down in a chair this time. "What has he to do with this?"

"You know him?" Tommy asked.

"Unfortunately, yes," Mindy replied. "He is unsavoury if you ask me. Always trying to pretend he is something more than he really is. I could hardly believe it when I heard he was engaged to Elaine DeVaughn, but in a way, I was relieved as it meant he would no longer be able to see Ariadne."

"You knew about their relationship?" Clara confirmed.

"I did. Not that I liked knowing. I told Ariadne that the man was using her, that he just wanted someone to go to parties with, someone with a little class. The moment he found a better offer, he would ditch her, and that is exactly what happened."

"We believe Fitzroy was the last person to see Ariadne on Christmas Eve," Gloucester said darkly, his words laced with implication. "He was seen taking her into his car and heading to Berkeley Square."

"On Christmas Eve?" Mindy blinked. "That cannot be. He told Ariadne he wanted nothing more to do with her after his engagement to Elaine DeVaughn. I knew that Elaine would ensure he did not wander, not if he wanted all the benefits marrying her would bring. Why would he risk being caught with Ariadne?"

"Perhaps, because they had to talk," Clara suggested. "Perhaps, because Fitzroy had found himself embroiled with some unpleasant people who he owed a favour to, and he had involved Ariadne in his troubles."

Mindy took all this in, slowly realising that whatever had gone on in her house last summer had been distinctly more sinister than she had first imagined.

"The people Fitzroy seems to consort with are the sort who would think nothing of murdering a woman, pregnant or not," Clara added to make her point.

She waited to see just how much Mindy truly cared for her friend. Was she prepared to risk her life to save face?

Mindy swallowed loudly, her throat dry as a bone and tight. She felt terrible and knew the feeling would only get worse. She shuddered as she thought of how she had become involved in all this, and how if she had just said no, perhaps Ariadne would be here with her right now – safe and sound.

"Fitzroy isn't allowed in my home anymore," she said at last. "I tolerated him while he was seeing Ariadne, though I told her time and again he was not good enough for her. Ariadne could not see it herself. I think she feared no other man would show an interest in her. Then he met Elaine DeVaughn at a dinner party and things changed. He proposed to her, and they were engaged. Ariadne was utterly broken by the news. He told her to never contact him again, never to see him."

"When was this?" Clara asked.

Mindy paused to think.

"About a month before the party when Chang was here. You know, I was a little confused by Ariadne's interest in Chang at the time, but she had been so distressed by Fitzroy's dismissal of her that I was just trying to do anything that made her happy."

"What reason did Ariadne give for taking notice of Chang?" Clara asked.

Mindy sucked in her lower lip and bit on it hard enough it turned white.

"She said she needed to get Chang alone to talk about her poems. She was so shy about her work and struggled to find the courage to push herself forward. She said that if she could just have a quiet place where she could speak to him about things, it would make all the difference."

"A quiet place, I understand," Tommy said. "But a

bedroom? Did you not wonder at such a suggestion?"

Mindy dipped her head.

"I am not naïve," she said. "I pretended not to guess what was happening, but I assumed Ariadne intended to seduce Chang to get his attention onto her poems. Had she not been so despondent of late because of Fitzroy, I would have refused, or tried to deter her. But her poems were all that was keeping her going and I would do anything to help her succeed.

"After I had agreed to her having a private meeting with Chang here, she said it would be in one of the bedrooms and I did not know how to refuse. I was scared that she might do something foolish if I scuppered her plans. She had been hysterical after Fitzroy threw her over and I had feared what she might do. I was trying not to unsettle her, which made me rather permissive. But I did not think they would do more than kiss."

"You really expect us to believe that?" Gloucester asked her.

Mindy failed to meet his eye. She had known exactly what was going to happen, and she had allowed it because she did not want her friend upset.

"Who is this Olivia who helped Ariadne?" Clara asked.

"Olivia Knepp," Mindy said at once. "She is the only girl called Olivia I know, and she was here that day. I never thought she and Ariadne were friendly."

"What can you tell us about her?" Clara added.

"She is brazen. The sort of girl who likes to shock. Her father was a painter who made a good deal of money. Somewhat novel for a painter. Her mother was the daughter of a wool merchant who was also wealthy. Olivia has no ambition, no purpose for her life, except to drift around and see whose attention she can draw. I only invited her because…"

Mindy suddenly stopped as a notion struck her.

"Ariadne asked me to invite her. She suggested it because, according to her, the girl had been rather down in the dumps of late and it would be a kindness to have her here. I never gave it a second thought. It was like Ariadne to think of someone else."

"We shall need an address for Olivia," Clara explained.

Mindy nodded; her fight gone.

"I deliberately stayed out of Chang's way at the party. I did not want to be involved, and the less I saw the better. I was a fool," Mindy placed a trembling hand to her lips. "Have I cost Ariadne her life?"

"Let us hope not," Clara said. "This goes far beyond you, Mindy. Someone has been playing a good game and you just happened to get caught up in it."

"I just wanted her to have something to focus on other than Fitzroy," Mindy said. "It really is all his fault for being such a cad."

Gloucester made a noise of scorn under his breath at her words.

Chapter Nineteen

Tracking down Olivia Knepp proved more challenging than they had anticipated. The address Mindy had for her was out of date, and when they arrived at the house, they were informed by the girl who had previously shared a flat in the property with Olivia that she had moved out some months before.

"She met a man," the girl said casually. "I think he was going to keep her as his mistress or something."

"Did she leave a forwarding address?" Clara asked, getting the impression the girl could care less where Olivia had departed to.

"She did," the girl sighed. "Do you really want me to find it?"

Clara's look carried the answer and with a groan the girl went off to search her flat for a piece of paper she had largely ignored and dismissed for the last few months. She returned with a face like thunder, handing over the paper and slamming the door in their faces.

"Well, that went well," Tommy observed.

Clara was more interested in the new address. It was in a better area, more upmarket. Perhaps the former flatmate had been correct, and Olivia had become the mistress of a wealthy man who was maintaining her in a lavish apartment. Clara showed the address to Gloucester.

"I know the area," he nodded, and they were soon back in the car and heading to their next stop.

They arrived to discover the apartment was unoccupied. The building concierge (the apartments being upmarket enough to warrant a specially employed person to oversee who came and went) explained that the young lady had only rented the apartment for a couple of months and had then moved on.

"And you can tell her, when you see her, that I could claim compensation off her for that burn mark on the rug, and the wine stains on the furniture," the concierge grumbled.

"I take it you do not have a forwarding address?" Clara asked, feeling they might be finally out of luck.

The concierge shook his head.

"She barely gave notice. I was expecting her to stay longer, that was the impression she gave, but suddenly she was off."

They had come to a dead end.

"Is there nothing you can tell us about where she went?" Gloucester asked the concierge. "It is urgent we locate her."

The concierge was sympathetic, assuming they were suffering from a similar situation as he was in, and that Olivia had rented property from them and then departed abruptly leaving a trail of stains and minor damage.

"The only thing I can suggest is you speak to Ernest Young. He comes in from time to time, to collect any post that has been left for Miss Knepp. He has refused to give me her address, but I did persuade him on one occasion to give me his address. There had been a situation of an important parcel for Miss Knepp being delivered here by accident and he did not know to come and collect it. It contained some expensive, perishable goods and by the time Mr Young came for them, they were virtually ruined. Miss Knepp was so upset that we agreed he ought to give me his address in case of future deliveries."

The concierge was pulling out a large address book as he explained all this. He thumbed through it until he came to the address for Young.

"I shall write it out for you. I don't have the time or liberty to go chasing after Miss Knepp, unfortunately. I wish you all the best in finding her."

He handed the new address to Clara and off the trio set once again.

"Seems to me, Miss Knepp belongs to that part of society known as the Bright Young Things," Gloucester said as he drove. "I happen to be too dull to qualify for such a title. You have to be something of a gadabout, flighty. Being a touch eccentric in a fashionable way does not hurt either."

"Bright Young Things move addresses often?" Tommy asked.

"Rather comes with the territory. They are usually either on an up, or on a down. More often than not, they are the sort of folks with expensive tastes and a lack of funds to support them. The sort of people who are trying to survive off a limited allowance from the parents or scrounging off friends and lovers."

"And so, they move around," Clara understood. "Depending on how the wind blows."

"Precisely," Gloucester said. "Ariadne almost fell into the category of a Bright Young Thing, except she has a bit more sense with her money and tends to avoid the sorts of extravagance that would have qualified her for the title."

They were drawing towards an area of modern flats,

the good quality sort rented by the upper middle classes. Not as lavish as the apartment they had just come from – far from it. That had reeked of old-world style and could have easily been mistaken for a suite in a smart country house. But these properties were still sumptuous and highly respectable.

They found the building where Young lived and had to hope he was in. They were calling relatively early in the morning and that meant if Young was associated with the Bright Young Things, he was probably the sort to still be in bed at this time of day, having been awake into the wee hours. Of course, Young might also have to work for a living, in which case, he could be out.

They took note of his flat number on the noticeboard in the entrance way and headed for the stairs. There was no concierge at a desk in this building, but the bottom flat on the left bore a plate that stated 'Manager' and was presumably where the person in charge of things at the flats resided. They headed up to the third floor.

"I hope Mr Young is in residence after all this trouble," Tommy groaned, finding the dashing around after Olivia was becoming tedious. It might also prove pointless if she denied drugging Chang.

Clara knocked on Young's door and waited impatiently. A few moments passed and then she knocked again. Gloucester was about to suggest trying to rouse the neighbours, who might know if Young was in, when they heard someone thumping up the stairs.

The person arrived on the landing and stopped to stare at them. He was in his twenties, carrying two large paper bags full of groceries and looking somewhat worse for wear. He was only dully interested in why three people were stood outside his apartment.

"Mr Young?" Clara asked.

"You have found him," Young sniffed, then he

coughed. "Horrid cold. Sorry, give me a moment."

Young put down his shopping and rummaged in his pocket for a handkerchief which he produced and blew his nose into noisily.

"Want a hand?" Tommy offered, grabbing up one of the shopping bags.

Gloucester copied him and picked up the other.

"Thanks," Young said. "It seemed quite a walk to the shops. I wouldn't have gone except I was getting desperate for food."

Young returned his handkerchief to his pocket and pulled out a house key instead. He opened his flat door and let them in.

"Why are you here?" he asked once they were all inside and his bags had been kindly carried through to the kitchen area of his flat.

"It is something of a long story," Clara began, hoping to ease into the reason they were there and avoid causing Young to shut down on them. If he refused to give the concierge Olivia's address, it was quite likely he would refuse to give it to them, unless Clara could make it appear as if they were only interested in Olivia in passing, due to her connection to Ariadne.

"A young lady vanished on Christmas Eve, and we are trying to locate her and ensure she is well. Her name is Ariadne Griffiths, and it was mentioned to us in passing that a young lady called Olivia Knepp knows her. We are trying to speak to anyone who knows Ariadne in the hope she has been in touch. For that reason, we have spent all morning trying to locate Olivia without much luck. It was suggested we come and speak to you."

Young seemed to accept the explanation. He felt too dazed by his cold to give it much thought. He wandered to a sofa near a gas fire and sat down heavily.

"I vaguely know Ariadne," he said. "I would not

really consider her a friend of Olivia's."

"We were informed they had spoken recently about a project together," Clara adjusted the truth, taking the handful of information she had regarding the party at the Bumptons' and extrapolating something from it. Surely, drugging and seducing Brilliant Chang constituted a 'project' together?

"I don't know anything about it," Young shrugged. "But, then again, I hardly know anything that Olivia is doing these days. We have been friends donkey's years. Though I think that Olivia considers more what I can do for her than our friendship these days."

They had caught Young in a depressed mood when he was feeling lonely and unloved. Sitting alone in his flat, suffering a cold with no one to take an interest in him, he had been dwelling on his friendship with Olivia and how she seemed to care nothing about his situation. He felt used in that moment of time, and that meant it was the perfect opportunity to approach him about Olivia's whereabouts.

"I am sorry to hear that," Clara told him, taking a seat opposite him. "Would you like us to make you a cup of tea? You look rather done in."

Young felt done in. The walk to the shops had exhausted him and there was a ringing in his ears. It would really be rather nice to have someone make him a cup of tea.

"I could not ask that of a guest," he said, recalling his manners, but also hoping Clara would not be deterred.

"Nonsense," Clara smiled, and she glanced at Tommy and Gloucester who reluctantly went to make tea. It would probably take the both of them to achieve the task.

"I am still trying to picture Ariadne and Olivia sharing a common purpose," Young frowned once they were alone. "They seemed so different."

"It can be surprising what unites us," Clara replied. "In any case, we only want to briefly talk with Olivia to see if she can offer us an idea where Ariadne might have gone, or what could have happened to her. It may be she cannot help us, but we have to try."

"Has Ariadne vanished of her own volition?" Young asked.

"We are not sure," Clara told him. "We are rather worried she has not."

Young absorbed this dire information.

"I hope she is all right," he said. "I shall give you Olivia's address and you can speak to her, but could you please refrain from telling her I sent you there? She might never speak to me again if she knew."

Despite his feelings of disappointment and hurt, Young was not prepared to lose Olivia.

"I promise," Clara reassured him.

Young was satisfied. He rose from the sofa and wobbled over to a sideboard, pulling out a drawer to produce a pad of paper and a pencil. He wandered back and with a trembling hand wrote out the address.

"She should be there today," he handed over the address, before adding as an afterthought. "But, if she isn't, you could try here."

He wrote out another address on a second piece of paper.

"But you must never let anyone know I gave this to you," he handed Clara the paper with the second address. "I am only doing this because a young lady is missing and that cannot be ignored."

Clara frowned at the second address.

"Buckingham Palace?"

"Well, it is not just the King who lives there," Young chuckled. "There are courtiers and servants and all manner of staff running the place. Plus, the guards. Look, Olivia has been seeing Lord Buckingham. It is not talked about because of his marriage, but if she is not at her flat, then the next likeliest place she will be is in his chambers at the palace. He has an office suite there, with a private bedroom and sitting room for when he works late."

"How convenient," Clara said wryly.

Young shrugged.

"I suppose it is obvious why I hold no interest for her these days. What am I but the son of a wealthy factory owner? I can hardly hold up against a lord."

"You are perhaps placing too high a value on rank, and too little on character."

Young smiled at Clara's words.

"You are very kind, but in the scheme of things, I find most women prefer rank over character. Perhaps I am a little jaded by this cold, or by Olivia's coldness towards me."

"The sort of woman deserving of a gentleman like you, sees beyond titles and wealth," Clara told him.

"Ah, you sound like one of those advice columns in the papers. It is a nice notion, but reality is somewhat more depressing."

Tommy appeared with a cup of tea at that moment. It was long past the stage of being over-brewed and at a point when it might be better referred to as bathwater. Fortunately, Young's tastebuds were currently not working, so he could not know how bad it was.

"You don't happen to know if Olivia has a connection to Brilliant Chang?" Clara asked casually as she was preparing to leave.

She had not expected much of a response and was surprised when Young choked on his tea.

"Chang? Is he involved?"

"Indirectly," Clara lied. "Then, he does have a connection with Olivia?"

"It is complicated," Young hid behind his teacup. "At one time, Olivia had this notion that she could…

well, I suppose you would say she contemplated seducing him and becoming his mistress. I thought I had dissuaded her of that notion, however."

"She fancied being the mistress of a criminal?" Tommy asked in surprise.

"A wealthy criminal," Young sighed. "With influence and good connections. Half the ladies of London are fawning over him, hoping to be in his good graces. Half the men, for that matter. He is dangerous and that attracts them. When you are so very bored with your life, it takes a man like Chang to brighten up your day."

"Unfortunately, I think I understand," Clara said, feeling it was all so ridiculous and also so sad. "If you get the chance, perhaps try to persuade Olivia to stay away from Chang in the future. It would be in her best interest."

Especially if she was responsible for feeding him a drugged drink, Clara added to herself.

"I don't think she will listen to me, but I shall try," Young nodded. "I don't want her ending up missing too, now do I?"

Chapter Twenty

Brilliant Chang had not thought it was possible to feel more exhausted than he already did. As it turned out, he had been wrong. The events of the previous day had taken the last drop of strength from him, and he lay in bed not caring if another assassin came for him. He doubted he would have the strength to fight off a second attempt on his life.

He stared at the ceiling and endeavoured not to move even a fraction, because any movement drew this deep ache from his bones and made him feel worse.

Annie appeared at the door of his room with more tea. He had failed to drink the last cup she had offered him, and she did not hold out much hope he would drink this one, but she was determined to try.

"I have locked the back door," Annie informed him. "So no one is bursting into the kitchen again."

Chang did not respond. He had his eyes shut and a pained expression on his face. Annie put down the cup of tea beside him, collecting up the untouched cup with its now cold contents. She looked at him for a moment, trying to think of something helpful to say.

When no words sprang to mind, she departed, not sure how to help him.

She was nearly at the bottom of the stairs when the doorbell rang. Annie went to answer it, slightly on guard. With yesterday's experiences still fresh in her mind she could not be sure who was there. When she opened the door, she found a lady dressed in a long, moth-eaten sheepskin coat, with wild auburn hair and a substantial pair of glasses perched on her nose.

"Aunt Tilly!" Annie said in delight, rushing to embrace the woman and nearly spilling tea over her.

"It has been too long, Annie, too long," the woman wrapped her arms around her.

She smelled a little musty, with a hint of rose oil.

"Come in at once," Annie said, allowing her through the door and then making sure it was shut and locked once she was inside. "Are you keeping well?"

"Never better," Aunt Tilly declared.

She was in her fifties. Skinny as a scarecrow and tall for a woman. But her skin had a youthful glow to it that always made people underestimate her age.

"This is a well-kept home, Annie," Aunt Tilly said.

Annie beamed with pride. Aunt Tilly never mangled her words and only said exactly what she thought.

"Now, what is all this about a curse?"

Annie's good humour disappeared in an instant.

"It is rather complicated. I did not want to say too much in the message I sent because it is a very private, and potentially dangerous, matter."

"That sounds serious," Aunt Tilly frowned. "The victim is not yourself?"

"No!" Annie said hastily, thinking it impossible she could induce a person to curse her. "It is someone we know. Actually, we are not even friendly with him. Look, I shall make you a cup of tea and explain."

For the next half hour, Annie was busy explaining to Tilly the circumstances that had led to Brilliant

Chang being under their roof, his connection to them and the alarming assault from the day before. She was pretty sure she had not missed anything when she came to a finish.

Aunt Tilly looked at her with deep anxiety in her eyes.

"I am not sure what I think about you helping this man," she said. "He is a criminal."

"Yes, well, you know how it is. Someone asks you for help and you just help. That is how we are."

Tilly nodded her head.

"True enough. I warred for years with Farmer Smith, but the day his granddaughter took ill I was the first person he came to, and I did not even hesitate to assist him. It was a fairy jinx, you know."

"Sorry?" Annie said, not quite understanding.

"On the granddaughter. She had been down by the brook and the fairies had cast a jinx on her. It amuses them."

Annie was not too sure about fairies. Once upon a time she would not have even paused at the mention of them, but back then she had lived in the countryside, surrounded by the ancient rural ways and customs. Living in a town with Clara had rather changed her perspective and she was not as willing as she once was to consider fairies real things.

However, fairies or not, she did have this nervousness about curses and that was why Tilly was here.

"You best come and meet Chang," she said next. "Do you think you can help him?"

"Maybe," Tilly said. "It will depend on how willing he is to work with me. A person can only be cured of their curse if they first trust the methods given to cure them and second, believe wholeheartedly they will work. Belief plays a big part in sympathetic magic."

"Of course," Annie nodded. "I think Chang is just so

scared."

"Understandable," Tilly said. "I would be scared too."

She followed Annie upstairs and to the bedroom where, as Annie had anticipated, Chang had failed to touch his cup of tea.

"Chang?" Annie said his name softly, not sure if he was asleep. "This is Aunt Tilly, the friend I mentioned who knows all there is to know about curses and magic."

"I know a fair bit," Tilly said modestly. "Not as much as your grandmother, Annie. She took a fair few secrets about the arts to her grave."

Chang opened his eyes a fraction, looking at them through narrowed lids.

"You can help me?" he asked.

Aunt Tilly stepped closer.

"I believe I can," she said. "The question is do you… has someone been burning sage in here?"

"That was me," Annie said sheepishly.

"It smells like it was dried sage, far too old for the purpose."

"I don't know, it cleared us from the room," Chang said with an edge to his voice.

Aunt Tilly's eyes turned on him and he found himself looking into her gaze. Her glasses were thick and magnified her eyes. She had an intense stare that burned into you. It reminded him a little of Clara and he felt himself falling silent under her gaze.

"I see," Aunt Tilly said, though it was not clear if she was referring to the sage incident, or to him.

Chang had a nasty feeling she was talking about him.

"Curses, Mr Chang, take belief. The belief in them when they are cast and the belief in the curing of them," she continued. "Resolving them is something we have to work on together and I expect you to be cooperative and amenable to my suggestions. Otherwise, I shall depart now."

Chang was feeling nervous enough about his possible curse that he was not going to allow this potential saviour to walk away. He wanted to feel like himself again.

"I shall cooperate," he said firmly.

"I shall give some tasks to Annie to fulfil once I am gone. I shall expect you to cooperate with her too."

"I will," Chang swore.

"Then, perhaps I can help," Aunt Tilly said haughtily. "The first question concerns the type of curse that was laid upon you."

"There are different types?" Chang flinched.

"Quite a number. Different cultures have different methods. I am sure there are ways in Asia of casting curses that we do not know of here in England."

"It's a long time since I was in my homeland," Chang shrugged. "I remember the barebones of traditions, not the details."

"Well, in any case I am hopeful we are looking at a British curse and those I know how to fix. The young lady responsible is of Irish descent?"

"She is," Chang said, his sneer returning at the mention of Ariadne. "You can fix Irish curses?"

"If that is what she used, yes," Aunt Tilly said, calmly. "Now, is there a possibility of her possessing either your fingernail clippings or hair?"

"What?" Chang said in alarm. "Well, of course there is, because she drugged me and I was in her company for several hours, though I don't remember a thing!"

"That was months before the blackmail, however," Annie pointed out.

"She may have prepared ahead, anticipating that normal means would fail to achieve the desired effect," Aunt Tilly said. "It is what I would do."

Chang looked at his nails, as if they would reveal

some sign of being cut.

"I don't recall noticing anything missing," he said.

"It is a possibility, however," Aunt Tilly nodded thoughtfully. "Well, we shall have to work with the notion that she did take something, just in case. My suspicion is this is what I call a verbal curse, one that does not use personal objects to achieve the result. It is one of the oldest sorts of curse, before people began to play with making wax dolls to represent a despised person or stealing fingernails and hair. A verbal curse is still nasty, but without the personal objects it is slightly easier to break."

Chang looked hugely relieved at this news.

"How do we break it?" he asked eagerly.

"You stop believing in it," Aunt Tilly said bluntly.

Chang's relief faded.

"I have tried that!"

"No, you have not," Aunt Tilly said. "You have attempted to ignore it, but that is a very different thing. Stopping believing in a curse is dreadfully hard, because the mind will cling to any scrap of belief, the smallest, smallest part. I shall show you how we train the mind out of that habit."

Chang was looking worried.

"What if I can't stop believing?" he asked.

Aunt Tilly was rummaging in one of the big pockets of her sheepskin coat. She had made the coat herself after receiving the skins from a local farmer she had freed from a curse on his livestock. She had made it with voluminous pockets so she could carry all she needed when she travelled for her work.

"If you cannot stop believing, then the only option is to find the person behind the curse and persuade them to remove it," Aunt Tilly explained.

"We are working on that," Annie said. "What if that person is dead?"

She gulped as she said the last part. Aunt Tilly

stopped searching her pockets.

"In some cases, it shall mean the curse is broken, in others, the curse can continue beyond the death of the caster. It depends on the magic used."

Chang was both horrified and disappointed. Aunt Tilly finally found what she wanted and produced a small stone wrapped with a sort of long, dried grass. The stone had a hole through the centre.

"A witch stone," Annie said authoritatively.

"Exactly. This one I have charged with healing energy, which I have sealed in with this grass wrapping," Aunt Tilly explained as if it was a perfectly ordinary thing to do, like describing how to make a suet pudding and wrap it in a cloth. "It is a protective object, but it cannot rid you of this curse alone."

Aunt Tilly gave Chang the stone. He folded it into his hand and looked as if he would cling to it for dear life.

"Now for the belief part. There is only one way to work on these things and that is to teach the mind to stop believing. This will take patience and dedication."

Chang groaned. Patience was not one of his strong points.

"You must work to gradually eradicate the belief that is powering this curse. First, you begin by clutching the stone and repeating three times 'I am not cursed.' Three is important. There is magic in threes. Do not repeat it just twice or go for four or five times thinking it will work quicker. It has to be three."

"I understand," Chang said miserably.

"For the first few days, you should repeat this once an hour through the course of the day. At night, before bed, I suggest you make a prayer to whatever deity is your choice, asking for release from the curse."

"I do not believe in any god," Chang said, sneering at the very notion.

"Ironic, as you clearly believe in curses," Aunt Tilly

brought him back down to earth sharply. "Personally, I have a healthy belief in God and the angels. I should be a hypocrite if I did not, considering I work with the spiritual side of life. If you cannot prayer to a deity, then send a prayer to the universe at large, or to some notion of 'otherness.' Something will hear you."

Chang was not amused by this.

"As the days progress, I want you to take heed of any sensations of change within you," Aunt Tilly continued. "Should you notice you have no pain in your big toe, for instance, or feel hungry or less sleepy, however small this change, note it and remember it is a sign of the curse's hold weakening. Focus on that sensation and repeat to yourself 'I am not cursed,' using even this small improvement as proof of that notion. Our minds like proof, and so we can help break this curse by focusing on these little things."

"That is all I do, keep thinking?" Chang asked, sounding annoyed. "I was hoping for something like a potion or you reciting some curse breaking stuff over me."

Aunt Tilly gave him a despairing look.

"Nothing is ever so simple. A doctor cannot heal a broken leg in moments, his medicines only aid the body to heal itself. Ultimately, it is our bodies that do the work, and they do that best when we are prepared to trust in the process and give ourselves time."

Chang was far from pleased with this, but he did not say anymore. Aunt Tilly had said all she needed to and had no desire to hang around. She was already feeling agitated at being away from the countryside for so long. The town was so full of people and brick buildings.

Annie escorted her back downstairs.

"Thank you for coming," she said.

"I did this for you," Aunt Tilly took Annie's hands in hers. "I shall work on a protection spell when I arrive home, to cast over you and this house. I am concerned for your wellbeing with that man upstairs."

"I shall be fine," Annie promised her, pretending not to notice Aunt Tilly's expression as she removed the chain and unlocked the front door.

She wished her a safe journey home and waved her off. Alone in the hall, she found herself considering what had just occurred. It had been a long time since she had dabbled in magic, and she found herself a little… underwhelmed. Annie was beginning to think Clara's cynicism was rubbing off on her. She just hoped her lack of faith in Aunt Tilly's ways would not stop the curse from being broken.

Chapter Twenty-One

Olivia's flat was empty – at least, no one answered the door, so they assumed it was empty. It was considerably smaller than the previous two flats they had visited and in an area that was less salubrious, though it still retained a Bohemian air, with the residents seeming to be largely of the creative time – budding writers, starving artists, and the odd actor. Clara tried to rouse someone in the flat across the hall from Olivia's but had no luck. She conceded defeat and suggested the next address.

"How are we going to persuade anyone to let us into Buckingham Palace?" Tommy said, frowning at the slip of paper Young had given them.

"I think, in that regard, I may be of assistance," Gloucester said seriously. "It shall mean a telephone call to my father, and I would rather avoid such a thing, however, for the sake of Ariadne, I shall do it."

He escorted them to a restaurant which he knew had a private telephone booth for the use of patrons. The restaurant owner recognised him and agreed to him using the telephone, while Clara and Tommy settled at a table at a window and ordered lunch.

What arrived at their table was far grander than the average lunch at Lyons teashop. There was a tiered stack of sandwiches of various fillings and all with the crusts cut off. A second tiered stand held dainty cakes and was accompanied by a cheese board with a selection of unusual cheeses in neat little wedges or circular slices, and some posh looking crackers. Clara, who had been mildly apprehensive about ordering lunch due to the potential price tag (there was no mention of prices on the menu, which was a sure sign everything was expensive) now gulped as she saw the array of food they had been delivered.

"I thought we ordered the small luncheon," Tommy asked in a whisper, thinking along a similar line to his sister.

They exchanged anxious looks as Gloucester returned from his telephone conversation and settled at the table. He glanced at the assortment of food and helped himself to a cucumber sandwich.

"Glasshouse cucumbers are never quite the same," he said. "But one must endure in winter."

There was nothing else for it but to eat what was before them. At least they would not go hungry.

"My father has agreed to make arrangements for me to speak with Lord Buckingham. He should be ready to see us when we arrive."

Gloucester looked glum.

"What did you have to agree to?" Tommy asked him.

"Nothing terribly dramatic," Gloucester sighed. "I shall be expected to attend a dinner and dance party my father has arranged for the middle of January."

"That is not so bad," Clara said gently.

"My father will ensure there are numerous eligible ladies in attendance, and they shall be thrust in my direction at every opportunity. More than likely, at some point in the evening I shall weaken and agree to marry one of them. I know my resilience and it is not great, not when father and mother are pressuring me."

"Sorry about that," Tommy said sympathetically.

"Oh, it's not your fault that Ariadne is missing, or that she has got herself into a pickle with this Chang fellow. I could have left her to it, but I feel a spur of responsibility," Gloucester picked up another sandwich, was about to bite into it when he paused and examined it suspiciously. "Excuse me."

He departed the table and was witnessed to be having a heated conversation with the restaurant owner. Clara watched him curiously. She picked up a sandwich identical to the one Gloucester had walked off with and examined it carefully. She could see nothing wrong.

Gloucester returned to the table.

"Do not touch the cheese sandwiches," he said with authority. "They tried to fob us off with regular Cheddar instead of the Double Gloucester described in the menu. I know those tactics, and I know very well the chef behind them. I just had words with the restaurant owner who confirmed, after some persuasion, I was correct. We shall not be paying for this lunch."

Clara did not mean to groan with relief, but it rather came out. She felt slightly guilty that they had found a way to wriggle out of paying for their food.

"You can tell the difference between Cheddar and Double Gloucester by just looking at it?" Tommy said, lifting up the top layer of a sandwich and eyeing the grated cheese inside.

"Can't you?" Gloucester asked. "Well, unfortunately most people cannot, which is why they get away with these things. Trying to save a little money, that is the crux of it all, and after they charge an extortionate fortune as it is."

Clara was doubly glad they had escaped paying.

They finished their lunch, minus the offending cheese sandwiches. The restaurant owner brought them a bottle of wine, on the house, to try to compensate for his mistake. Clara was uninclined to drink at this time of day, especially on a case. Gloucester graciously accepted the wine for later.

It was almost two o'clock when they finally headed in the direction of Buckingham Palace.

"How does your father come to have such a close connection to Lord Buckingham?" Tommy asked as they drove along.

"Ah, he happens to be my uncle," Gloucester admitted sheepishly. "Complicated family politics. My grandmother was first married to Lord Buckingham, thus her eldest son inherited the title when his father died, then she married my grandfather, Lord Gloucester. As such, she ended up with two sons who are both lords."

"That is somewhat complicated," Tommy agreed, trying to get his head around the aristocratic marriage arrangements.

"Grandmother was quite a salt," Gloucester chuckled. "She never let such a thing as a husband's death stop her ambitions. I am afraid I rather disappointed her."

Clara reached forward from the back seat of the car and squeezed his shoulder.

"A true grandmother would never be disappointed with you," she assured him. "There are far greater things a man can be than merely a lord."

"You are very kind," Gloucester said, touched.

They arrived at the gates of Buckingham Palace. Gloucester drove the car right up to them, as if it were the most natural thing in the world. Clara had never been this close to a royal palace, and she found herself slightly nervous under the circumstances. Gloucester did not share her unease and when the guards came to ask his business, he gave his name and his uncle's name without hesitation.

The guards appeared to have been apprised of his intended arrival and they opened the gates. Gloucester drove through into the great forecourt of the palace and circled around to the front door with its massive pillars and steps. Clara had to admit she was in awe – and that did not happen often.

Gloucester parked the car at the bottom of the steps, unconcerned that it was rather in the way and probably should have been parked somewhere more discreet. He got out and opened the passenger door for Clara and Tommy.

"Don't be nervous," he told them. "I have been coming to the palace since I was a boy. I know where all the secrets are kept."

He winked at them. Clara was not convinced by his words, but she had no intention of being cowed just because this was a palace. She braced herself and followed him up the stairs. The guards at the palace doors stopped them and politely asked their business. Gloucester gave his uncle's name once again, and one of the guards left his post to escort them to the offices of Lord Buckingham.

They went deep into the palace. The corridors seemed to stretch for miles and Clara was utterly certain she would never find her way out again without a guide. She had soon lost track of the turns they had taken, the rooms they had passed and whether they were on the east or west side of the palace. The only thing she was sure of, was that they had not gone upstairs.

They reached a grand set of doors that looked much like every other set in the palace and stopped before them. The guard knocked and a moment passed before they were asked to enter. The guard showed them into a tall-ceilinged chamber, decorated with wallpaper that was at least a century old and furnished with objects of a similar age. A pair of stately windows opposite the door looked onto a garden.

Standing beside a giant fireplace, reading some papers, stood a man in his sixties. He was slender and handsome, with more than a hint of a resemblance to Gloucester, which must have come through Gloucester's grandmother.

"Uncle!" Gloucester said cheerily. "We missed you at Christmas."

"I had a lot of work to do," Buckingham replied, sounding annoyed at their interruption. "Your father insisted it was urgent I see you. What is it?"

"First, may I introduce my associates Miss Clara Fitzgerald and Mr Thomas Fitzgerald," Gloucester had become very formal in his attempts to win over his uncle. "They are assisting me on the matter of a missing friend."

"A missing friend?" Buckingham said dismissively. "Really, Alfie, this is tiresome."

Gloucester fell silent in the face of his uncle's anger. Clara stared at the gruff man who had not even bothered to greet them. He was rude, surly, and clearly thought he was more important than them and that their business with him was an unnecessary interruption to his day.

His response to them was the antidote Clara needed to her nerves. She no longer found herself on edge because she was in a royal palace, it was just another old house, after all, and Buckingham was just another person she had to question to solve a case. Clara did not like being dismissed as unworthy of someone's time, it had a tendency to flare her temper. She stepped forward now, past Gloucester, to confront Buckingham.

"Lord Buckingham, we actually do not need to bother you at all, and you can be rid of us swiftly if you would just kindly inform us if Olivia Knepp is here?"

Lord Buckingham feigned a puzzled look.

"Who?"

"Your mistress," Clara said politely. "Surely you recall her? We need to speak to her. We have been all over London looking for her and at last her trail leads us here. Do not be concerned, this has nothing to do with you, as such, but rather involves your mistress in a scheme against a dangerous criminal. A woman is missing because of this scheme. A thug with a knife burst into my kitchen because of this scheme and my patience in the matter is wearing thin. So, please, tell me where Olivia is."

Buckingham's puzzlement was replaced with a frown.

"Do you realise who you are talking to?" he demanded.

"Yes," Clara said. "Do you realise who you are talking to?"

Lord Buckingham was so astounded by her words he hesitated – a fatal move when dealing with Clara in a temper.

"I am tired of wasting my time rushing about London," Clara carried on. "All because a group of people thought up a scheme for blackmailing a very dangerous man. One of those people was your mistress, and trust me when I tell you Lord Buckingham that you do not want to be caught up in the trouble she is in. The scandal of her associations and what she did could ruin your career. No more offices in Buckingham Palace, no more power, no more importance. You will just be another lord rattling around in his overly big country mansion."

"Are you threatening me?" Lord Buckingham said nastily.

"No. I am giving you a warning. Olivia Knepp has conspired to blackmail a dangerous criminal, who is now out for her blood. And he has connections too, connections to powerful people who owe him more than they care to admit. One woman has already disappeared because of this drama. Whether you care for Olivia, or whether you merely care for yourself and keeping your reputation untarnished, you must speak to me and tell me where she is."

Lord Buckingham did not have the words to explain what he was feeling in that moment, though outrage was part of it. Outrage at being confronted by this ordinary woman, and outrage that his mistress had potentially placed him in a vulnerable position. He glanced at his nephew in desperation.

"It is true, Uncle. This is a very serious matter. You do not want to become involved in it, if you can help it, which is why you must tell us where Olivia is."

Buckingham was not used to being placed under such pressure, at least not when it came to his own personal position and reputation. He was stubborn, however, and stubbornness can make a man stupid.

"I think you should all leave," he said firmly.

Clara stared at him defiantly.

"You best summon a guard, then," she said. "Actually, summon three, one for each of us. And then I shall return home and pass on the information I have about Olivia and her association with you to the person who she has wronged. I doubt he shall be much troubled by the palace guards when it comes to getting to you."

"That is a threat!" Buckingham growled.

"Yes," Clara said sternly. "It is."

She stared at Buckingham, and he stared back. Their eyes locked and a battle of wills began. Both were as stubborn as each other, to the point of irrationality. Tommy watched on as his sister and a nobleman engaged in a staring contest. He looked at Gloucester with a gasp of exasperation. Gloucester was a little embarrassed by his uncle's behaviour and shrugged.

There was a hiss from Buckingham as he had to turn away and blink.

"Fine!" he declared; some unspoken accord having been reached. "I do not want to be caused trouble by a girl I have merely been dabbling with. Girls like her are ten a penny."

There was a sudden clatter as a pair of doors next to the fireplace where jerked opened and a pretty young woman marched through.

"You uncaring scoundrel!" the woman yelled at Buckingham, who was unmoved by her words.

"My dear, I have better things to do than worry about you or what you have become embroiled in," Buckingham told her coldly. "It was fun while it lasted, now, if you please, gather any belongings you have here and depart."

The woman was stunned. She turned to Clara, seeking out a spot of sympathy wherever she could find it. Clara nodded to her.

"Olivia Knepp?"

Olivia indicated silently that was who she was, then the reality of her situation came over her and with one last look at Buckingham, she burst into a shower of tears.

Chapter Twenty-Two

The extraction from Buckingham Palace of the weeping Olivia proved somewhat trickier than had been anticipated by Lord Buckingham. She was making a scene; a very, very, vocal scene and was not going to desist. She was not going to leave quietly or without alerting everyone in the building that she had been unceremoniously ditched. Buckingham was both exasperated and embarrassed. In the end, he managed to find a back way out of the palace which limited how many people saw Olivia singing her woes.

"Just get her away from here Alfie!" he snapped at his nephew as they found themselves outside again.

Olivia had cried herself out and was reduced to hiccupping sobs, though there was a look about her that suggested at any moment she could start up the waterworks again if it suited her.

"Don't tell anyone about this," Buckingham warned his nephew, before slamming shut the door he had just ushered them through.

Gloucester sighed.

"And apparently he is a better example of nobility

than I am, according to my father," he said ironically to Clara.

Clara patted his arm.

"We know better," she promised.

They walked around the palace, getting wet as none of them had an umbrella. Olivia was clutching at a bundle of belongings that Buckingham had hastily gathered up for her, sniffing to herself and contemplating another failed romance.

"It was never going to last," Tommy told her, failing to appreciate this was the last thing you told a woman who has just been cast aside.

She glowered at him.

"Who are you anyway? And why are you interfering in my life?"

"We would rather not be," Clara assured her. "But we have been tasked with finding Ariadne Griffiths and we hoped you might have some information."

"Ariadne?" Olivia looked at them puzzled. "I haven't seen her since the summer."

"You are not close then?" Clara asked.

Olivia was clearly confused by the question.

"We are not friends, if that is what you mean. We just happen to know each other."

"Then there was some other reason why you assisted her in a scheme to seduce and subsequently blackmail Brilliant Chang?"

Olivia came to a sharp stop. Her mouth was open to make a denial, an automatic response from Olivia, but Clara was ahead of her.

"Brilliant Chang knows it was you who drugged his drink at the Bumptons' party," Clara said plainly. "He is not very happy right now and is looking to have revenge."

That was pushing the truth as Chang was in no fit state to be considering revenge, but it was the sort of thing to spark Olivia to speak honestly. Olivia was looking alarmed, contemplating the position she now found herself in. No lord to protect her, in fact, Buckingham had been only too keen to throw her to the wolves, all alone and with a murderous criminal mastermind blaming her for his misfortunes. It was slowly dawning on her how desperate her situation was.

"We better talk," she said, which was music to Clara's ears. "Out of the rain."

They all agreed to that and hurried back to Gloucester's car. He drove them to his home where they could speak privately and without being disturbed.

Olivia had recovered from her indignation and took an interest in Gloucester's accommodation, noting the large Christmas tree with an air of approval. Clara suspected she was the only one to notice the cogs whirring in Olivia's mind and to realise she was considering the possibility of tempting Gloucester to be her next keeper. Clara was pretty certain she would be disappointed in that regard.

Gloucester made sure they were all comfortable by the fire, and warming up again, and then started things off.

"Where is Ariadne?"

Olivia glared at him.

"How should I know? I told you. I saw her last summer and not since."

"Where were you on Christmas Eve?" Clara asked. "The Bumptons' party?"

"No," Olivia sneered, blithely avoiding the trap she had been set. "I was with Lord Buckingham, attending a drinks party at the palace."

She held her head up, clearly intimating that she was above the Bumptons now. Clara wondered how long it would take for her to remember that was not the case.

"All right," Clara said. "Then, tell me about the last time you saw Ariadne. That was at the Bumptons' home, yes?"

Reluctant to admit she had ever been to a party hosted by someone without a title, Olivia hesitated before she finally spoke.

"Yes, it was."

"And that was the day you spilled Brilliant Chang's drink on purpose and offered him yours. He took it without any suspicion that it was drugged."

Olivia shuffled in her seat.

"Yes," she sighed.

"What I really want to know is who came up with this scheme to blackmail Chang. Who had the audacity? I don't think you and Ariadne plotted this. It does not seem your style."

Olivia tipped her head forward, abashed at what she had done.

"I have never done anything like that before," she said. "It would not really do for the men in my circles to think I was a common blackmailer."

"It would most certainly limit your options," Tommy said wryly. "What lordship would dare to keep a mistress who had demonstrated herself adept at blackmail."

Tommy earned another glare from Olivia.

"Who came up with this idea, then?" Clara drew back her attention.

Olivia looked uneasy, not sure she could risk saying the name aloud. She was already in trouble, but it was the distant, vague sort of trouble that you could pretend was not real. If she named names, trouble drew a lot closer to her.

"Perhaps I can assist you," Clara said. "Benjamin Fitzroy. You know him?"

Olivia chewed at her lower lip anxiously, then she nodded.

"He was walking out with Ariadne, until he thought he had found a better prospect in Elaine DeVaughn," Clara continued.

"I heard he had proposed to her, and she had accepted," Olivia replied. "I don't know him well either, because, in the scheme of things he is not my type."

"Then, how on earth did you become caught up in his plans?" Clara asked. "Because he did ask you to help him."

Olivia had run out of lies and ways to wriggle around the truth. All she could do was nod her head again.

"I was having a bad time," she said. "I had been thrown over by a man and I had rather overextended myself financially. I was not sure how I would pay my rent or buy food. It was all looking rather dire, and I went to this party and got rather drunk. I spilled my story to a friend, just wanting a shoulder to cry on. Fitzroy overheard me, and later in the evening he came to me and offered a potential solution for my crisis.

"All he needed was for a young lady to swap drinks with a particular gentleman. It was such a minor thing, and he was going to pay me a sizeable fee for my efforts. I could hardly refuse something so innocent. I did not realise the drink was drugged."

"Come now!" Gloucester snorted in disbelief. "What did you think Fitzroy wanted the drinks switched for? Just as a lark?"

Olivia shuffled uncomfortably again. She had realised there was something amiss, because no one paid the sort of money Fitzroy was offering without a good, and likely illegal, reason.

"I suppose I thought it was a prank," she said.

"A prank played on one of the most dangerous men in London," Clara remarked sinisterly.

She wanted Olivia to remember the potential

trouble she was in. Olivia shuddered involuntarily and clasped her hands together in her lap.

"It was rather stupid, I admit that. But all I did was stumble into him and swap drinks. If anyone were to ask, I could always act shocked and suppose the drug was meant for me."

"Which has the potential to be a reasonable conclusion," Tommy spoke. "Except for what occurred afterwards."

"I wasn't around for that part, I swear. As soon as I swapped drinks, I made an excuse and left. I spent the rest of the party outside in the garden and never saw Chang again."

This, Clara believed.

"What about Ariadne," she asked, "did you speak to her about what was to happen?"

"You make it sound as though we were all very organised," Olivia remarked. "As if we had meetings to plot things out. That was not the case. Fitzroy told me what to do and I did it. I knew Ariadne was to do something after I had swapped drinks, but precisely what I did not know, nor did I care. I did my bit and then I took my money."

Clara felt she was telling the truth, which was disappointing because it brought them no closer to finding Ariadne.

"What do you know about Benjamin Fitzroy?" Gloucester asked suddenly.

Olivia turned her attention in his direction.

"He is ambitious, and he wants to be wealthy. Ridiculously wealthy. The sort of wealthy it is impossible to spend through," she said. "In that regard, he is rather like me. His only hope for wealth is through marriage. I don't know much more about him than that. We did not associate."

Gloucester was frowning.

"If this all comes back to Fitzroy, then what is his

connection to Brilliant Chang and who encouraged him to attempt this scheme?"

"Good questions which I think only the man himself can answer, if we can persuade him to talk," Clara was staring at Olivia intently. "Olivia, I think I can persuade Brilliant Chang you were a dupe in all this too and should be left alone, on the condition that you come with us right now to confront Benjamin Fitzroy."

Olivia hardly gave the matter any thought before she replied.

"Yes. I will do that. I don't want Chang resentful towards me. I don't need the difficulty."

"You are thinking that with Olivia's evidence, Fitzroy may break?" Tommy asked his sister.

"I am hopeful," Clara said. "It is the only thing I can think to do right now to try and find Ariadne. I am convinced he had something to do with her disappearance that night."

"He made Ariadne disappear?" Olivia asked in alarm. "Wait a minute. I don't want to be made to disappear too."

"You have nothing to fear from Fitzroy," Clara told her firmly.

"How can you say that? If he has plotted against Chang and made Ariadne vanish, he is clearly a dangerous man to cross!"

"Olivia, if we are to find Ariadne alive, we need your assistance," Gloucester leaned forward in his seat to emphasise his words. "You must not back out now."

"It is all very well you asking me for assistance," Olivia snapped, "but once you have all gone your own ways, I shall be alone again, and if Fitzroy wants to harm me, he can. I saw something in him when he made that offer to me, something dark and cruel. He would come for me, I know it."

"Then, you shall just have to come under my protection," Gloucester said, a touch frustrated by the situation.

Olivia paused.

"You mean that?"

"Yes. You can come and live here," Gloucester said carelessly, having not considered what he was suggesting. "Fitzroy will not trespass here. He would not dare."

Olivia was perking up at this idea. Clara would have liked to have taken Gloucester aside and explained how his notion would seem to the girl and the complication he was getting himself into. But the offer was made and there was not anything more they could do about it.

"Yes," Olivia said swiftly, before anyone had a chance to consider what had been said too hard. "I shall confront Fitzroy as long as I have a promise of protection."

Gloucester was satisfied. Clara exchanged a look with Tommy, but they both remained silent.

They headed straight to Berkeley Square, Gloucester eager to confront Fitzroy and force him to speak the truth at last. Clara was not sure what to expect when they arrived on the man's doorstep. She hoped Fitzroy would be jarred into speaking the truth at last, but she was a cynic and knew they could be flogging a dead horse.

Fitzroy opened the door himself when they rang the bell and glowered at them. He was about to slam the door in their faces when Clara spoke.

"You recall Olivia Knepp, Mr Fitzroy? She has kindly explained the arrangement you had with her."

Fitzroy paused. He looked angrily at Olivia who shrunk back from his gaze. Only the fact Tommy was stood behind her, prevented her from departing back down the steps.

"Whatever she has said, it is all lies," Fitzroy barked. "I am tired of your impositions on me. If you come again, I will summon the police."

"What about Bruno?" Clara asked, in a last attempt to draw him out. She could see now that Fitzroy was a harder nut to crack than they had hoped.

"I don't know anyone called Bruno," Fitzroy said, though the fact he had not slammed the door in their faces seemed to bely that statement.

"He knows you," Clara said, pushing her luck. "You have been useful to him in his attempts to be rid of Brilliant Chang, but his assassin failed yesterday, and Chang is alive and well."

She hoped to spook Fitzroy, have him realise the deadly waters he was swimming in. Her hopes were in vain. Fitzroy was not so easily gulled.

"I know nothing of this Bruno, nor about assassination attempts. What sort of person do you think I am? Go away and never come back, or I shall summon the police!"

This time he slammed the door. In the span of a few hours, it was the second door that had been slammed shut in Clara's face.

Olivia was heartily relieved.

"I did as you asked," she said, turning woeful eyes on Gloucester. "And you promised to protect me!"

"Yes, yes," Gloucester said, not really paying attention. "You are under my protection."

Olivia was satisfied and was clearly planning her next move to entangle herself further in Gloucester's life. Clara was busy with her own thoughts.

Fitzroy was proving tougher to break than she had imagined. They might have to try drastic action to get him to open up, because right now they had nothing.

"What now?" Gloucester asked her.

"Back to Brighton," she said.

Gloucester was appalled.

"You are giving up?"

"No," Clara reassured him. "I am trying another

course of action, but the person I need is back in Brighton and he might not be so easily convinced to come to London."

"In the meantime, Ariadne's chances are fast fading," Gloucester sunk his head. "I know how these things go."

"Poor Gloucester," Olivia cooed, petting his arm in sympathy.

Gloucester was horrified and turned to Clara, having suddenly and belatedly realised what he had let himself in for.

Chapter Twenty-Three

Annie was surprised and elated to see Clara and Tommy arrive home before dinner that day.

"I expected you to have to catch the late train," she said, eagerly heading to the kitchen to make arrangements for a larger dinner.

"Well, we have pleased Annie, at least," Tommy remarked.

He shrugged off his coat and hung it on the stand.

"Clara, do you think Ariadne is still alive?"

Clara had been endeavouring not to think too hard about Ariadne's condition, when she did, she naturally veered into unhappy thoughts.

"I think it depends on why she vanished and who took her," Clara said. "Assuming she was taken, and that she did not disappear of her own accord."

"I suppose that remains a possibility?" Tommy said vaguely hopeful.

"I am open to any possibility," Clara assured him, though deep down she believed the evidence indicated Ariadne had been snatched against her will.

"We need to speak to Chang," she said, at which

point she turned and spotted him standing on the staircase.

He looked pale and the way his hand rested upon the banister suggested he was not convinced he would remain upright if he let go. It was subtle, but the indications of a sick man were there.

"Have you found her?" he asked, his eyes narrowed and a look of ferocity on his face.

It was a look that had a tendency to chill the hearts of those he normally worked with. Clara just resented it.

"I am doing my best under trying circumstances," she informed him. "I don't suppose you have worked out who this Bruno person might be?"

"No," Chang snapped. "Clearly he is using an alias so if I did learn his name, I would not recognise it."

"Sensible," Tommy said. "Could be anyone. Someone close to you, maybe."

"Yes, yes, I have considered all that," Chang let his temper take over.

Annie heard the commotion from the kitchen and appeared promptly in the hallway.

"None of that!" she pointed a finger at him. "We had this discussion, remember?"

Chang pulled a face.

"Remember!" Annie persisted.

"Yes," Chang groaned. "I remember."

Clara exchanged a surreptitious look with Tommy, both slightly stunned and amused by Chang and Annie's change in relationship.

"Now, think peaceful and hopeful thoughts," Annie told the criminal.

Chang sighed, then he made the effort to lighten his expression.

"You are doing your best, Clara," he said, though he was speaking through gritted teeth. "I am sure you will succeed, for you are remarkably persistent."

Clara tried to work out of that was sarcasm.

"Much better," Annie said. "Don't you feel better too? Anger is an emotion that locks us all up inside and makes us miserable. Goodness does the opposite."

"I feel the same," Chang said defiantly.

"Then you best keep at it," Annie said. "You have a long way to go compared to most."

She turned her attention to Clara and Tommy.

"I remembered something my grandmother used to say," she explained.

"The one who cast the Evil Eye on people?" Clara said.

"The same," Annie said, ignoring the catch in Clara's voice. "My grandmother once told me that the people who are most affected by bad influences are those who are unhappy in their soul, and who allow negative emotions to fester within them. Jealousy, anger, resentment, bitterness, all these emotions feed into a pot of unhappiness within a person and make them more susceptible to malign influences. A person with a happy, generous soul is much harder to cast the Evil Eye upon, because their nature acts as a natural barrier to such things."

"And also a happy, kind soul is unlikely to cause a problem that would result in the Evil Eye being cast on them," Clara pointed out.

Annie ignored her logic.

"I think, if Chang begins to change his heart and replaces his anger with hope and kindness, it will have an impact on his wellbeing."

"Clara is now going to inform us that as there is no such thing as curses, my mood has no bearing on things," Chang said, with a hint of satisfaction.

Personally, Clara thought a change in Chang's demeanour would be rather pleasant and had no intention of giving him an excuse to remain the uncaring, miserable soul he was currently. Even if the change was superficial and made in an effort to improve his health, she felt it would make his time here much more bearable.

"One thing all nurses know is that a patient with a positive and hopeful outlook is more likely to recover than one who confines themselves to doom and gloom," she said. "The mind is a powerful tool and sometimes it is the patient's attitude that makes the difference as to whether they recover or not."

Chang glared at her, which in turn earned a glare from Annie.

"What do you have to lose?" Annie demanded of him. "Don't you want to feel better."

"Yes," Chang said in exasperation.

"Then make this effort," Annie berated him.

She headed back to her kitchen.

"You have encountered Annie at her finest, when she is nursing a person to health," Tommy said with a grin to Chang.

"It feels more like bullying a person back to health," Chang grumbled.

"The end result is the same," Tommy chuckled. "The point is, you are stuck with her for the time being, at least."

Chang let out a deep breath and sagged a little. He was too tired to argue anymore.

"Come into the parlour, there is something we need to discuss," Clara said.

He followed her and Tommy into the front room and settled onto a sofa with some relief. His body felt heavy with exhaustion yet again. Clara and Tommy took an armchair each.

"We have now determined three of the main players in the scheme against you," Clara told Chang. "Ariadne, of course. Benjamin Fitzroy and Olivia Knepp. Fitzroy seems to be the ringmaster in all this. Olivia claims he just paid her to swap drinks with you and she did not even know the drink was drugged."

"You believe that?" Chang asked with a raised eyebrow.

"No," Clara replied. "Olivia had to have guessed there was something in the drink, else why be asked to swap it? She says she thought Fitzroy was playing a prank."

"On me?" Chang said, finding that preposterous.

"Olivia Knepp is somewhat gullible," Tommy interjected. "She is also permanently short of cash. Not to mention, she was rather hoping to become your mistress and may have taken your rejection somewhat personally."

"I do not recall her beyond the incident with the drink," Chang said. "She sounds like the sort of girl I would do all in my power to avoid."

"In any case, Olivia has told us all she knows, which is not a great deal," Clara explained. "We hoped that if Fitzroy was faced with her, he would be forced to tell us the truth. He has proved far more resilient to persuasion than we had hoped."

"You are not using the right sort of persuasion," Chang said darkly.

"Pleasant thoughts, Chang," Tommy caught him out. "Remember?"

Chang cast up his eyes in defeat and flopped back against the sofa.

"I do have another idea," Clara said, drawing back his attention. "Fitzroy is plainly working for this Bruno person, who scares him enough to keep his mouth shut despite the evidence we have so far presented to him. You are correct Chang, that our persuasion has not proven sufficient up to this point and the odds of us getting near Fitzroy again now he knows what we are about are, well, pretty non-existent. That is why we must set a trap. Confront him in a manner that makes him feel he has more to lose by failing to speak to us, than he has to gain from his silence."

Chang was listening intently.

"A confrontation?"

"I think it may be the only way. Unless we can determine who this Bruno person is and thus use that information against Fitzroy," Clara continued. "My suggestion is that we confront Fitzroy with you, Chang."

A smile crept onto Chang's lips.

"You think my presence will be sufficient threat to get him talking."

"I think having the man before him who he has been working against, and knowing just how dangerous that man is, will be a shock to Fitzroy's confidence. He is currently living in the notion he is untouchable, because of where he lives and also because of his denials of doing anything. He is arrogant, but arrogance can be shaken."

Chang was enjoying this notion, the idea of indulging his power against someone, to putting the fear of God into them, made him cheerful.

"Nice thoughts, Chang," Tommy reminded him. "Nice thoughts."

"To enable this confrontation, you will need to come with us to London," Clara added.

"I surmised that," Chang remarked with his familiar sneer. Then he remembered himself and endeavoured to pull his features into a warmer expression. "You are wondering if I will come?"

"You fled London for a sound reason. Returning could put you are risk," Clara replied. "Also, we have to consider your health."

Chang became quiet. He was contemplating his health a lot lately.

"We shall need to consider the arrangements carefully," Clara added. "We cannot expose you to view, so all must be done as much in secret as possible.

I have an idea of where we can lay our trap and it should be a safe place for you."

"I want to know who is behind all this," Chang said firmly. "I want this malaise lifted off me. Ariadne needs to be found for that to be achieved and so I shall confront this Fitzroy."

"The supposed curse is the least of things," Clara said, unable to resist dismissing once again the idea that a curse was behind Chang's problems. "Someone has plotted against you and has done so very cleverly and deviously. They are a dangerous threat to you and determining who they are has to be a priority."

"I did not think you would care if one of my rivals took me out," Chang sniffed.

"I do care, just not for the reasons you suppose. First, you are a known quantity to me and, much to our mutual dislike, we do have a sort of working relationship. You don't step on my toes. I avoid stepping on yours. If someone takes your place, I cannot be sure of the same arrangement," Clara elaborated. "Second, your rival was prepared to send an assassin into my home and threatened Annie's safety, thus he has crossed a line and made himself my enemy. Third, we have Ariadne to consider. Whatever her involvement in all this, we have to find her and make sure she and her baby are safe."

"On that I am agreed," Chang said. "I was told today that Ariadne dying does not necessarily mean the curse will be broken and I shall be stuck this way."

Clara opted not to argue about the nature of 'curses' for once.

"That settles things," Tommy smiled. "Tomorrow you will come with us to London and maybe at last we can get what we need from Fitzroy."

"I shall be at my most fearsome," Chang said proudly. "He shall be so terrified, he will reveal all."

Clara was not sure that would be quite the case.

Right at that moment, Chang did not look the vicious criminal he usually aimed to portray himself as. He looked... ordinary, just another man going about his life. Something about his presence had changed, though she could not think how to properly explain the difference to herself. It was as if some of his energy was gone, like he was diminished somehow.

It was a complicated notion and started to sound a little too much like all this curse and magic talk for her liking.

She noticed at that moment that Chang was clutching a stone in his hand.

"What is that?" she asked.

Chang, who was no fool, wrapped his fingers tightly around the stone and palmed it.

"It is a gift. A token of good will," he said. "I think we can agree I need all the good will I can get right now."

Clara could agree with that.

"I shall organise the arrangements through Gloucester," Clara said to her brother. "My feeling is we should have the meeting at Elaine DeVaughn's. It is the only place we can be sure Fitzroy will go and where we can conduct ourselves in private."

Annie appeared in the doorway of the parlour.

"You are all abandoning me tomorrow then?" she said, not without a hint of delight to be free of her patient and to have the house to herself.

"I have to get away in case you try to poison me with burning sage again," Chang retorted.

"I told you, it cleared the room wonderfully," Annie said without an inch of regret. "I dare say this house is completely free of evil spirits now. Or at least it will be once you are gone tomorrow."

"Oh, very droll," Chang snorted. "And after I have endured your beef tea too."

"You have not drunk it!"

"I am meant to drink that stuff?" Chang pulled a face of disgust. "I thought it was like the sage, placed there to create such a stink nothing with any sense would stay in the room."

"You should watch your tongue. That beef tea recipe came from my grandmother."

"Then I am even more convinced it is poisonous!"

Clara and Tommy were watching the exchange with curiosity. Despite the seeming argument, it was plain that this was all banter between the pair and something they had been doing for the past couple of days without taking any of it to heart. Clara had the ominous sense of warmth growing between the unlikely pair. A friendship forming.

She found that the most alarming thing she had encountered all week. Just as well to get Chang out of her house tomorrow and away from Annie.

"At least I have not hit you over the head with a coal shovel," Annie was saying to Chang. "Though, there is still time, and I don't think the inspector would blame me for doing it."

"I must confess, that was a side to you I had never expected to see," Chang replied.

"He was just lucky he had not upset my chickens," Annie said stoutly. "Or things would have gone a lot worse for him."

Tommy decided it was time to interrupt them.

"Now, Annie, I must tell you about our lunch at this ridiculously expensive restaurant and the drama Gloucester made over cheese, so we ended up eating for free. Your blood will boil!"

He hastened his wife away to the kitchen to tell her the story, leaving Clara alone with Chang.

"I will be glad when you are out of my home," she informed the man once Tommy and Annie were gone.

"Me too," Chang replied with sincerity.

Chapter Twenty-Four

The next day, Benjamin Fitzroy received a missive from his fiancée, asking him to come over for lunch. Things had been tentative between him and Elaine since she had learned he had seen Ariadne on Christmas Eve. He was desperately trying to resolve the situation, because Elaine was his safest bet for a financially secure future. Fitzroy had big ambitions, which required money. Unfortunately, his family lacked the means to propel him into the future he desired. The only thing they could offer him was their name and the respectable reputation that came with it.

Fitzroy had been looking for a wife with means ever since he was old enough to consider marriage. He was practical about the whole business. He needed to marry money and any other consideration was minor in comparison. He had floated around the correct parties for years trying to find a woman who was prepared to take on a poor husband – more importantly, a woman who was not controlled by her family, for more than once his plans had been dashed when an irate father, brother or uncle had refused permission for him to marry their respective female relative.

Elaine was different. She was independent and she thrived off offending her family. Marrying him pleased her because it would upset her parents. Her defiance was the thing that cinched the deal.

She was also not bad looking, reasonable company and relatively undemanding when it came to what he must agree to for the match.

Ditching Ariadne had been a little awkward. He was fond of Ariadne, and they had hung around together on and off for years. But needs must.

Fitzroy would be loathed to lose Elaine because of Ariadne and he was going to do everything he could to salvage their relationship. He might have blustered about things the day Gloucester and that annoying woman, Miss Fitzgerald, had accosted him, but he had the sense to know it was not wise to burn bridges so freely.

He attended lunch at Elaine's home in the hopes that everything could be restored to the way it had been before and that Ariadne could, at long last, be completely forgotten about.

He was welcomed into the house by the butler. Fitzroy was a little unnerved by this formality. Elaine often opened the door herself, especially when she knew he was coming. He could see no sign of her as he entered.

"Miss DeVaughn asks that you head through to the Blue Drawing Room, sir," the butler said. "She has been delayed but will join you shortly."

The Blue Drawing Room was Elaine's private space and Fitzroy felt a little happier that she had mentioned he should go there. He relaxed and walked through the front drawing room, and to the connecting doors. He did not pay attention to the butler closing the drawing room doors behind him. He opened the doors of the

Blue Drawing Room and strode inside. There was a decorative screen arranged near the doors to stop the draught that tended to blow in when they were opened. Behind the screen, shielded from view, was a suite of furniture – two soft couches in blue satin and an armchair to complement them.

Fitzroy could not see the chairs, but he could see that a hearty fire was burning in the hearth. He was cold from his walk to Ariadne's house (his car was low on petrol and his finances for the month did not extend to buying more fuel) and the warmth of the fire called to him. He strolled over and stretched out his hands to the flames with a sigh.

It was a several moments before Fitzroy sensed he was not alone. It was a strange sensation, like a tickle between the shoulder blades or a feeling of heat burning into the back of his skull. The longer he stood paying attention to these signs, the clearer the feeling became and the more certain he was someone was sat behind him. Someone who had not bothered to declare their presence.

He turned, half expecting to see Gloucester sitting there, or that Fitzgerald woman. Who he actually saw made his blood run cold.

"I do not believe we have been formally introduced," Brilliant Chang lounged on a sofa, smiling pleasantly. "Brilliant Chang."

"I know who you are," Fitzroy said coldly. "Why are you here?"

"I have been invited for lunch," Chang said calmly.

Fitzroy did not believe a word of it and he was not going to be placed in a position to have accusations thrown at him once again. Angered that Elaine had duped him into coming there, he marched back towards the doors and went to fling them open. It was then he discovered they had been locked behind him.

His blood ran cold a second time, as a sensation of

hopelessness slipped over him. He had to remain calm. He could not allow Chang to see his fear.

"It appears someone has locked the doors in error," Fitzroy said, his eyes going to a second set of doors at the far side of the room. He tried to recall where they led to and if it was a dead end or not. "I shall ring for assistance."

"I wouldn't bother," Chang said placidly. When Fitzroy turned to him, looking alarmed, he shrugged. "Miss DeVaughn will be here shortly and will unlock the doors. In the meantime, we can talk."

"I don't believe we have anything to talk about," Fitzroy said angrily.

"That is rather rude," Chang tilted his head. "Do you say this because I am foreign? Or because you have been working against me?"

Fitzroy felt his breath catch in his throat.

"You are mistaken," he said.

"Am I?" Chang removed the 'Bruno' letter from his coat pocket and placed it on a low coffee table that filled the space between the sofas and armchair.

He pushed it towards Fitzroy with a sharp jerk. Fitzroy stared at the paper, unable to bring himself to look at it closer. He recognised the writing. He knew where it had come from, but how had it ended up in the possession of Brilliant Chang?

"Someone sent an assassin after me the other day," Chang continued calmly. "The gentleman is now unconscious in a hospital bed. No one is sure if he will wake up."

Fitzroy was starting to tremble. The man before him was more dangerous than he could even contemplate, and he had been locked in a room with him. He was starting to understand that Elaine did not care what became of him, that she had decided he was not worthy of her forgiveness. All because he had been stupid enough to stop and speak to Ariadne the other night.

"What do you want?" he asked Chang, hoping he might be able to talk his way out of this.

"You can begin by telling me who Bruno is," Chang said.

"Who he is?" Fitzroy said in surprise. "I only know of him as Bruno. That is how he introduced himself to me."

"All right," Chang said calmly, "then why don't you tell me how you came to be associated with him."

Fitzroy was uneasy; that was not a story he liked to tell. Squirming out of speaking the truth, however, looked impossible. He glanced around the room, desperate for an exit, wondering if the windows might be easy to clamber through, except they only led to the enclosed garden and he would just be exchanging one cage for another, colder one.

"Well?" Chang demanded.

His gaze seemed pleasant enough but there was something in his demeanour that made Fitzroy aware his patience was running out. Fitzroy was cornered. He had no other option left but to speak. He just hoped Elaine was not somewhere listening to all this, otherwise he might not be able to salvage anything from this disaster.

"I had been gambling at a club in Soho," he began. "I ran up some debts to some rather unpleasant people. I looked to be in serious trouble when Bruno stepped in and paid off my debts, just like that. Of course, I knew he would want something in return."

"Yes," Chang nodded. "He had been watching you, ready for his moment."

Fitzroy gulped as he saw how stupid he had been.

"I thanked him profusely and naturally said about repayment, and he said he would forgot my monetary debts if I helped him with a project. Just a small favour or two, was all he would need. I knew at once that there was no option to refuse," Fitzroy felt his arrogance slipping as he saw the terrible depths he had fallen into through his energetic pursuit of money.

"What did he ask you to do?" Chang said.

Fitzroy tried not to look at him as he spoke.

"He said he needed to deal with someone who had hurt him. I did not ask any questions, it seemed better I did not know too much. He did eventually reveal that person was you, but after I had already started to put a plan into action. He needed me to recruit a woman to act as a stooge for a blackmail scheme he had in mind. I knew Ariadne would agree because she would do anything for me."

"You persuaded her to seduce me and get herself pregnant?" Chang asked, mildly impressed by the depths the man had stooped to.

"Not precisely," Fitzroy admitted. "She was to pretend to seduce you and we would fake her pregnancy. Ariadne would never have agreed to anything else and there was no certainty she would actually fall pregnant."

Chang stared at him. It was a penetrating stare, the sort that seems calm on the surface but that suggests beneath there is a churning river of anger and fury. Fitzroy took a step back from him and started to think about how to defend himself if the need arose.

"It was all fake?" Chang demanded in an icily calm voice.

Fitzroy was struggling to catch his breath.

"Yes," he said weakly.

Chang clenched his fists together, barely holding onto his temper. He could have lashed out and dismantled the whole room if he let himself go, that was the pitch of his outrage.

"I knew she was lying!" he declared, a sudden insight coming over him.

He had been right all along!

"Bruno wanted you to be made vulnerable, maybe forced to leave London. He knew how diligently you avoided associating with single women for the reason you did not want to be responsible for any unplanned children. He also knew the dent it would make on your reputation if people learned how you had been drugged and seduced. He wanted you weakened."

"And the curse?" Chang said. "Who thought of that?"

"Bruno," Fitzroy replied. "He told Ariadne that if you would not react to the blackmail threats then she had to pretend to curse you. He said you were superstitious enough to take such a thing seriously."

"And he was right," Chang said bitterly.

He was quiet a moment, then looked up.

"Bruno is someone I know and who knows me well," he said. "He knows my plans, my intentions. He is part of my inner circle."

"I cannot help with that," Fitzroy said quickly. "I do not really know much about him."

"But he comes to you, to tell you what to do?" Chang said quickly.

"Sometimes he comes to my home, or he arranges for us to meet somewhere. Other times he sends letters like that one," Fitzroy pointed to the one on the coffee table. "I ought to have burned that."

Chang was uninterested in his failure to cover his tracks.

"When did you last speak to him?" Chang asked.

"Christmas Eve," Fitzroy closed his eyes as he whispered his answer. "Ariadne was having... second thoughts. She was tired of being the centre of a scandal and she realised she was not going to get me back through her efforts. I think she was angry at me as much as anything. On Christmas Eve, I spotted her walking home, and I pulled over to speak to her. I wasn't really thinking about the situation, I just wanted to wish her a good Christmas, is all. I was a little merry, I suppose.

"She flew into a rage at me, yelling how I had ruined her life and that she was finished with all this nonsense. She was going to go to you and tell you the truth. She wanted to hurt me, to make me say I would take her back. Neither of us were thinking straight.

"I managed to convince her to get into my car and we would talk about things at my house. She came with me, and I thought she would sleep off the drink and be in a better mood. But when I tried to help her into bed, she grew angry again, we argued, she threw things. Things got a little rough and for the safety of us both I rushed out of the room and locked the door behind me. Then I sent a message to Bruno. It was all I could think to do. I hoped he would say it was all over and Ariadne could stop playing her part."

"But he did not," Chang guessed.

"He turned up. I never expected that. I have a telephone number for messages I need to send him which I can use any time of the day or night. It was not even dawn when he appeared on my doorstep with two other men. He said he had come for Ariadne. I just let them take her. I never even asked what he meant."

Fitzroy hung his head. A click announced that the far doors were opening and when Fitzroy looked up, Clara, Tommy, Gloucester, and Elaine had all emerged from the other room. He winced at the sight of them.

"You are a cad!" Gloucester told him. "You cast her to the wolves!"

Fitzroy had nothing he could say to that and just hunched his shoulders further and kept his eyes on the floor.

"We need to know how to find Bruno," Clara said, stepping forward and trying to be practical. "Do you know where he might be right now?"

"I can give a good guess," Fitzroy said. "But he will

know I sent you there."

"Your alternative is to refuse to speak and face my wrath," Chang told him coldly. "As you may have noticed, I am in the room with you right now, not this Bruno fellow. My immediate retribution will be swift and painful if you do not talk."

Fitzroy knew he was done for. He looked briefly at Elaine, knowing it was over between them. He was finished.

"All right," he groaned. "For Ariadne's sake, I will tell you."

Chapter Twenty-Five

"There is a nightclub," Fitzroy explained. "It is called *The Fiddle*, which rather describes what playing at any of its tables is like."

Chang pricked up his ears.

"I know that place," he said. "I know who runs it!"

"Bruno owns the place," Fitzroy continued. "That is what he told me."

Chang launched himself up from the sofa suddenly and scared the life out of Fitzroy who jumped back nearly into the fireplace.

"Mateus Vinkler!" Chang said aloud. "He must be Bruno! He runs The Fiddle, and he would know all that information about me."

"He is one of your inner circle?" Clara asked him.

"No," Chang said. "At least not for a long time. He sided with my sister when she decided to turn against me."

Chang's energy suddenly abandoned him, and he swayed on his feet. Memories of the deep betrayal by his sister and the nightmare it had sparked, ending in her death, swam through his mind. Fitzroy was watching him curiously. He was sharp enough to note a man's weakness. The last thing Clara needed right now was Fitzroy getting the idea that Bruno's plan against Chang was working and he was truly vulnerable. She stepped forward.

"How can we be sure Bruno will be at the club?" she said, distracting Fitzroy.

"He is always there," Fitzroy shrugged his shoulders. "I mean, he is there a lot."

"Ariadne will not be held there," Chang said, his voice quiet but sinister. He had regrouped and remembered what he was about. "Mateus is no fool. Well, he is a pretty big fool for going up against me, but in some regards, he is not so stupid."

"How come he is still in operation when he sided with your sister?" Tommy asked.

Chang gave him the sort of look reserved for a schoolboy who was being very dense.

"If I was to go after every person who sided with my sister, I should be mounting a vendetta for the rest of my life," he said as if it was obvious. "I needed to get my organisation back into line, to secure everything. Mateus did not seem like someone I needed to worry about. He had slunk away back to running his nightclub and had even made cautious enquiries about working with me again. He seemed cowed, but clearly not enough."

"He is trying to take over your empire," Clara remarked. "That is the mark of an ambitious and brave man."

"Don't get carried away, Clara. Empires like mine are not so easily conquered," Chang liked the word empire and enjoyed saying it.

Fitzroy was watching them all with tentative hope.

"Now I have told you where to find Bruno, that is me out of the picture," he said lightly, aiming to make it a statement rather than a question. "I have learned my lesson about getting involved in such affairs. I shall be more cautious about favours in the future. I shall be going now."

"You are going nowhere," Chang pointed a finger at him. "You have assisted in making my life miserable and now try to usurp me. That is not something I intend to let go unpunished."

Fitzroy went pale and glanced to Elaine in desperation for help.

"Chang, I did not help you find out the truth to have you taking justice into your own hands," Clara intervened. "Whatever justice might be considered in this case. We shall hand Fitzroy over to the police."

"What?" Fitzroy said, more alarmed than when Chang was threatening him.

"You participated in an attempt to blackmail a man," Clara explained to him. "You also drugged him. And you are involved in the kidnap of a young lady. I imagine the police will be interested in your association with Mateus Vinkler too."

Chang was catching her drift and liking where she was going.

"Mateus has been on the police's books for years. They have been trying to arrest him, but no charges have ever stuck. He is linked to a number of murders ordered by my sister, but no one has been prepared to stand up and speak against him. I think in this situation they will find things a lot easier, because I am a witness for them, and I shall gladly speak up against Mateus."

Chang was grinning from ear-to-ear. He knew when he could use the police to serve his own ends. Clara was not exactly keen on him manipulating the justice system; however, her primary concern was finding Ariadne alive and since bringing Mateus into police custody was going to play a part in that, she would allow things to happen.

"I can't go to prison!" Fitzroy said in horror. "My

family reputation would be ruined."

"You committed a crime, old boy. Several, actually. The natural consequence of that is prison," Tommy told him.

Fitzroy was aghast.

"But, but…"

"It is better than what I would have had done to you," Chang sniffed.

Fitzroy met his eyes. Whatever weakness Chang might have displayed earlier, it was long gone, and he looked the confident, cocky gangster again. Self-assured, certain of himself. He was once more in charge, and he was decidedly dangerous.

Fitzroy was trying to think how he could talk his way out of the situation. Desperate to avoid facing criminal charges. His mind was blank.

"We need to get going," Clara declared to break the stalemate. "Elaine, will you be all right keeping Fitzroy confined somewhere in your home until we return?"

Elaine gave her an amused look.

"You have no concern on that front," she promised her. "Fitzroy is going nowhere. I shall be keen to see him arrested."

"Elaine!" Fitzroy said in horror.

Elaine looked at him stonily.

"You conspired to have your former lover kidnapped, after using her for your own malicious purposes. A blackmailer, a gambler and a man who runs with criminals. You have disappointed me."

"Elaine, I made mistakes…"

"These were more than mistakes. Character flaws I could accept, tolerate, even, but the sheer stupidity you have demonstrated is something I cannot abide. I could never marry such a foolish man."

Fitzroy's bluster was finally lost. He stared at them all, trying to work out a means of escaping his fate. He found no sympathy in any quarter.

"Come on," Clara said, moving towards the doors. "We need to find Ariadne and end this drama."

Chang, Tommy, and Gloucester followed her. Gloucester had been remarkably silent during the entire affair. He had watched the dismantling of Fitzroy's various lies, seen his enemy brought low and he had not said a word. Now he walked past Fitzroy to leave the room and paused right in front of him.

"She best be alive, old man," he hissed at Fitzroy nastily. "Or else I will be the one the police want, for murder."

Something in Gloucester's tone, or his expression, sent a chill down Fitzroy's spine and he believed, wholeheartedly, that the lord's son meant everything he said and would gladly kill him. What little colour he had left drained from his face as Gloucester departed after the others.

"How are we going to handle this?" Tommy asked as they climbed into Gloucester's car and set off for The Fiddle.

"I shall handle it," Chang said calmly. "Mateus will not expect me to walk into his nightclub."

"He will have guards," Clara pointed out. "You only have us."

"That is not a problem," Chang was smiling. "While I am speaking to him, someone shall call the police and ask that a message be given directly to Chief Inspector Monroe. He shall be informed that Brilliant Chang is prepared to give evidence against Mateus Vinkler, if he hurries to get down here to arrest him. Monroe has been after Vinkler for a series of murders. He is after me too, but Vinkler has caused him so much bother, I think he will overlook that."

"Still sounds like a risk," Tommy said, uneasy about things. "Maybe we should have the police arrive first."

"Mateus will be long gone at the first hint of police

involvement," Clara said. "We need to have him suitably distracted."

"Quite right, Clara," Chang was amused. "You are learning."

"Sadly, it has become necessary to do my job, but I agree with Tommy that we are stepping into dangerous territory."

"You will be fine," Chang said dismissively. "I have seen you in action."

Clara was not convinced, though his praise was satisfying. However, there was nothing else they could do, and it seemed unlikely they would be able to persuade Gloucester to stop from heading to the nightclub on his own if they did not go with him.

Gloucester was a man on a mission, his entire focus on rescuing Ariadne. He was her knight errant, determined to find her and whisk her to safety. Clara hoped for his sake they found the girl alive.

After some doubling back and forth, and stopping to ask directions, they located the area where The Fiddle was situated. To access the club, it was necessary to head down an alley between two buildings, where a side door allowed people to enter discreetly and kept the club's existence largely unknown to passers-by. There was not even a sign to declare its name.

Nightclubs were a complicated issue for the police. They were often shutdown for violating a licensing law, or because of some more serious crime. Criminals were known to haunt them and in London, at least, there had been more than one incident of a major gunfight within a nightclub. They were dubious places to hangout and so naturally attracted the rich adventure-seeker who liked to try his or her hand at illegal gambling.

Chang led the way down the alley. There was no one about. Guards on the door would just make it more obvious something was there. Chang hammered on the door, confident that he would be allowed straight in when he was recognised. A hatch in the door slammed across and a pair of eyes peeped through.

"Brilliant Chang, here to see Mateus Vinkler," Chang stated.

"I don't have your name listed to see Mr Vinkler," the eyes replied.

Chang did not blink.

"Tell Bruno, I know his secret and we best talk."

The eyes blinked.

"I am not sure…"

"Just tell him," Chang suddenly reached into his pocket and produced a small pistol which he pointed through the eye slit in the door.

Clara had not known Chang was carrying a gun. She tried not to act surprised. Beside her Tommy stiffened. Quietly, Gloucester dug into his own coat pocket and retrieved a service revolver, which he carefully checked for bullets in plain sight of the door attendant.

Clara was even more surprised by this. When had everyone decided to carry guns?

"Have you anything in your pocket I should know about?" she asked her brother.

"Only a tin of mints," Tommy answered. "Ever feel you have missed some important message everyone else received?"

"You mean like, 'make sure you are armed?'" Clara sighed. "Yes, rather."

The door attendant tried to slam shut his little hatch, but Chang had put the gun muzzle far enough in that the hatch could not close.

"All right!" the door attendant yelled and then darted away.

Chang removed his pistol from the slot, amused, and tried the door, which proved to be unlocked. He headed inside, not waiting to see if the others followed.

Gloucester was close on his heels. Clara was right behind with Tommy.

They entered a narrow hallway that turned left and took them into a large open room that was buzzing with music and the chatter of conversation. People were sat around gambling tables, under electric lights with green glass shades. Others were lining a bar which had a vast selection of drinks behind it and three barmen endeavouring to keep up with the orders. The room was hazy with smoke and smelt of alcohol and other unfamiliar substances.

"Now would be the time for calling Chief Inspector Monroe," Chang said, addressing Clara pointedly.

Clara was not about to leave, not with Chang and Gloucester both armed and determined to cause trouble. She could see chaos erupting and innocent people getting hurt if she did not do something to keep them in check.

"Tommy, can you go find a public telephone and summon the police?" she whispered to her brother.

"Clara…"

"Please, Tommy, I need to keep these two in my sights. If we are to find Ariadne, I need to prevent Chang or Gloucester doing anything stupid."

Tommy still hesitated, reluctant to leave his sister alone in this dangerous place.

"I will be fine," Clara promised him. "The quicker the police are summoned and arrive here, the sooner we shall all be safe again."

Reluctantly, Tommy conceded and headed off to find a telephone. Chang and Gloucester were now stood in the middle of the room, looking around them and sticking out like a sore thumb. Unconsciously, several people had already moved away from them, causing a circle of space to form around them. Clara joined them just as a man appeared from a back doorway.

He was tall and dark-haired, with a thick moustache and unpleasant eyes. The way he walked, with a swagger of confidence, told you he was in charge. Behind him came two muscular, brutish men who were doing a good job of looking mean and sinister. Clara was in no doubt Mateus Vinkler had arrived.

Mateus saw that Chang was already in his club and his eyes narrowed.

"Hello Mateus," Chang said cheerfully. "I must say, the hospitality at your club is somewhat shocking. I have not been offered a drugged drink as yet."

His comment was intended to inform Mateus of just how much he knew. Mateus had the sense not to flinch at the words.

"I don't have an appointment to see you," he said. "But feel free to have a drink, just remember to pay for it.

"I wouldn't drink any swill you are serving," Chang sneered.

Before Mateus could respond, Gloucester stepped forward and aimed his revolver at the man's head. This instantly resulted in the room falling silent, except for the odd feminine shriek as people scurried for cover. Mateus' guards drew their own guns and pointed them at Gloucester.

"Enough!" Gloucester yelled. "I want to know where Ariadne is! And if you have murdered her, heaven help you!"

"Who is this madman?" Mateus growled. "Guards..."

Before he could order his men to fire Clara was stood before him.

"This man is the king's nephew," she lied quickly. "His uncle is Lord Buckingham, who you will find in his offices at Buckingham palace at this very moment. He is a high-ranking member of the nobility and one of his dearest friends is a woman called Ariadne

Griffiths."

Mateus paused, considering the consequences of having the king's nephew shot in his club.

"Oh dear," he said.

Chapter Twenty-Six

There was a moment when it was not plain what was going to happen, a moment when everyone held their breath expecting chaos to ensue, for bullets to fly and for someone to end up dead. Clara was not sure which way things were going to go, but she decided her safest bet was to fix her gaze on Mateus and not let him look away. In that terrible fraction of a second, all she could do was hold his stare and to hope he had the sense to back down.

Mateus took a long breath. His guards were ready to fire, and they would need little excuse to do so. Brilliant Chang had slightly more restraint, but Gloucester was an unknown quantity and the proximity of his revolver to Mateus' head meant that even if his men opened fire there was a good chance Mateus would die along with Gloucester.

Mateus did not want to die. He had survived this long because he was quick-witted and did not take unnecessary risks. He also could control his temper, and in many regards that was the key to his success. Cool headedness was a gift he shared with Chang; in many ways they were very alike.

Mateus forced himself to relax, sending a subtle signal to everyone – especially Gloucester – that it was not necessary for them to resort to violence. He had not taken his gaze from Clara. Who she was, he was not sure, but he sensed she wanted this to remain a peaceful affair as much as he did and, in that regard, he was glad to side with her.

"I guess we need to talk," he said carefully to Clara.

"We do," Clara said.

Mateus tilted his head towards Gloucester.

"Could you ask him to lower his gun?"

"Could you ask your guards to lower theirs?" Clara replied.

"All right," Mateus said, taking a chance because Clara seemed sensible. "Lower your guns."

He called the order over his shoulder. Clara glanced at Gloucester.

"Lower the gun," she told him softly.

He did not respond, there was a pained look on his face, his anguish pouring from him. Clara gingerly reached for his forearm and slowly pulled his arm down. He suddenly seemed to realise what he had been on the cusp of doing and he stepped back, almost falling onto a card table. Chang quietly restored his gun to his pocket and then extracted the revolver from Gloucester's limp hand. Somewhat pointedly, he gave the revolver to Clara, who took it more because she preferred Gloucester unarmed and Chang with only one weapon, rather than because she wanted it. Mateus relaxed further now that the gun was in Clara's possession.

"Shall we talk in my office?" he suggested.

"Yes," Clara answered. "Your guards will wait outside, however."

Mateus paused.

"That would put me at a disadvantage."

"Yes," Clara said. "I rather fancy it would."

Mateus considered the situation further.

"However, to shoot me in my office would guarantee your own demises and I do not think you would want that."

"I certainly do not," Clara promised him. "I don't want anyone getting shot."

Mateus believed her and agreed to her conditions. They headed to his office.

"How much do you know?" he asked as soon as they were in the room and with the door shut.

Mateus had moved behind his desk, treating it like a barrier between him and the others.

"You have been plotting against me," Chang said simply. "You have been attempting to make me vulnerable through blackmail."

He avoided saying anything about the curse because he felt foolish mentioning it here. It also made him feel weak that he had succumbed to such a thing.

"I have been," Mateus admitted freely. "And it worked, you left London."

"And you sent an assassin after me, figuring I would be an easy target without my usual security arrangements."

"Yes," Mateus nodded. "What happened to the fellow?"

"He is unconscious in the hospital," Clara told him. "With the police keeping a close watch on him. You see, I do not take kindly to assassins in my home, and I also do not dabble in criminal activities. That is why I was quite happy to involve the police in this affair."

Mateus was uneasy. Policemen hovering around his assassin was not a good thing, not if the fellow awoke and thought it would save his bacon by speaking to the police.

"You see, Mateus, when I realised what was occurring, I sought assistance from a person who was not involved in criminal gangs, quite the opposite. A person who technically despises me, but who is so disgustingly good and honourable, she will help out anyone who asks for her aid. Even her enemy," Chang was grinning from ear-to-ear. "My associate here, would much rather I was wallowing in a prison cell and would do all in her power to see me there. She was the one person in all this I knew I could truly trust."

Mateus was trying to understand all he had just heard. He looked at Clara with a frown.

"Ok, you have caught me out," he said, deciding making denials would achieve little. "I suppose Fitzroy has told you all about me. I always knew it was a risk involving him. He does not have a lot of nerve."

"Fitzroy also failed to dispose of the evidence of your association. He has kept the letters you wrote to him under the name Bruno," Clara added. "He is rather a fool, if you ask me."

Mateus winced.

"I won't deny that. But he was useful and, rather like Chang here, I was looking to find someone who was not involved in a criminal gang to do my dirty work. I wanted an outsider, someone who could go to the right parties but would be overlooked as a potential threat," Mateus considered his failure further. "I took a chance, and it came very close to succeeding. Now what do you want from me?"

"I want nothing," Chang said calmly, causing Mateus to look at him in surprise. "Except for the woman, Ariadne Griffiths."

Mateus did not mask his confusion.

"Why would you want her?"

"Just tell us where she is!" Gloucester barked, his self-control leaving him again.

Clara was very glad she had his gun safely in her pocket.

"Is she alive?" Clara asked Mateus.

"I believe so," Mateus answered. "I told my men to take her to a secure place while I decided what to do with her. She was making things difficult by threatening to reveal to Chang that she had lied about her pregnancy. She was going to tell him about my scam. Killing her was inconvenient just now, because Fitzroy might have started gabbling if he thought she was dead."

"You found yourself with a lot of loose ends," Chang said, smirking. "And you were not sure the best way to deal with them."

Mateus shrugged his shoulders.

"It would become messy to start murdering everyone. In hindsight, involving someone who was a part of the higher echelons of society was unwise. It meant that Fitzroy's disappearance or death would be noticed. Had things only just carried on as they were, none of that would have mattered."

"Where is Ariadne?" Gloucester demanded.

Mateus looked at him calmly.

"My men will know. I shall have them take you to her, but first we have to discuss what you plan on doing after that."

His gaze was directed at Chang. Chang was smiling. It was not a pleasant sight.

"I should shoot you for what you tried to do to me," Chang said. "This is not the first time you have worked against me. When you sided with my sister, I accepted it as a mistake and allowed you to carry on unharmed, believing there were more urgent threats to deal with. Now it turns out I was wrong and leaving you to carry on with your business would be foolish."

Mateus stared at him, a hard, cold gaze.

"I will only order my men to take you to Ariadne if you give me your word you shall not harm me."

"I can hardly make such assurances," Chang replied.

Gloucester glowered at him.

"This is not about you!" he declared. "Give him your word and let us find Ariadne!"

"Or I just kill this traitor and end things here and now," Chang sneered.

"Except you won't," Clara remarked to him mildly.

Chang cast his eyes at her, and they exchanged a look. Chang was thinking she was referring to what he had been told about curses potentially surviving a person after death. Clara was actually referring to her intention of having the police deal with Mateus.

"Chang, give him your word," Clara said steadily. "Think about Tommy."

Chang frowned.

"Think about..." he slowly remembered that Tommy had gone to give a message to Inspector Monroe, the man he said would be the keenest to see Mateus behind bars. He recalled what they had discussed in the car. Being faced with his betrayer, he had forgotten their plan and had been contemplating his own revenge. Even now he wondered if he could quite live with doing things 'properly' and allowing justice to take its course. It was altogether tempting to put a bullet through Mateus' head and be done with it.

The one thing that swayed him was the thought that he might never be free of this malignant force hanging over him if he failed to find Ariadne alive and have her remove his curse. Clara would have been disappointed to know it was superstition in the end that convinced Chang to do as she said.

"Mateus, I give you my word I shall not take revenge upon you," Chang said, he stretched out a hand for him to shake on the matter.

Mateus looked somewhat unconvinced. He glanced at Clara.

"Precisely what hold do you have over him?" he asked her.

"None," Clara replied. "I am just a good influence on him."

"I told you, she despises me," Chang said cheerfully.

Mateus was even more confused, but he did accept Chang's hand and shook on the arrangement.

"I shall tell my men to take you to Ariadne," he added. "She is of no further interest to me, anyway."

"I will be watching you," Chang told him sinisterly. "One step out of line, one hint you are working against me again, I shall come for your blood. I do not often give people third chances."

Mateus nodded at him.

"I hate to say it, but you are more generous than your sister. I cannot decide if that makes you weaker than her or just more cunning."

"Perhaps it would be best to recall which one of them is still alive," Clara told him, her own tone dark as she spoke. "I had the misfortune of meeting Chang's sister and was partly responsible for ending her reign. She was too impulsive for her own good."

"I suppose I should take your words as a compliment," Chang sniffed, trying to appear unoffended by her talk.

"It is as near a compliment as you will ever get from me," Clara told him. "My point to Mateus is that he has chosen the wrong side once already, and he might be advised to recall that the next time he gets ideas. Of course, that suggests there is a right side, which there is not. There are two wrong sides, and he chose the worst of them."

"How do you tolerate this woman?" Mateus asked Chang, confused. "Does she not irritate you?"

"She irritates me to distraction," Chang replied. "I find it surprisingly refreshing. In a world of sycophants and dishonest men, she is quite the relief."

Mateus did not understand, but they had made their arrangement and now all he wanted was for Chang to leave. He showed them to the door. As he opened it, his guards tensed, ready in case there was to be trouble. Mateus held up a hand to indicate all was fine.

"I want you to show them where you took Ariadne," he told the guards. "Both of you do not need to go. Pick one of you and take them there."

The guards looked between them and then one shrugged, indicating he was happy to be the escort.

Mateus was glancing out at his club, relieved to see his clients were returning to their gambling and drinking. Things were not quite as settled as before, but they were a lot calmer.

"Pleasure doing business with you Chang," Mateus said insincerely, holding out a hand for him to shake.

Chang wanted to bite it off rather than shake it, but he accepted it, nonetheless. He knew when diplomacy was the best bet for his ongoing survival.

They drifted back across the nightclub, Mateus' guard leading the way. People gave them uneasy looks, but the worst was over. Clara was just hoping they could get out of the nightclub before the police arrived.

They emerged in the alley as Tommy came dashing towards them. He saw the guard and fell silent.

"Gloucester, can you show the guard to your car," Clara took charge.

Gloucester was still twitchy.

"I want to get to Ariadne swiftly."

"I will be right behind you," Clara promised him. "But I have something in my shoe and if I do not deal with it, I shall be in agony. Tommy, could you help me?"

Clara leaned against a wall and started taking off her shoe. The guard did not seem to suspect anything, and he headed off with Gloucester. The moment they were out of earshot, Clara glanced at Chang.

"You have to remain here to speak to Inspector

Monroe and ensure Mateus is arrested."

Chang was only too pleased to oblige.

"I would not normally be happy waiting for the police, but on this occasion, I do believe I shall enjoy it. I understand now, Clara, why you wanted me to give my word. It did not matter, because we had planned something else for Mateus, and I am finding it more satisfying than a quick death for him."

Clara felt Chang was enjoying himself too much.

"Tommy, I think you should remain here and help the police. Someone with a strong sense of right and wrong ought to be about, at least," Tommy nodded at her.

"I thought that might be the case. I had to give the police my name, anyway."

"I shall fetch Ariadne and we shall take her back to Gloucester's house, then we shall come back for you."

Clara gave her brother a quick hug.

"Stay safe," she told him and hurried up the alley.

Gloucester had the car engine going, and she was barely inside before he started to drive off. It was just as well they left when they did, for as Clara glanced back, she saw several vehicles pulling up near the alley, both motorised and horse drawn.

She allowed herself a sly smile. Mateus Vinkler was going to be in for a shock.

Chapter Twenty-Seven

"Can the King order people executed?" the guard asked as he sat next to Gloucester giving directions to where they were keeping Ariadne.

"I would have to ask him," Gloucester said coolly, playing up to the notion Clara had placed into everyone's heads that he was the King's nephew. "It would depend on the circumstances and just how upset he, or someone in his extended family, was."

The guard was not the smartest penny in the pound. He did not need to be for the work he did and having a man who lacked the intelligence to be ambitious was always an advantage for men like Mateus. The guard absorbed this information slowly.

"I never laid a finger on her," he said, clearly worried now and trying to extract himself from the situation as best he could. "We were just told to put her somewhere she could not cause trouble until Mr Vinkler had decided what to do with her."

"She is still alive?" Clara asked from the back seat.

"Last I checked," the guard responded nervously.

"Which was when?" Clara demanded.

The guard was started to picture himself being executed in the courtyard of the Tower of London, by a Beefeater with a big axe.

"Day before New Year's," he said. "We have been busy since."

The car jerked forward as Gloucester sped up.

"Did she have food and water?" Clara asked the guard, feeling a trickle of doubt creep into her stomach.

"Probably," the guard said, hazy in his recollection. "We were meant to make sure she had something."

"Are we close?" Gloucester demanded through gritted teeth.

"Nearly there," the guard promised.

They had turned into a rundown area of industrial warehouses and other buildings. There were few people around, as most of the properties were used for storage. Several appeared empty and had broken windows. The guard pointed at a place for them to pull over the car, outside a warehouse that stood end on to the road and had a narrow door leading onto the pavement.

"This is it," the guard said, producing a key from his pocket.

He was looking more anxious by the minute. Clara could hardly blame him. Gloucester looked likely to be out for blood and no doubt the guard was still thinking about the possibility of being executed by royal command.

The guard unlocked a hearty padlock on the door and showed them inside. They followed him to a second, inner door, which was secured by a bolt. This the guard pulled across and revealed a room minimally furnished. There was a bed with grey blankets, a chamber pot that told its own story and an armchair that looked likely to be home to a family of mice. There was no obvious sign of Ariadne.

The guard stepped into the room, astonished that his prisoner was not there. The door had swung inwards to his right and almost slammed against the wall.

Almost.

Clara noted it and caught Gloucester's arm before he also entered the room. He looked at her in surprise, but she just smiled and indicated he should wait. The guard was now fully into the room and from behind him, they both could see the door swing back a fraction and then a woman burst out from behind it holding a length of wood in her hands. Swinging the wood back over her head she brought it down as hard as she could on the guard's skull.

It proved a disappointing blow because he moved at the last moment and Ariadne was not very good at violence. It hit his shoulder rather than his head and he stumbled sideways but was not knocked unconscious.

Things would have become nasty very quickly if Clara and Gloucester had not been on the scene. As the guard turned on Ariadne, his outrage at the assault overcoming his fears of Gloucester's royal influence, they dived forward to step between him and the unfortunate girl.

"Ariadne!" Gloucester cried, scooping her into his arms with a joyous look on his face.

"Gloucester!" Ariadne burst into tears and lolled in his arms, weakened by her recent experiences, and exhausted emotionally.

Clara stood purposefully before the guard, who was rubbing his shoulder and slowly remembering his concerns about the possibility of axes and chopping blocks. He glared at her.

"For your sake, I think it is good Ariadne was healthy enough to try what she just did," Clara told him firmly.

The guard opened his mouth to protest, then took heed of her point.

"Yeah," he said, moodily.

"You came to rescue me!" Ariadne wept weakly in Gloucester's arms. "I thought I would die here!"

"Let's not hang around here any longer than necessary," Clara suggested. "We can talk properly once we are back at Gloucester's house."

Gloucester was only too pleased to agree to that and helped Ariadne out the door. Clara turned to the guard.

"You might not believe this, but this is your lucky day," she told him.

The guard looked at her confused.

"Right at this moment, Inspector Monroe is raiding The Fiddle. With Brilliant Chang's assistance he will be arresting Vinkler and anyone else involved in his organisation who is there. Chang will gladly testify against Vinkler and, I suspect, with assurances of Chang's ongoing protection, so will Fitzroy and Ariadne. In Fitzroy's case, it will be the only way he can ensure his safety. In short, by coming here with us, you have escaped the disaster befalling your boss."

"You tricked us!" the guard said, a rather slow reaction to her explanation Clara felt.

"Please! Vinkler intended to double-cross Chang and you know it. This way, at least he will not die horribly. At least, not today."

The guard was rubbing his shoulder and trying to fathom what had occurred and what he was going to do now.

"You should count yourself lucky," Clara reminded him. "You are not under police arrest and now have the chance to get away from here."

"What will I do?" the guard asked her, as if she was some sort of oracle for his future.

"Well, I would suggest you find a job that is legal,

but that might be a vain hope. I am sure you will figure something out."

She walked away from the building, glancing back just once to point at the warehouse.

"At least you have a roof over your head."

The guard was more confused than ever, not sure if she was lying about the police raid and whether he should wander back to see his boss. Some sense of self-preservation suggested to him it would not hurt to leave it a while before he went back to The Fiddle, just in case.

Clara entered the front passenger side of the car. Ariadne was laying across the back seats, under a blanket Gloucester had produced for her. She appeared asleep. Gloucester was eager to get her back to his house and he barely waited for Clara to close the car door before he drove off.

A short time later, they were at his home, helping Ariadne into the drawing room with its beautiful Christmas tree. She was settled before the fireplace, which was burning brightly, its warm glow restorative.

Gloucester called for tea and sandwiches, while Clara tucked a warm wrap around Ariadne and told her to rest.

"I believe this is yours," she produced the brooch Ariadne had lost on Christmas Eve.

Her eyes lit up at the sight of it.

"Oh, I thought it was gone for good," Ariadne took it and sighed. "I have had a terrible time. I thought they were going to murder me or leave me to starve."

Tears welled in her eyes again. Clara aimed to distract her, along with getting a clearer picture of what had happened between the girl and Brilliant Chang.

"How did Fitzroy convince you to help him?" she asked.

Ariadne sniffed and felt in her clothes for a

handkerchief. She was still dressed in the gown she had worn at the Bumptons' party, with her warm coat over it. She would need a change of clothes promptly, but Gloucester and Olivia could attend to that. Clara had to discover the truth and then get back to Chang.

"It was not very hard," Ariadne admitted. "All it took to convince me was that if I helped, he would come back to me and forget about Elaine DeVaughn."

Ariadne spat the name.

"Did you really believe him?"

"I was desperate to have him back," Ariadne whispered. "I missed him so much."

"Fitzroy is a rotten soul and does not deserve you," Gloucester said fiercely. He had settled onto one of the sofa's and was watching Ariadne with a pang of concern, convinced she was about to expire before his very eyes.

Ariadne had no response to his statement. It was true, of course, but love rarely saw the truth.

"What really happened at the party?" Clara asked.

"Not a lot," Ariadne replied. "Fitzroy arranged for Chang to be drugged and when he was dopey, we took him up to one of the bedrooms with Mindy's permission. He was almost unconscious. We undressed him and laid him on the bed. I undressed down to my slip so that it would seem as if we had slept together. Then they left me with him, alone.

"He was so doped up, that at one point he rolled over in the bed and fell onto the floor. I could not get him back onto the bed by myself, so I just left him there, in the blankets. When he finally woke, he saw me and all I had to do was smile and act loving to make him suppose we had been intimate."

Ariadne groaned at the memory.

"I hated every second of the ordeal. Chang jumped up as soon as he saw me. He looked horrified, as if being with me was his worst nightmare. It was awful to see his face, to know how much he despised what he thought had just occurred. I felt worse than a whore because I felt his disgust…"

Ariadne stumbled over her words.

"You didn't have to keep up the façade after Chang left," Clara said. "You did not have to continue with the deceit."

"But I did, for Benjamin's sake," Ariadne insisted. "He told me he was in desperate trouble, and he had to do this, or his life would be over. I could not allow that to happen."

"He was happy enough to allow you to vanish and not care what became of you," Gloucester said bluntly. "If he had spoken honestly to us, we would have found you so much sooner."

Ariadne did not want to hear that her lover had been so callous about her disappearance. She shut her eyes, as if to shut out the truth.

"You risked a lot for Fitzroy," Clara said softly. "Your reputation, your life."

"I know," Ariadne replied. "I was a fool."

Clara had no answer for that. She had been a fool, and it was impossible to change that fact. Gloucester reached out for Ariadne's hand.

"It is over now," he promised.

"Not quite," Clara intervened. "Chang believes you laid a curse upon him."

Ariadne frowned.

"I beg your pardon?"

"He thinks you laid a curse on him," Clara repeated, then she paused. "Didn't you?"

"No. Well, yes," Ariadne said. "At least, not a real curse. Fitzroy said the plan was to blackmail Mr Chang and expose him as weak. It wasn't working, though, because Chang kept refusing to listen to me. We were trying to destroy his reputation and make people realise he was not as indestructible as so many believed. If we could weaken his hold, bring doubts into the minds of his men, then he could potentially be removed. When he remained stoic, Fitzroy told me to pretend to curse him. I thought it was the stupidest thing ever. I did it, but I never supposed he would believe me."

"He did believe you." Clara said.

Ariadne was astonished.

"But curses are nonsense!"

"Just to be on the safe side, would you mind writing out a note that states you remove any curse from Chang," she asked. "It would help to ease tensions."

Ariadne was confused.

"I don't understand."

"It would be for the best," Gloucester said, grasping what Clara was thinking. "Here, I shall get some paper."

Ariadne was writing out her note as the tea and sandwiches arrived. She was relieved at the sight of food and warm tea. Clara took the note and left her to recuperate. She had learned all she could from Ariadne.

"Gloucester, could you drive me back to The Fiddle to collect Chang and Tommy?"

"Of course," Gloucester assured her. "You have my deepest thanks, Clara, for finding Ariadne."

Clara smiled at him.

"I am glad she is safe, and I am glad I know what was at the heart of this ridiculous saga."

"What a strange Christmas this has been," Gloucester said. "Still, it has all worked out for the best. At last Ariadne shall be free of Fitzroy's influence."

Clara was not so sure of that; men like Fitzroy had a habit of being pernicious and difficult to get away from. She sensed that despite it all, Ariadne would gladly go back to Fitzroy if he asked her to, and therein lay the real tragedy of it all.

Gloucester drove her back to the nightclub which was still busy with the police. They were having a whale of a time finding all manner of illegal things inside. Inspector Monroe was going to be busy for days.

Clara waved to Tommy who was loitering at the corner of the building. He turned and called to Chang who was out of sight, then they both headed to the car.

"Ariadne?" Tommy asked.

"She is safe and well," Clara replied. "She sent this for you, Chang."

She handed Chang the note. He read it carefully and his shoulders dropped in relief. Then he scowled.

"If I am not cursed, why do I still feel so awful?"

"Perhaps because what is wrong with you is not magical, after all?" Clara suggested.

Chang glowered at her.

"You haven't fixed me."

"I am not a doctor!"

"Then I am coming back to Brighton to see Dr Cutt again," Chang sulked, getting into the car. "He promised me answers."

Clara tried not to groan – just when she thought she was going to be able to get rid of him...

Chapter Twenty-Eight

It was the end of the first week of January 1924 and they were back in Brighton, keeping an eye on the news from London and the consequences of their recent foray into the city. The newspapers were having a field day over the arrest of a notable gangster and the dismantling of his string of nightclubs and other illegal organisations. There was going to be a lot of fallout from the drama, and it looked like Inspector Monroe would make his name from this.

Chang was gleeful over the news, he confessed to Clara that he was finding Vinkler's fall from grace and police difficulties far more satisfying than if he had simply killed him. Clara did not care to speculate whether this would change the way Chang dealt with his enemies in the future.

As for Benjamin Fitzroy, he had been gladly handed over to the police by his former fiancée who was taking his betrayal and poor judgement with grave stoicism. It helped that Elaine had never really loved the man. It was easier to distance herself that way.

Fitzroy was a small cog in a far larger affair and had

agreed to testify against Vinkler after Chang reported he wanted to drop all the charges of drugging against Fitzroy. Seeing as the police could not pursue the matter without Chang's testimony against Fitzroy, it meant they had to let him go. Chang, of course, had his sights set on Vinkler and Fitzroy had to earn his freedom by telling about his involvement with the man, what he knew about his schemes and also about the kidnapping of Ariadne on Vinkler's orders. In exchange, Chang had assured Fitzroy he would have his full protection.

Trapped between two men who would both do him considerable harm if he fell afoul of either of them, Fitzroy was stuck and had to agree to aid Chang, as it was his only way of keeping himself safe from both gangsters.

Miserable and scared, Fitzroy was currently residing in a property owned by Chang, closely watched over by the gangster's most trusted men.

Olivia Knepp had settled into Gloucester's home and did not look as though she would be leaving in a hurry. She was tired of playing mistress to men who discarded her as soon as they were bored or inconvenienced by her presence. Clara had chatted to Gloucester a few times on the telephone since she had left the Capital, and he was perplexed as to what to do with his house guest. Clara suggested she might eventually grow tired of living under his roof and would leave of her own accord. She just needed some breathing space to determine the direction her future lay in. Gloucester was less convinced. He rather fancied Olivia had settled in his house to stay, at least for the foreseeable future.

He had other things on his mind, however, to distract him. It did not come as a complete surprise when he told Clara he had proposed to Ariadne, and she had accepted.

"I did not think you were the marrying kind," she said to him.

"I don't think I am," Gloucester admitted. "But under the circumstances it seemed the best thing to do. I do care about Ariadne and that, surely, is a better foundation than many a marriage is based upon?"

Clara was not sure if he was making a sound decision, but she had to agree that many marriages were made under worse circumstances.

"Ariadne is delighted with the idea," Gloucester insisted. "At last, she is free of Fitzroy."

Clara could not share his optimism. When it came to relationships, things were never that simple, but she was pleased for him, nonetheless.

They had nearly endured a full week of the new year with Chang under their roof, when Dr Cutt arrived at their door with news concerning his tests. Clara was relieved to see him. Chang was not an easy house guest and had become moody over the last few days. He had travelled home in elation from their adventure. After initially being concerned he still felt unwell, he had convinced himself that his body just needed time to recover after the lifting of the curse and the best place to do that was in Brighton, away from prying eyes and any further potential usurpers.

As the days passed and his health did not improve, he became more and more despondent. On several occasions Clara had come across him clutching the slip of paper Ariadne had written her removal of the curse upon and glaring at it, as if it held some sort of power. Clara opted not to mention her thoughts on curses at these times, as it seemed unlikely to help.

Remarkably, it was Annie who proved Chang's consoler, making sure he was well fed and watered, and often sitting with him and just talking. He had become quiet and withdrawn, not even interested in making his usual snide comments.

When Dr Cutt arrived, his typical happy smile on his face, Clara was at once glad and fearful. She took him into the front parlour to have a quiet word before he met with Chang.

"Is he dying?" she asked.

"Well, that is a rather relative question and dependent on context. Technically, we are all dying, seeing as we get older not younger and with each passing year our bodies deteriorate a fraction further. However, if you mean is he dying from this condition, well, that will very much depend on whether he is prepared to accept my diagnosis and the treatment that should follow," Dr Cutt said cheerfully.

There was never a simple answer from the doctor.

"You know what is wrong with him, then?" Clara said.

"I do," Dr Cutt was amused she thought he might not have determined an answer. "I had my suspicions, however, I had to await the results of my tests to be sure. Unfortunately, there was quite a delay due to the festive season, but now I have the answers I anticipated."

"You best come see Chang," Clara motioned for him to follow her, and she took him through to the morning room where Chang was moping in an armchair by the window.

He rarely moved from this position, and looked far from the feisty, energetic criminal Clara had first encountered. The sight of Dr Cutt did little to cheer him.

"What news have you brought me? Am I to perish soon? At least then this will be over," Chang spoke.

"Quite a maudlin fellow, isn't he?" Dr Cutt smirked at Clara, before addressing Chang. "My dear fellow, I have my diagnosis and I can assure you that if you follow my advice, you shall recover and live many more years in good health."

Chang noticeably perked up.

"Say that again?"

Dr Cutt moved closer to his patient.

"I know what is wrong with you."

"What is it?" Chang demanded.

Dr Cutt suddenly became hesitant.

"Possibly it would be best if we discussed this in private?"

The doctor glanced at Clara who took the hint and departed. She ended up in the kitchen with Annie and Tommy, who were both also eager to discover what Dr Cutt had learned.

"Perhaps it is his heart," Annie speculated. "I mean, he has been such a bad person, maybe that is because there is something wrong with his heart?"

"An interesting theory, Annie, but I do not believe any medical man has proved that a certain illness can make a man bad or that curing him will make him good," Tommy told her gently. "Of course, long-term illness can affect the way a person feels emotionally and may have an impact on the way they treat others, but only as a reflection of their already existing personality."

Annie frowned.

"It could be something to do with his brain, then," she argued. "He is a clever man, but he uses his wits in a very despicable manner."

Annie had a deep held conviction that everyone had some good in them, if you could just find it. Clara thought it was a charming way to be and did not consider it naïve. She sometimes thought it was a better conviction than her perpetual cynicism.

"Whatever is wrong with Chang, I just hope it can be cured swiftly," Clara said. "I would rather like him away from my home."

"It is a nuisance having him here," Tommy agreed. "The police give the house shifty looks when they walk by on the beat."

"Do they?" Clara asked, having not noticed this.

"Oh yes," Tommy told her. "I saw a constable just the other day quite glower at our front door. They don't like that he is here."

"Well, they can cut out such antics," Clara said, annoyed to learn of the behaviour of the local constabulary. "It is not my fault, nor the fault of my front door. If they keep glaring at it, they will make the paint peel."

Tommy was going to respond, but at that moment a yell rang out from the morning room and made them all silent.

"Syphilis!"

The fury in Chang's tone had Clara rushing back to the other room to make sure he had not decided to vent his anger on the ageing doctor. She found he was still seated in the armchair, his fingers digging into the padded arms and an expression of horror and outrage on his face. Dr Cutt looked as cheerful and mild-mannered as always.

"The tests are conclusive, and your symptoms had me considering the possibility even before I took your blood," Dr Cutt was explaining. "Though it is rare these days, syphilis is still a condition medical men see from time to time. Why, when I was a young man, I recall seeing the condition rather regularly, but a lot of work has been done in educating the population and controlling the disease since then."

"Educating?" Chang said, an edge to his words. "Are you inferring I am uneducated and thus I contracted this disease at my own doing?"

"Of course not," Dr Cutt tutted at him. "I am merely explaining why the condition is less well-known than once it was. It is still about, for sure, and many people become infected and do not show symptoms immediately."

Chang was contemplating all this and what it meant for him.

"But, all my female friends..." he caught himself as he realised he was about to start talking of his love life before the elderly doctor.

Dr Cutt was too worldly to be troubled.

"Mr Chang, I take it you are a man who has enjoyed companionship with the opposite sex, and it would seem to suggest that one of these companions was carrying this condition."

"I do not use ladies of the night," Chang glowered at him. "If you are implying such a thing."

"I was not," Dr Cutt smiled.

Chang's horror was turning to shame as he realised what he was being told. He had always been so careful in his choice of women, he had said as much to Clara, but this proved he had not been careful enough. He dropped his head in his hand.

"The good news is I can treat you," Dr Cutt told him. "A number of new treatments have been discovered in recent years. Some are arsenic based, while others involve infecting a patient with malaria to induce a high fever."

"You treat me by making me sicker?" Chang said, mortified.

"Well, in essence, yes," Dr Cutt shrugged. "But the important thing is I can make you better."

Chang was defeated, his choices lay before him and were extremely limited. He nodded his head.

"Very well."

"I should prefer you to stay in a private hospital where your treatment can be monitored," Dr Cutt continued. "I have already made arrangements with a local cottage hospital where you shall have a room and be well taken care of. You can come with me now and we shall get started if you wish?"

"Why not," Chang groaned. "I shall just pack my

belongings."

"I'll help," Annie told him.

He left the Fitzgerald household within the hour. Clara was rather glad to see the back of Chang and hoped he would soon be safely out of her way in London. Dr Cutt had not mentioned how long the treatment would take, but she was just glad he was out of her hair.

Things gradually returned to normal over the next few days. There was news from the inspector that the assassin who had come after Chang had regained consciousness, but was currently unable to remember his name, let alone what he had been sent to Brighton for. The doctors were not sure he would ever regain his memory. Clara wondered if that was for the best. Could a man begin a new life after all? One where all memory of being a thug and working for men like Vinkler was eradicated? Or was she being overly optimistic, like Annie?

The case was truly closed, and Clara was quite relieved. For once, she had been involved in a mystery where no one had died, and that was cheering.

It was a couple of weeks after Chang had departed her home that Clara received an envelope with familiar handwriting. Chang had good penmanship, but something about the way he wrote reminded Clara of the oriental symbols that made up the Chinese alphabet. She opened the envelope cautiously, wondering what she would find inside. There was no letter, but a cheque fell out. She picked it up from the floor where it had fluttered and observed the amount with surprise. Chang had clearly appreciated her efforts to aid him and the inconvenience he put her to. The lack of any correspondence suggested he was content to allow their working relationship to return to the way it had always been – they kept their distance unless their paths had to cross.

Clara felt that was satisfactory. She tucked away the cheque and smiled to herself. She would not forget this case in a long time, and nor would Chang. She rather liked the idea that he might just feel a little indebted to her after this.

Who knew what that could mean in the future?

Printed in Great Britain
by Amazon